D1355752

Wishes and Dreams

Wishes and Dreams

Jeanne Whitmee

ROBERT HALE · LONDON

© Jeanne Whitmee 2006
First published in Great Britain 2006

ISBN-10: 0-7090-8208-8
ISBN-13: 978-0-7090-8208-8

Robert Hale Limited
Clerkenwell House
Clerkenwell Green
London EC1R 0HT

The right of Jeanne Whitmee to be identified as
author of this work has been asserted by her
in accordance with the Copyright, Design and
Patents Act 1988

2 4 6 8 10 9 7 5 3

Typeset in 11¼/14pt Sabon
by Derek Doyle & Associates, Shaw Heath
Printed and bound in Great Britain
by Biddles Limited, King's Lynn

CHAPTER ONE

W E'RE closing now so you can make a start on the cleaning.'
Ada Griggs, the owner of Maison Griggs was already pulling
off her overall. 'You can start sweeping up and then I want all the
cubicles scrubbing out,' she went on. 'And remember to pay special
attention to the basins. I want everything sparkling when I come
in on Monday morning.'

'Yes, Mrs Griggs.' Laura sighed resignedly. It was eight o'clock
and she had been hard at it since half past eight this morning,
running errands, fetching and carrying, making tea and sweeping
up the hair that constantly littered the floor.

'And you needn't look like that either,' Ada went on. 'You
might think yourself a leading light with the "Players" but here
you're just the dogsbody and don't you forget it.'

'No, Mrs Griggs,' Laura muttered.

'And make sure you lock up properly before you go.'

'Yes, Mrs Griggs.'

As Ada left by the back door along with the other two hairdressers, Shirley, the sixteen-year-old apprentice, gave Laura a sly
wink. 'Take no notice, duck,' she said. 'Miserable old cow! If I
was you I'd just give the floor a quick once over and nip off
home.' She pulled on her coat and eyed Laura through the
mirror. 'Going to the dance down the drill hall tonight? They
reckon Sid Willis and his lads can really swing it.'

Laura shook her head. 'I've got no money to spend on dances,' she said. 'What I earn here only just pays for my lessons with Miss Seymour.'

Shirley leaned closer to the mirror and coated her full lips with scarlet lipstick. 'Learning to talk posh?' she said, her voice distorted by her pout. 'I don't know why you bother.'

'It's more than that. I want to be an actress,' Laura told her. 'A professional one.'

'Yeah, so you're always saying.' Shirley tossed her blonde curls. 'Oh well, rather you than me. You wouldn't catch me staying on at school neither. I was really glad when I failed the scholarship. All them exams is a boring waste of time if you ask me! I'm just putting up with old mother Griggs till some good-looking fella comes along and pops the question. Nice little semi and two kids. That'll do me.' She patted Laura's shoulder. 'Ta-ra, kid. Take my advice and give the place a lick and a promise. No one won't notice the difference.' And with a swirl of her skirts she was off out the door.

Laura worked at Maison Griggs every Friday after school until closing time at eight o'clock and all day on Saturdays. Most of the time she was run off her feet and by closing time all she wanted to do was fall into bed, but it was the only way she could pay for her lessons with Rosa Seymour.

Rosa was the Millborough Players' producer. She had been a professional actress until a tragic accident had crippled her when she was twenty-five. She gave voice and acting lessons at the large house near the park that had belonged to her parents. She also rented out her basement studio to her friend Frances Grey for ballet and tap lessons. When Laura first joined the Players, Rosa had seen how keen she was and had offered her lessons at a reduced fee. Laura was overjoyed. But her parents saw things rather differently. As for shelling out for acting lessons, discounted or otherwise, they made their feelings all too plain.

'You should be paying more attention to your schoolwork like your sister does,' Harry Nightingale told her. 'And if it's work you want you can put in a few hours here at the shop after school to help your mother.'

Laura didn't point out that she already helped in the shop whenever she could and, anyway, it was not the work but the money she needed.

Her mother, however, was well aware of what was in her mind. 'Work for us? Oh no, that wouldn't suit, would it, lady?' she said, folding her arms and regarding her younger daughter. 'You can't help your mum and dad of a weekend out of the goodness of heart, can you?' She shook her head. 'I don't know. It's all money with you. We let you stay on at school and this is all the thanks we get. Why can't you be more like our Moira? She's worked hard and got her matriculation. *She's* off to train to be a teacher. Her head isn't full of rubbish about going on the stage – *and* she still finds time to give us a hand on a Saturday.'

'I help too!' Laura protested. 'As much as I can.' She was sick of having her sister's saintliness rammed down her throat and she knew it was useless to try to change her parents' minds, so when she saw the notice in the window of Maison Griggs for a girl to help part-time, she applied for the job. Mrs Griggs paid her just enough for two acting lessons a week and one dancing class.

She thought about what Shirley had said. She hadn't wanted to stay on at school after School Certificate, but her parents had insisted that she must be given the same chance as her sister. However, they made sure at every opportunity that she knew what a sacrifice they were making and that they expected her to do as well as Moira. For Laura the pressure was intolerable. Her dream was to go to RADA but when she tentatively broached the subject, her parents had looked at her as though she was suggesting a trip to the moon.

'Rarder? What's that when it's at home?' her father asked.

'It stands for the Royal Academy of Dramatic Art, Dad,' Laura explained. 'It's another college – in London, one that teaches acting.'

Meg shook her head impatiently. 'You've got to get your head out of the clouds, our Laura. That kind of thing's not for the likes of us. It's a nice little hobby, acting, and I'm sure you do it very nicely – at school and with the Players, but it's not a proper *job*.

Everyone knows that.'

'You have to remember that them who does it have private means,' Harry put in. 'It's a – I don't know – a sort of *playing about* occupation, for folks with money. You can't earn a proper living doing it.'

'Besides,' Meg went on with a sniff, 'I'm not at all sure it's respectable. You hear all sorts.'

Laura knew when she was beaten. Her mum and dad were way behind the times with their views. This was 1938, not the 'gay nineties'. No one could be more respectable than Rosa Seymour. She was a lovely person. Miss Grey too. And until her accident Rosa had earned a perfectly good living. She'd even been in one or two films. Silent ones it was true, but just the same. . . . It was so frustrating. But Laura refused to be put off. She was determined to make her dream come true somehow. She would be seventeen in a few weeks' time and she planned to leave school at the end of term come what may.

It was past nine by the time she had finished her chores at the salon and it was already growing dark as she walked home through Millborough's high street. It was halfway through September now and the signs that summer was over were all too evident. The melancholy scent of distant bonfires hung on the evening breeze, sharp in her nostrils, and there was a chill to the air. The lamplighter was on his rounds, lighting the gas lamps with his long pole. On they came, one by one with the familiar pop, their yellow light sending Laura's long shadow bounding ahead of her as she walked.

Acting was her dream. Ever since she'd appeared in the nativity play at St Mary's Elementary School at five years old it had been all she wanted. Every year she had been in the school play and since she'd been at Millborough High School she had played several leading parts. Juliet, Portia, Rosalind; Shakespeare had been a revelation to her, the poetry and rhythm of the words and the enchantment of the stories set her imagination on fire.

Then last year she had been invited to join the Millborough Players. They were putting on a production of *Daddy Longlegs*, a play about an orphan girl who has a mystery benefactor, and they were looking for a young girl of Laura's age. That was when she first met Rosa. Being directed by a professional had been so exciting. Laura learned so much and received rave reviews in the local press for her performance. It had been the most thrilling time of her life and when Rosa had offered to coach her, her happiness had been complete. She ran home that night, determined to coax her parents into letting her take up Rosa's offer, only to find, to her disappointment, that they did not share her enthusiasm.

Nightingale's Tobacconist and Newsagent's Shop was in Jessop Street, close to the market square. Harry Nightingale had built up a flourishing paper round and employed a willing team of young lads to help him deliver, mornings and evenings. Most of the workers at Shearing's shoe factory passed the shop on their way to work and called in for their Woodbines or pipe tobacco, and later for an evening paper. The family lived in the flat above the shop which boasted a living-room, kitchen and two bedrooms, one of which Laura had to share with Moira, her sister. There had been three bedrooms but the previous year Harry had had the smallest converted into a bathroom, something of which he and his wife, Meg, were inordinately proud.

This evening when Laura arrived home the family had already started supper.

'Thought you'd got lost,' Harry remarked, one eye on the evening paper which he had propped against the tea cosy.

'We started because Moira's going to the dance,' Meg said, getting up from the table to fetch Laura's plate from the oven.

'David's picking me up at half nine,' Moira said smugly. 'Don't want to get there till it's in full swing.' She had her father's sandy hair which she wore very short and which she 'finger waved'. Her short-sighted hazel eyes looked up at Laura through her glasses. 'Don't you want to come?'

Laura shook her head and applied herself to the plate of mutton stew that her mother had put before her. 'I'm too tired. It's been really busy at the salon.'

9

'I don't know why you want to work for that woman,' Meg remarked.

'I've told you, Mum. It's to pay for my lessons,' Laura said wearily.

'Well, I don't know, I'm sure,' Meg complained. 'Here's your father and me, going without God-knows-what to keep you on at school and all you can think of is working yourself silly for some common hairdresser woman to pay for highfalutin acting lessons. Seems to me you might as well go and work for her full-time and save us some money!'

'Don't start, Mother,' Harry said. 'Let's have our supper in peace. We've gone over this till I'm fair sick of it.' He jabbed a finger at the paper. 'We'll have a lot more to worry about soon if I'm any judge. This business with Czechoslovakia looks bad. If you ask me we're in for another war.'

Meg's eyes widened. 'Oh, Harry, don't say that! It doesn't bear thinking about. It doesn't seem any time at all since the last one. Surely Mr Chamberlain wouldn't let it happen?'

'I don't know as he'll have much choice,' Harry said gloomily. 'France has already sent troops to the Maginot Line.'

Moira was reading the back page of the paper, partly visible over the top of the tea cosy. 'Ooh, look. It says there that the BBC is showing its first television film next Monday. I wish we had a set.'

Laura kept her head down, only too glad that the subject of her remaining at school had been averted.

After supper Laura helped her mother with the washing-up and then joined her sister in the bedroom where she was getting ready to go out. Moira had changed into her best black skirt and the pink silk blouse she had embroidered herself. Regarding her from the bed where she sat Laura observed idly how the black skirt flattered her sister's wide hips, yet the blouse over-emphasized her ample bosom, making it look as though the embroidered butterfly was about to be torn in two. In her opinion pink didn't suit Moira's colouring either, but she knew better than to say anything.

10

Moira looked at her sister through the dressing-table mirror as she applied face powder to her pale skin in an attempt to disguise her freckles. 'Is it really worth it, slaving at that place?' she asked. 'You never seem to have any fun.'

'I'm happy enough,' Laura said. 'And it will all be worth it eventually.'

'Will it though?' Moira ran a comb through her hair, licked her fingers and pushed the tight waves into place. 'It all seems so hit and miss,' she said. 'I mean, when *I've* done my training and qualified as a teacher I'll have no trouble finding a job, whereas you. . . .'

'You don't know anything about it,' Laura said.

'Poor Mum gets so tired,' Moira went on. 'Did you know she's taken a girl on to help in the shop?'

'No. Has she?'

'Yes. Well, she had to, didn't she, now that you work for that hairdresser? When I go off to college the week after next she'll have no one to help her on Saturdays. It's that Vicky Watts from Artillery Street. She used to be in your class at St Mary's didn't she?'

Laura remembered Vicky very well: a scrawny little girl with huge grey eyes who always seemed afraid of everything. Because of this she was often bullied.

'Vicky, yes I remember her,' she said. She remembered a particular occasion when the child was in tears because one of the bigger boys had hit her and run off with her pencil case. Laura remembered watching from a distance as Vicky cowered against the wall, her little face crumpled and stained with tears. She could easily have made the boy give it back, or at least have comforted the unhappy child, but she hadn't. Partly because she was afraid of being associated with a girl everyone saw as pathetic and partly because a part of her despised the girl for not fighting back. Looking back now she felt deeply ashamed and wondered if Vicky remembered the occasion too.

'I daresay Peter will be at the dance,' Moira said, taking Laura's silence and concerned look as guilt for letting their mother down. 'He's not at all bad looking, you know.' She gave her sister a sidelong glance. If you're not careful he'll find himself another girl.'

Laura shrugged. 'It's up to him what he does. If he wants to go out with someone else he's free to. We're not joined to each other.'

Moira got up from the dressing-table. 'Oh well, if that's your attitude, it's your funeral,' she said, gathering up her coat and bag. 'If you want to ruin your life you'd better get on with it. It's Mum and Dad I feel sorry for. You're a real disappointment to them.'

'Oh listen to Miss Goody-goody,' Laura taunted. 'It's a wonder to me you're not snatched up to heaven, you're so perfect!'

'No need for that. I'm sure I'm only trying to point out—'

'Well *don't*.' Laura interrupted. 'Just get off your soap box and go to your silly dance. Keep your opinions to yourself, Moira. I don't tell you how to live your life!'

Scarlet-faced, Moira stood up and flounced to the door. 'Have it your way, our Laura,' she said. 'And much good may it do you.'

When Moira had gone Laura lay back on the bed and closed her eyes. The Peter Moira had referred to was Peter Radcliffe whom she had known since her early schooldays. He was a nice, sensitive boy two years older than her and about the only person who seemed to understand her desire to act. Moira's remarks about him had caught her on the raw. He too belonged to the Millborough Players and often helped with backstage jobs and painting scenery. She wondered whether he really would be going to the dance. He had certainly asked her if she was going when she had seen him earlier in the week. Would he really ask someone else out as Moira had said? Contrary to her protestations she knew she would feel disappointed and let down if he did.

'Oh well, it can't be helped,' she told herself. 'I won't achieve my goal without making some sacrifices.'

She got up to stare critically at herself in the dressing-table mirror. Toffee-brown eyes looked back at her out of a pale oval face. Her hair was dark copper, like a polished chestnut and she wore it in a smooth jaw-length bob with a fringe that partly covered her deep forehead. She leaned forward and studied her complexion. She'd been lucky. Moira often suffered quite badly from spots, not to mention the dreaded freckles, but her own skin remained smooth and unblemished. When she smiled a dimple appeared close to the corner of her mouth. She'd always considered it her best feature.

'You're nothing to write home about, Laura Nightingale,' she told her reflection. 'Still, you're not fat and freckly like our Moira, thank goodness!'

She went downstairs a little later and found her parents engrossed in the news on the wireless. Dad was going on again about Hitler and uttering dire warnings about what country he might threaten next. They didn't notice when Laura fetched her coat and slipped out through the side door. A walk in the fresh air was what she needed.

Down by the canal a stiff breeze ruffled the water. The gas lights gave a mellow glow so that the rubbish people deposited along the banks dissolved into the shadows and the full moon turned the brackish water to rippling black satin. Laura walked for a while then turned into the little cobbled lane that led up into the high street. All the lights were on at the drill hall at the top of the street and the sounds of Ted Willis's band floated out every time the door was opened. Laura picked out the tune of 'Smoke Gets in Your Eyes' and hummed it as she walked along.

The shops were so familiar to her that she could have seen them with her eyes closed. Williamson's, the grocer's, open till late on Saturday evenings, with its rich scents of coffee and cheeses floating out through the open door. Next door was Drew's, the cobbler's – its window full of sturdy work-a-day boots. Then there was Maxwell's, the draper's, with its tasteful display of corsets and underwear. Then Laura's favourite, Phillips, the chemist's. As a child she had been fascinated by the bulbous jars with their pointed stoppers that stood on a shelf at the back of the window, the light making the red, blue and green liquid gleam like jewels. At the front, Icilma face creams and Drene shampoo were exhibited cheek by jowl with Jeyes Fluid and Beecham's pills.

At the far end of the street was the Plaza cinema with its modern Art Deco façade resembling sun rays. It was Millborough's newest building, replacing the old cinema and its tin roof. Laura paused at the foot of the steps to look at the photographs displayed outside. They were showing a Greta Garbo film. Laura would have loved to go, but all her spare money had to be carefully saved for her lessons.

'*Anna Karenina*. Have you seen it?'

The voice behind her made her spin round in surprise. '*Peter*! You made me jump. Where did you spring from?'

'I waited for you outside the drill hall. I thought you might just turn up.'

She shook her head. 'Couldn't afford it.'

'I'd have treated you.'

'I'm sure you've got better things to spend your money on,' she said sharply.

He grinned good-naturedly. 'I think I can be the judge of that. Do you want to go? It's not too late. Your sister's in there with David Simmons.'

'I know she is.' Laura began to walk on. 'I'm not dressed for a dance and anyway, I'd rather have seen Greta Garbo. She's such a wonderful actress and so beautiful. But don't let me spoil your fun.' She began to walk down the street, remembering her sister's remark about Peter finding another girl. 'You go to the dance if you're so keen on it.'

'Hey! Slow down a bit, can't you?' Peter said, hurrying after her. 'Where's the fire?' Catching up with her he grasped her arm and pulled her round to face him. 'What's up?' He bent a little to look into her eyes. 'Why are you so angry?'

Laura sighed. 'Sorry. I didn't mean to snap at you. I just get so tired of everyone disapproving of what I want to do. They all think I'm mad spending my money on acting lessons instead of having fun. Moira says I'm ruining my life, but I know I'm not.

No one understands. They want me to be just like her. They think it's just a silly young girl's dream, wanting to act. No one believes I can make it happen.'

'I do,' Peter said softly. 'And anyway, you don't really need anyone to believe it, do you? Believing in yourself is enough.'

'But it's so hard, trying to earn money for lessons. Mum and Dad think I'm selfish and stupid and Moira – well, she thinks I'm deranged.'

They'd reached the market square and Peter led her over to the bench next to the drinking fountain. 'Let's sit down a minute.' He drew her down beside him and slipped an arm round her shoulders.

'I've made up my mind,' she told him. 'I'm going to leave school at Christmas.'

'What do your folks say about that?'

'They don't know yet. I'm going to leave though. I've had enough. I'm not doing any good there. I've got my School Cert. and I don't need anything else. It's a waste of time – and their money.'

'What will you do?'

'I don't know. If the worst comes to the worst I could always ask Mrs Griggs to take me on as an apprentice.'

He laughed. 'You're not serious.'

'Well, it'd only be temporary. I'll get something. You just see if I don't.'

He pulled her close to his side. 'You don't have to convince me,' he said. 'I'm on your side, remember.' He leaned forward and kissed her softly. 'As far as I'm concerned you've got a great future ahead of you. Just think, I'll be able to say, "I knew her before she was famous".'

Laura laughed and relaxed against him. 'Oh, Peter, what would I do without you?'

CHAPTER TWO

VICKY Watts stood proudly behind the counter in Nightingale's shop. It was Monday, her first morning. She had arrived at half past eight, allowing Mrs Nightingale, who had been in the shop since it opened at seven, to go upstairs and make breakfast.

'Now, you'll be all right, will you dear?' Meg had asked kindly. 'If there's anything you're not sure of just give me a shout.'

Vicky had nodded eagerly, but she was determined to show her new employer that she could cope. There was a list of prices on the shelf under the counter and she had always been good with figures and money. The cash register was slightly unnerving, with its loud bell and the drawer that flew open, but she was sure she'd soon get used to it. She had worn her best frock so as to make a good impression on her first day. It was one she had made herself from a remnant of material she had found on the market. She thought that the sky-blue fabric brought out the colour of her eyes. She had edged the collar with lace and sewn some tiny pearl buttons she had found on an old dress of her mother's, down the front.

The doorbell tinkled and two customers came in. Vicky's heart beat faster as she said, 'Good morning. What can I get you?'

She served the man a packet of pipe tobacco and a *Daily Herald*, the lady a quarter of humbugs. This was what she had looked forward to – meeting all the different customers who came in.

Alone again, she looked around at the colourful packets of

cigarettes and sweets. There were Players and Woodbines, Capstan and Craven A on the shelves behind her, whilst on the counter was a mouth-watering selection of chocolate bars, bottles of fruit jellies, pear drops and striped humbugs to weigh out on the shiny brass scales. There were tins of Radiance toffee complete with a little hammer to break up the slabs and a big jar of aniseed balls at four for a penny for the children. On the door was an enamelled advertisement for Nestlé's chocolate and above it hung a wire rack holding an array of daily papers and magazines. Vicky thought it was magical.

This was the first proper job that Vicky had had. So far all she'd done was a few hours of cleaning work, fitted around her household duties and looking after her invalid father. He had taken a lot of persuading to allow her to take this job. She'd be out of the house all day, from eight till five apart from an hour's break for lunch. But when she had told him how much she would be earning he had begun to relent. It was a big improvement on the pittance she could earn from 'charring' and would make a difference to their meagre income.

Vicky had been born when her mother had almost given up hope for the longed-for child. It had always been obvious that her parents' feelings on the arrival of a baby girl in the spring of 1922 had differed. Her mother had adored Vicky from the first moment she set eyes on her, but her father never tried to hide the fact that he resented the intrusion of a demanding infant when he had grown used to having the house and his wife's undivided attention to himself. A few months after Vicky's birth he'd become disabled in an accident at the factory where he worked, making him unemployable fifteen years before his retirement age.

When Vicky was little she and her mother were inseparable.

Margaret Sowerby was the only daughter of middle-class parents; an accomplished young woman of twenty-five when she married. She was well versed in genteel manners, a good needle-woman and a proficient pianist. Her parents had cherished great hopes that she might meet a well-to-do young man, maybe a doctor or a lawyer, and make an appropriate marriage. So, when she had announced her intention of marrying 35-year-old Daniel Watts, a machine fitter from Shearing's shoe factory, they had been shocked and disappointed. As well as considering him too old for their daughter, they thought him uncouth and ignorant, and when she refused to give him up they threatened to disown her. Nothing Margaret could do or say would make them change their minds and after the wedding – which they refused to attend – they hardened their hearts and closed their door to the couple unreservedly.

The marriage was not a success. Once the initial euphoria had worn off it was painfully plain that she and Dan had nothing in common. Even as a young man, Dan was short-tempered and intolerant and he soon began to despise his wife's elegant taste and her refined way of speaking, calling her a snob and a toffee-nosed bitch, especially when he had spent the evening at the Ship Inn, drinking himself almost insensible.

Vicky's birth made up for everything as far as Margaret was concerned. As the baby grew into a little girl, Margaret taught her everything she knew: to cook and sew and to appreciate the books and music that she loved, all of the finer things in life. She also taught her to play the old upright piano that her grandmother had left her; the only thing she had been allowed to take with her from her parents' home when she married. Most important of all, she taught her to speak nicely. Margaret abhorred the ugly Midlands accent that her neighbours spoke and was determined that her daughter would not acquire it.

Sadly Margaret caught influenza in 1932. It turned quickly to pneumonia and when Vicky was barely ten she was left without a mother. After that she was forced to grow up quickly. In her mother's absence she became her father's slave and, later, his nurse. The pain from his injured leg, coupled with the frustration of having no work and limited mobility did nothing to sweeten Dan's temper and at times Vicky's life was hard to bear.

When Vicky passed the scholarship examination at eleven he refused to let her take up her place at Millborough High School, arguing that educating girls was a waste of time and money. Vicky's place was in the home, taking care of him now that her mother was gone. He didn't hold with girls of her class getting ideas above their station. Besides, he had no money to waste on fancy uniforms and hockey sticks.

As her teens approached she was forbidden to go to dances or the cinema. Father's word was law and she didn't dare to disobey. As soon as it was legally permissible Dan insisted that she leave school and get a job to augment the family budget. There was little hope of getting the kind of job she would have liked – perhaps in a library or a music shop. All she knew was domestic work, of which she had plenty of experience. She took a variety of cleaning jobs which she found tedious and boring, but the houses she worked in allowed her to see for the first time how squalid her own lifestyle was.

The little terraced house in Artillery Street was cramped and run down, freezing in winter, hot and claustrophobic in summer. There was no bathroom, the only sanitary facilities being the outside lavatory and the tin tub that hung on a nail in the yard, used to bathe in once a week in water laboriously heated in the copper. The weekly wash was done in an outside wash house and hung to dry on wet days on a pulley rack in the living-room, filling the air with suffocating steam. Then there was the black leaded range that refused to draw when the wind was blowing in the wrong direction. Vicky longed for independence, but saw no escape from her drudgery. The years stretched ahead of her like a long dark tunnel with no light at the end.

Dan relaxed his clampdown on her social life a little after her sixteenth birthday, allowing her to go out once a week as long as she was in by nine o'clock, but Vicky had no friends with whom to share her leisure time. Instead she would go to the cinema, losing herself for a couple of hours in the 'ninepennies'. It was a glimpse of another world, one where anything was possible. But she could never get away until the second house and frustratingly she always had to leave before the film was over in order to be home by nine. Once she had tried to reason with Father that nine o'clock was too early, but he had accused her suspiciously of being 'up to no good' which soon silenced her on the subject.

When Vicky saw the advertisement in the evening paper for a girl to help out in Nightingale's shop, her heart had leapt. The diversity of shop work appealed to her. She remembered Laura Nightingale from her early schooldays. Her memories of that time were not pleasant. She'd been constantly bullied because she was small for her age, because she 'spoke posh', because she always came top in arithmetic. It seemed that any excuse would do. Laura had never joined in the taunting and jeering though. Vicky had always been grateful to her for that and she had always admired and envied the pretty auburn-haired girl.

When she begged her father to let her apply for the job he'd been reluctant.

'Nightingale's? They stay open all hours,' he'd pointed out. 'What about me? You know I need you here – to see to me leg and get me meals and that.'

'Jessop Street is only ten minutes' walk away, Dad,' she'd pleaded. 'I'd easily be able to run home and get you something to eat in the lunch hour, make sure you're all right.'

Dan's bad leg had become ulcerated and infected. He refused to let her send for the doctor, insisting that all doctors were 'money grubbing quacks', and he didn't trust them as far as he could throw them. He insisted that 'nature would take its course'. But things had gone from bad to worse, and for the past three months he had been confined to bed, unable to put any weight on the leg. Every afternoon Vicky would have to wash him and change the dressing on his leg before making his evening meal. She was becoming seriously worried about its condition. Although she did her best, it was not clearing up. The foul odour from the ulcers made her gag every time she took the bandages off and the stained sheets had to be changed and washed every day. She knew he must be in a great deal of pain but every time she tentatively suggested getting medical help, he flew into a rage, accusing her of wanting him taken into hospital and 'out of the way'.

'You're not getting rid of me that easy, lady,' he'd growl. 'All the years I've kept you. You owe me that at least!'

She guessed that as well as being in agony he was frightened, and in spite of his harshness to her over the years she couldn't help feeling a stab of pity for him.

'Managed all right, have you, love?'

Vicky smiled and nodded as Meg reappeared through the door at the back of the shop. 'I'm fine thanks, Mrs Nightingale,' she said. 'I'm enjoying myself. You needn't have hurried back. There haven't been many customers.'

'It's always quiet after the early morning rush,' Meg told her. 'There's still some tea in the pot. Why don't you nip upstairs and have a little break?'

Vicky blushed. 'Oh no, I'm all right, really.'

'Well, if you're sure,' Meg said. 'Don't want to overwork you on your first day.'

Vicky smiled. She'd loved serving the customers and she certainly didn't call this overworking. More like a holiday.

The day passed pleasantly. Vicky managed to go home and make her father some lunch, getting back easily in time for the afternoon shift. Soon after four that afternoon the shop doorbell tinkled. Vicky looked up.

'Can I help you? Oh!' It was Laura who had come in. She wore her dark green school blazer and felt hat and carried a bulging satchel. Seeing Vicky behind the counter she smiled.

'Oh, hello, it's Vicky, isn't it?'

'That's right.'

'How was your first day?'

Vicky blushed. 'Lovely. I've enjoyed it. Your mum is ever so kind.'

'Good. I remember you from St Mary's.'

'That's right.' Vicky blushed and Laura bit her lip at the small silence that followed, wondering what was going through the other girl's mind.

'Well – we'll have to have a proper talk sometime,' Laura said.

'But I've got to go and get ready now so I'll have to hurry.' She turned and almost collided with her mother in the doorway. Meg was carrying a cup of tea.

'Watch out! You nearly knocked me flying!'

'Sorry Mum.'

Meg shook her head at Laura's retreating back. 'Nearly had this tea all over me! Honestly, that girl! Off to her *acting* lesson if you can believe it. Lot of nonsense. Wouldn't catch a girl like you hankering after that kind of life, eh?' She handed Vicky the cup. 'Drink that down while it's hot. You've hardly stopped all day,' she said.

'Thanks.' Vicky hid her face in the cup. She envied Laura her independence and her talent. Who knew what excitement lay ahead of her, whereas it sometimes felt to Vicky as though her life had been cast in stone from the moment she was born.

Laura stood in the middle of the studio and put everything she had into the soliloquy from *Hamlet*. She'd been practising it all week, in the privacy of her bedroom. Rosa believed in teaching the speeches Shakespeare had written for both sexes so that her students could feel both male and female emotions.

'We should all know what it is to feel a man's pain as well as our own,' she insisted. She sat now at her desk, watching and listening to Laura, occasionally closing her eyes. When the speech came to an end she looked up.

'Come and sit down dear.' When Laura was seated she said, 'That was very nice. I liked the way you deepened your voice and your stance was good. But you must remember that Hamlet is a very disturbed young man. He is suffering the loss of his father very deeply. He feels betrayed by his mother and his uncle, and he trusts no one around him – not even his own feelings. In the soliloquy he is looking for an answer, a way out. But he's desperately afraid of the consequences of his actions.'

'I didn't get any of that into it, did I?' Laura said unhappily. 'You're saying that I just – said the words.'

'Sometimes we have to think of it in modern-day terms in

order to understand it better,' Rosa said. 'Imagine it happening to someone you know. It's easy to get carried away by the Bard's beautiful language.' She smiled. 'Your breathing and delivery are improving enormously.' She laughed softly and patted Laura's shoulder. 'Don't look so despondent, darling. We mustn't expect miracles. You're coming along very nicely. Rome wasn't built in a day.'

'It's a lot harder than *Daddy Longlegs*.'

'Of course it is. There's no comparison between an orphan girl and the Prince of Denmark!' Rosa closed her book. 'I think that had better be all for this evening.' She got up from behind her desk and reached for her stick. 'Now, I shall make you a hot drink before you go.'

'Thank you, Rosa. That would be lovely.'

Rosa Seymour was a handsome woman of fifty. Tall and upright in spite of her crippled leg. She had long, jet-back hair, olive skin and dark perceptive eyes, a legacy from an Italian grandmother. She wore her hair in a heavy chignon low on her neck and dressed rather eccentrically in long skirts and shawls in rich colours.

In the kitchen of the rambling old house she had inherited from her parents, she made cocoa, heating the milk on the ancient range. Bringing the mugs to the big chenille-covered table in the centre of the room she reached up to the mantelshelf for the tin of biscuits with the coronation picture of the King and Queen on the lid.

'Have a ginger nut,' she invited. 'Nothing like a ginger nut to lift the spirits.'

Laura loved this kitchen with its huge dresser, its shelves crammed with massive meat dishes and copper pans. There was a big chintz-covered sofa against one wall and opposite, a large old-fashioned desk where Rosa did all her accounts and paperwork. She did quite well out of her business, teaching deportment and elocution at two local private schools and giving individual lessons to a growing number of private students.

'People are beginning to realize the benefits of speaking well,' she told Laura in her sonorous voice. 'The wireless has shown people that it's important at least to *sound* educated. It's good for business and for one's social life.'

Until now though she hadn't had many students who were serious about a career in the theatre and she had high hopes for Laura. She saw her own youthful self in the girl and understood very well how much a career in the theatre would mean to her. When her own career was shattered by the accident she'd considered her life over, but now she knew that if she could nurture the talent, fan the flame of aspiration, even in one young girl, the pain and disappointment she had suffered would not all have been in vain.

'Are your parents any happier with your ambitions?' she asked as they sipped their cocoa.

Laura shook her head. 'Not really. I'm just going to have to prove it to them, aren't I? I've made one decision though. I've made up my mind to leave school at the end of this term.'

'Is that wise?'

Laura looked at her teacher. 'I thought I might get a job – in the theatre somewhere.'

Rosa shook her head. 'My dear, you're not ready yet. Is there any chance that your parents might agree to your going to RADA?'

'None at all. I wondered if there might be a company that would take me on as a student?'

'Only if your parents were prepared to pay a premium.'

Laura sighed. 'Then it's out of the question.'

Rosa reached out to pat her arm. 'Don't look so downcast, darling. We'll think of something. In the meantime there's an awful lot for you still to learn.'

When Laura got home that evening Moira was sitting with her parents in the living-room mending a pile of stockings. She looked up as Laura came in.

'Here comes Greta Garbo,' she joked. 'When's your next film, Greta?'

'Put a sock in it, can't you!' Laura snapped.

'Oh dear, things not go so well this evening, did they? Did the Lady Rosa give your knuckles a rapping?'

'Of course not, don't be silly.' Laura threw herself down into a chair. She was so sick of her sister's mocking. Her nerves on edge she decided on a sudden impulse to drop her bombshell. Now was as good a time as any.

'Mum, Dad – I've decided to leave school at Christmas.'

The announcement certainly silenced her sister. Moira stared at her, open-mouthed, whilst her mother dropped her knitting into her lap and her father took his pipe out of his mouth.

'That you will not, my girl,' he said.

'I'm doing no good there,' Laura went on. 'You've often said that it's a waste of money and I agree. I'll get a job.'

'What kind of job?' Meg asked.

Laura shrugged. 'I don't know yet, but I'll get something.'

Moira sniggered. 'Seems you wasted your time taking on that Watts girl, Mum,' she said. 'You had the perfect shop girl right here under your roof all the time.'

'It's not a joke, our Moira,' Meg said sharply. 'Perhaps you'd like to go and put the kettle on while we talk about it, seeing that you can't be serious.'

Red-faced, Moira got up and went towards the kitchen, giving Laura a look of pure disdain as she went.

Harry was refilling his pipe, thoughtfully tamping down the tobacco. 'You'll regret it if you do leave, you know,' he said. 'I don't think you realize what a privilege it is to have a good education. You mother and I never had the chance. . . .'

'I know, Dad, and don't think I don't appreciate all that you've done for me,' Laura said. 'But I've got my School Cert. and I know I won't get my matric. I haven't got the same kind of brain as Moira and I don't feel I need it anyway. I'd never make a teacher or sit behind the counter in a bank. It would drive me mad in a week. I want a career in the theatre and staying on at school really is a waste of time.'

Harry and Meg looked at each other. Harry lit his pipe and drew on it for a moment. Then, puffing out a cloud of aromatic

25

smoke he said. 'Listen – how about this? Leave school and get a job here in Millborough for a year. I'll go and have a word with your headmistress. I'm sure if you changed your mind she'd take you back. If you don't and you're still sure about what you want at the end of a year, then we'll think again.'

'I won't change my mind,' Laura said. 'Thanks, Dad. I'll do as you say. I can keep on with my lessons with Rosa.' She got up. 'I think I'll go to bed now. Goodnight.'

When she'd gone Meg glanced anxiously at her husband. 'What made you give in like that?'

'I didn't give in.' Harry smiled. 'Let her see what it's like in the real world. She'll soon realize what side her bread's buttered,' he said. 'All I'm doing is buying us a bit of time.'

Laura was still awake when her sister came to bed. Neither spoke as Moira undressed, but when she got into bed she turned to her sister.

'So – what are you going to do with your new-found freedom?' she asked. 'I hear they're looking for girls at Shearing's and of course there's always Woolworth's.'

'I'm not too proud to do either,' Laura said rebelliously. 'Anything will do until I can get a job in the theatre.'

Moira laughed. 'That'll be the day! You'll finish up with no job and no prospects like that pathetic Vicky Watts.'

Laura stared at her sister. 'She's not pathetic! Perhaps you'd like to live the kind of life she has.'

'I'm sure I don't know what kind of life she leads,' Moira said. 'And I don't care either. All I know is that she's a freak with her stringy hair and her old-fashioned, home-made clothes.'

'Her mother died when she was ten and I heard that she has to look after her father. By all accounts he's a horrible man.'

'Oh dear, how *sad*,' Moira jeered.

Laura turned over abruptly. 'You really are as hard as nails, aren't you?' she said.

Moira punched her pillow. 'It doesn't do to be too soft if you want to get on in the world,' she said. 'You have to think of number one. That's something you're going to have to learn.

You're the one with all the chances and you're chucking them away for some daft dream of turning into Greta Garbo.' She raised herself on one elbow and looked down at her sister. 'You're going to wish you could turn the clock back, Laura. Believe me, you will, so don't say I didn't warn you!'

CHAPTER THREE

IN October Laura celebrated her seventeenth birthday and at the end of term she left Millborough High School for Girls. She left with no regrets at all, seeing it as a rite of passage, her first step on the road to adulthood and her new career, though she knew that it could not begin just yet. Mrs Griggs gave her more hours at the hairdresser's enabling her to increase her lessons with Rosa, and in the months that followed she took and passed RADA's bronze, silver and gold medals. The regional exams were held in St Mary's church hall in Millborough and when Laura took the gold at the end of the summer she was delighted to receive a pass with honours.

Rosa was thrilled. 'I've never put a student in for all three medals in one year before,' she said. 'But I knew you could do it – and you have. Congratulations, darling. Surely now your parents will take you seriously.'

But Meg and Harry Nightingale were more dismayed than delighted at their younger daughter's success.

'We'll never get her to go back to school now,' Meg complained. 'It's all that blooming Seymour woman's fault, filling her head with impossible ideas.' But in spite of their misgivings they grudgingly congratulated Laura, acknowledging the fact that she had worked extremely hard.

'Rosa says I should try for my LRAMDA next year,' Laura told them.

Harry shook his head. 'What's that when it's at home?'

'It stands for Licentiate of the Royal Academy of Music and Dramatic Art,' Laura explained. 'If I get that I'll be qualified to teach speech and drama.'

At this Harry perked up. 'Really? Oh well, that sounds sensible at least,' he said, nodding his head approvingly at his wife.

Although he hadn't said a lot to his family Harry was becoming increasingly worried about the situation in Germany. Hitler seemed set on conquering the world. The man was dangerous and mad. When Mr Chamberlain had returned from Munich last September brandishing the agreement he'd got Hitler to sign there had been a brief period of relief, but then in November there had been the disturbing news about the horror referred to as 'Crystal Night': the appalling abuse and victimization of the Jewish population and the confiscation of all their property. In Harry's opinion it was a crying shame that nothing was being done to stop Hitler. Where would he choose to strike next? Now there were rumours that Londoners were being supplied with air raid shelters. It was all very worrying. Although Nightingale's shop sold newspapers Harry was thankful for once that his wife and daughters only seemed to read the women's page. Meg would occasionally express her concern when they listened to the news together on the wireless in the evenings, but he always reassured her that everything would be all right. Now he wondered if perhaps he should have prepared her for the worst.

In April there was talk of the conscription and training of young men. Harry was glad he only had daughters. In May Italy signed a pact with Germany after Mussolini occupied Albania, and in July Hitler was at loggerheads with Poland over the vitally important port of Danzig.

Meanwhile Laura had begun studying hard for her LRAMDA. Now, with Moira away at teacher training college in Wales, she had her bedroom to herself to practise aloud as much as she needed to. The examination date was set for November and Laura was working hard, determined to pass.

She saw Peter infrequently these days. They were both busy, she with her job at Maison Griggs and he with his engineering studies at the technical college. He had joined the Air Training Corps the previous year and was full of enthusiasm for planes and flying. On Saturday evenings they would go to the pictures or a dance and occasionally Peter would borrow his father's car on a Sunday afternoon and drive Laura out to the airfield at Lansdowne Moor to watch the planes taking off.

'I've almost done my stint of flying with an instructor,' he told her. 'Just you wait till I get to do my first solo flight.'

But as the summer drew to a close, a crisis arose that no one, even the most optimistic, could ignore. Hitler seemed determined to invade Poland. The newspapers were full of it. Plans were set in place for the evacuation of British city children and gas masks were distributed to every household. Hitler was served with an ultimatum which he arrogantly chose to ignore. Then on Sunday, 3 September 1939, everyone's worst fears were realized. Great Britain declared war on Germany.

During the initial weeks apprehension and uncertainty reigned. Millborough received its share of evacuees from London, the pathetic hordes of bewildered children with their gas masks and name labels throwing the community into confusion. All places of entertainment were closed, throwing many people out of work. Iron railings were removed, ostensibly for the manufacture of guns and bombs, and monstrous, brick air-raid shelters and blast walls were hurriedly built in the streets.

Householders were instructed to black out their windows and everyone waited with bated breath for bombs to start dropping like rain out of the skies. But as the days and weeks passed and none of the expected horrors came to pass, things gradually settled back into a normal everyday pattern. Theatres and cinemas opened their doors to the public again for limited performances and the children even started making use of the shelters and blast walls in their street games. In many cases London parents came to take their children home again and the initial panic subsided.

Full of patriotism and determined to do his bit. Harry announced his intention of volunteering for the army.

'Surely you're too old!' a horrified Meg argued. 'You did your bit in the last lot.' She watched helplessly as he got ready to go to the recruiting office, knowing by the determined set of his jaw that nothing she could say would change his mind. 'What am I going to do here on my own without you?' she said in an attempt to appeal to his responsibility as father and husband.

Harry's expression remained resolute. 'The same as thousands of other wives will have to do, get on with life and make the best of it,' he said. 'You've got the shop so you'll always have an income and Millborough isn't an industrial town. Apart from the shoe factory there's nothing the Germans will want to knock out. You and the girls should be safe as long as you sit tight.'

'What about our Moira?'

'Moira's college in Wales should be safe enough, out there in the wilds,' Harry told her. 'If not they'll evacuate.'

But Meg needn't have worried. Much to his humiliation Harry was turned down for the army. The wound he had received as a young soldier on the Somme had resulted in arthritis in his hip and he failed his medical. Instead he was directed to the ARP and two weeks later he joined the Millborough section. Returning home after his enrolment he put on the dark navy battledress and paraded for Meg and Laura in the living-room, proudly donning the tin hat with ARP written in big white letters across the front.

'What's ARP stand for, Dad?' Laura asked.

'Air Raid Protection. The letters are so that people will recognize us easily in an air raid,' he explained. 'We'll be doing first aid and everything in the event of a raid 'cause we'll be first on the scene, see – before the fire or ambulance services. There's lots of training courses to go on.'

'And what about when there are no raids?' Meg asked.

'We'll be taking turns at manning the post,' Harry told her importantly. 'We'll be getting the early warnings, soon as the enemy planes are spotted flying over the Channel. And we'll have to patrol the streets, making sure that folks have blacked out their windows properly.'

'Sounds really important.' Meg smiled indulgently, saying a silent prayer of thanks that she could keep her husband safe at home. After all, it looked as though Millborough was going to be a safe area.

*

Laura was disappointed when she heard that her exam was cancelled.

'Don't worry. They'll get back to normal in a few months' time, like everything else,' Rosa assured her. 'Wouldn't surprise me if it wasn't all over by this time next year. Bullies like Hitler always cave in when people stand up to them. Anyway, look on the bright side. You'll have more time to study for it now.'

Laura was full of the news when she met Peter the following evening, but he had his own, more immediate news to impart.

'I've been called up.'

She stared at him. 'You mean you've got to go – to the war?' Somehow she hadn't expected him to be called up as soon as this. 'Will you go into the RAF?'

'You bet!' His eyes were bright as he turned to her. 'They can't get enough young pilots and I've already done quite a bit of training so they've snapped me and all the rest of the chaps in my group up.'

Laura swallowed hard. 'When will you have to go?'

'Next week.'

'*Next week*?' Her face dropped. 'Oh, Peter.'

He smiled down at her. 'Don't tell me you'll miss me.'

'Of course I'll miss you, silly. Now that my exam has been cancelled as well there'll be nothing to look forward to.'

'Well, you can fill your spare time writing long letters to me,' he told her.

'Oh, I will.'

He stopped and turned to look at her. 'We've known each other a long time, haven't we Laura?'

She laughed at his suddenly-grave expression. 'Yes, of course we have.'

'What I'm trying to say is, that I – well, I'm asking really – can I look on you as my girl, my *special* girl, I mean?'

Touched, she reached out to touch his cheek. 'Peter. Of course you can. I mean, there's no one else, is there – for either of us?'

'It'd mean an awful lot to me.' He took the hand that lay against his cheek and pulled her closer. 'As far as I'm concerned

32

there never will be anyone else, Laura. I've loved you for almost as long as I can remember.'

'Oh, Peter.' She slipped her arms around his neck and returned his soft kiss. 'I love you too. And I'll write to you every week – promise.' She looked anxiously into his eyes. 'And you will be careful, won't you?'

'You bet!' He grinned. 'Take a tough Jerry to catch me napping.' After a moment he pulled off the signet ring he wore on his little finger. Taking her hand he pushed it on to her index finger, the only one it fitted. 'There, wear it for me,' he said, pulling her close. 'It'll do till I can get you a proper one.'

Laura laid her cheek against his. 'I'll think of you every time I look at it,' she whispered.

At Maison Griggs the senior stylist joined the ATS and Shirley was promoted to be a fully-fledged hairdresser. Mrs Griggs asked Laura if she would like to take Shirley's place as apprentice.

'You know the salon and the way we work here,' she said. 'And if you want the place I'll waive the twenty pound premium and pay you a small wage. After all, you could almost say you've served an apprenticeship already.'

Laura had no illusions about her prospective position. Mrs Griggs knew which side her bread was buttered. Most of Millborough's young single women were more interested in joining the women's services or going into well-paid munitions work than paying the likes of Ada Griggs to teach them the craft of hairdressing. She would be little more than a general dogsbody – at everyone's beck and call all day long. On the other hand, she would be paid, albeit poorly. It would do as a stopgap. When she consulted her parents they were all for it.

'You'd have a trade at the end of it,' Meg pointed out. 'That would always come in useful. And it's generous of her to let you off the trainee's premium.'

So Laura began to work full time at Maison Griggs as a trainee hairdresser soon after her eighteenth birthday.

One Friday evening a couple of weeks later, when she was on

her way to Rosa's for a lesson, Vicky walked along with her on her way home. The other girl was quiet as they walked and suddenly she said, 'I feel a bit guilty about you taking that job at Griggs's.'

Laura turned to her in surprise. 'Why on earth should you feel guilty?'

'Well, if it wasn't for me you could have been working with your mum and dad at the shop.'

Laura laughed. 'I see enough of Mum and Dad and I'm sure you're a lot better at the job than I'd be,' she said. 'I know how much you like it.'

'Oh I do,' Vicky assured her. 'I love it; meeting all the people who come in and everything.' She glanced at Laura. 'But what about you? Do you like hairdressing?'

Laura pulled a face. 'I hate it to tell you the truth. I'm only doing it to help pay for my lessons with Miss Seymour. I hope to get a job in the theatre as soon as she thinks I'm ready.'

'You'll make a lovely actress,' Vicky said shyly. 'I wish I had your looks and – and talent.'

Laura was pleased and slightly taken aback by the remark. 'Oh, Vicky, what a nice thing to say. But you do have nice looks. You could. . . .' She broke off. She had been going to say, 'You could be very pretty if you made more of yourself,' but she stopped herself in time. 'You could do anything you wanted,' she said. 'You speak nicely and Mum says you're really bright and quick to learn.'

'I'd quite like to have joined one of the services,' Vicky said wistfully. 'I've never had the chance to go anywhere but Millborough. It would have been nice to meet people and see the world – make some friends of my own age.'

'So, why don't you?'

Vicky shook her head. 'I can't. There's Dad you see. I have to look after him now that he's bed-ridden, but he'd never have let me anyway even if he wasn't ill.'

'What's wrong with him?' Laura asked.

Vicky shrugged. 'It's his leg. It was badly injured in an accident at work years ago. It's ulcerated now. He can hardly bear to stand on it, but he won't see a doctor. It worries me.'

'Couldn't you just send for the doctor?'

Vicky shook her head. 'He'd be furious with me if I did that. He's never joined a panel you see, so he'd have to pay. He hates having to part with money. I'd never hear the last of it.'

'So you have to look after him? Do you have any help?'

Vicky shook her head. 'No, there's just me. Dad'd never trust anyone else.'

'It can't be easy.'

'No. It isn't. Sometimes it's. . . .' She stopped and in the dim evening light Laura saw that Vicky's eyes were bright with tears. She told herself that she was lucky. Maybe her parents didn't approve of her acting aspirations but it was only because they cared about her. At least she'd had every chance in life and a mum and dad who did their best. On impulse she slipped her arm through Vicky's and gave it a little squeeze.

'Cheer up,' she said. 'And if you want to have a good moan any time I'm always ready to listen even if I can't do much to help.'

Vicky stared at Laura in amazement. Hers was the first real offer of friendship she had ever had. 'Well – same here of course, though I don't suppose *you* ever have anything to moan about,' she said.

Laura shook her head. 'Peter, my boyfriend, has just been called up. He's gone into the air force. I hope he's going to be all right,' she said.

'Oh, so do I, but I'm sure he will.'

Laura opened the top button of her coat and pulled out Peter's ring which she wore on a chain round her neck. 'He asked me to wear his ring for him,' she confided. 'He put it on my finger but it kept slipping off. Anyway, I didn't want people asking questions about it.' She slipped the ring back inside the neck of her jumper. 'It's nice, knowing it's just between him and me and feeling it there.'

Vicky's heart lifted. It was so good to have another girl of her own age to talk to. And being trusted with her special secret was the best compliment she had ever had.

Every Friday evening Vicky's father had a visitor. Sid Taylor was a man in his early thirties. He was tall and thin with greasy, slicked back hair and his jaw was permanently dark with bristly stubble. Vicky hated the shifty way he looked at her, with his oddly colourless eyes. She felt instinctively that he wasn't to be trusted. But Dan seemed to like him well enough and, as he was the only visitor her father ever had, Vicky kept her opinions to herself.

He arrived as usual that Friday evening at six o'clock. Vicky answered the door and stepped aside for him to go upstairs to Dan's bedroom. As he brushed past her, closer than necessary in the narrow hallway, his eyes swept over her.

'Lookin' lovely as always, Vicky,' he muttered.

Vicky shuddered. She did not look lovely and she was all too aware of the fact. She'd been scrubbing the scullery and had a rough sacking apron on over her skirt. Her hair needed washing too, so why was he paying her compliments? 'Dad's waiting for you,' she said abruptly as she closed the street door. 'Go on up.'

Sid did not stay long. It was barely twenty minutes later when he appeared in the kitchen doorway, eyeing her as she stood peeling potatoes at the sink, her back to him.

'Yer dad don't seem too good tonight,' he remarked.

She hadn't noticed him standing there and his voice made her start. She wished he wouldn't creep about so. 'No,' she said. 'His leg's bad.'

' 'As he seen the doctor?'

Vicky felt like asking him what business it was of his. Instead she shook her head. 'He won't let me send for him,' she said.

'Maybe you should just do it anyway.'

Vicky put down her knife and turned to look him in the eye. 'I do the best I can,' she said.

Unperturbed, he took out a crumpled packet of Woodbines and stuck one between his lips, his eyes on her as he lit it. 'I'm sure you do,' he said, blowing out a cloud of smoke. 'He's a lucky

fella, 'avin' a lovely young daughter like you lookin' after ''im.'
His shifty eyes swept over her from head to foot, making her
flush with embarrassment. 'Doin' anythin' special tomorra night,
are you, Vicky?'

'I've always got plenty to do,' Vicky told him, her flesh crawl-
ing at the thought of spending an evening with Sid. 'And if you
don't mind, I've got Dad's tea to see to now, so if there's nothing
else. . . .'

'Oh, hoity-toity.' He grinned, displaying crooked, tobacco-
stained teeth. 'Be like that then. Still, I like a girl with a bit of
spirit. See you next Friday, Vick. Be good.' He turned on his heel
and left the kitchen.

She waited, holding her breath until she heard the front door
slam then hurried through to turn the key in the lock. What her
dad saw in that man she'd never understand.

Half an hour later she carried the tray upstairs. Dan's bed
looked rumpled and she put the tray down and began to
straighten the bedclothes.

'Don't fiddle, girl!' Dan snapped. 'Leave things alone, can't
you. I want me tea. I thought you was never comin'.'

Vicky ignored him, tucking in the sheets and plumping up the
pillows. 'Sid didn't stay long tonight,' she said. 'Everything all
right, was it?'

'What d'yer mean?' Dan asked suspiciously.

'Nothing. He said you didn't seem well. I wondered if you'd
fallen out.'

'Oh, you'd like that, wouldn't you?' Dan began to tuck into
the stew and potatoes. 'Never did go much on Sid, did yer? You
can bet yer life he won't fall out with me though. Knows which
side his bread's buttered, does Sid.'

Vicky frowned. 'What do you mean?'

'Never you mind, girl. None o' your business.' He stirred the
bowl of stew with his spoon. 'Not much meat in this, is there?'

Vicky shook her head. 'It's all I could get at the butcher's. We
don't get much on the ration.'

Dan snorted. 'You'd think a man who's an invalid would be

entitled to a bit more. As if I don't 'ave enough to put up with without being slowly starved to death by the bleedin' government.'

Vicky took a deep breath and said daringly, 'As a matter of fact, Sid thinks you should let the doctor look at your leg.'

'He *what*?' Dan's face turned purple. 'Had the bloody nerve to say that, did he? Cheeky bugger! You should'a told him to mind his own flamin' business.'

Vicky leaned forward to wipe a trickle of gravy from his chin. 'But he's right, you know, Dad. I'm sure the doctor would give you something to ease the pain. You'd like to get up and about again, wouldn't you?'

Dan pushed her hand away roughly. 'Leave *orf*! I'm not tellin' you again. I'm not 'avin' no quack pokin' me about. So just shut yer mouth about it and go and get me puddin'.' He glared at her. 'That's if there *is* a puddin'? Or 'as the soddin' government done me outta that as well?'

After Vicky had eaten a solitary supper and washed up she went into the rarely-used parlour and sat down at the piano. Playing the music her mother had taught her was her only form of relaxation. Dad didn't like it but he had looked asleep when she fetched his supper tray. If she applied the soft pedal she wouldn't disturb him.

Taking out the music from the piano stool she selected a Chopin waltz that had been a particular favourite of her mother's and began to play. The old instrument was badly in need of tuning but as the tinny notes echoed round the room she could almost imagine that Mum was sitting beside her again. She came to the end of the piece, paused a moment, her eyes closed, then began the lovely melody again. But she had only played the first few bars when there came a loud thumping on the ceiling. Getting up, she went to the door and called up the stairs,

'What is it, Dad? What do you want?'

'Shut up that bleedin' racket, can't you?' Dan's voice rang out. 'Hammerin' away just like yer ma used to. It's enough to drive a bloke barmy.'

'Sorry, Dad.'

'You got no consideration, bangin' away on the bloody pianner when I'm lyin' up 'ere in agony! Just make yerself useful and get me a cup of tea, you stupid tart!'

Vicky turned back into the room, her eyes pricking with tears, a lump in her throat. Was she never to be allowed a life of her own?

CHAPTER FOUR

'THANK you, dear. That looks very nice.' Mrs Gittings smiled as Laura held up the mirror for her to see the rigid waves and rows of tiny curls at the back. 'My Fred's got a forty-eight hour leave,' she said, patting her new coiffeur with satisfaction. 'He'll be home tonight so I thought I'd better make the effort.' She slipped her arms into the sleeves of the coat Laura held out for her.

'Well, I hope you have a nice weekend with him,' Laura folded the used towels and gathered up her scissors and comb.

'Got to make the best of it. It'll be the first leave he's had since he was called up,' Mrs Gittings complained. 'I dread him telling me it's embarkation leave. So many of my neighbours have got hubbies or sons going off to fight abroad.' She heaved a sigh. 'Never know when you'll see them again do you – or even *if*. All them poor fellas at Dunkirk last year. Thank God my Fred wasn't in that lot.'

'Best to look on the bright side, eh? 'Bye then, Mrs Gittings.' Laura finally closed the door behind her last customer and drew a deep breath Another week over, thank goodness.

She had just completed her first year working full time at Maison Griggs. It had taken a while to master the finger waving and reverse pin curling that most of Ada's customers requested and Ada Griggs would allow no one to use the electric permanent waving machine with its countless wires and clips. But although Laura had become quite a capable hairdresser she still found little fulfilment in the job. It was true that she found a certain satisfaction in work well done and got along with her clients well enough – apart from the ones for whom nothing would ever be right. But her ambition to be an actress and her frustration with the time it seemed to be taking to achieve her dream grew stronger as the months passed. Many of the small repertory companies up and down the country accepted students, but as with other apprenticeships it was usual for them to demand a premium and most of Laura's meagre earnings went on acting lessons. She knew it would take years to save enough money for the longed-for day when she would actually step on to the stage of a real theatre.

'Old mother Gittings hung about a bit, didn't she? I thought you'd never get rid of her.' Shirley was still busily backcombing the front of her hair at the cracked mirror in the cramped little back kitchen that Ada Griggs insisted on calling 'the staff room'. Along with most of the younger generation of women she had adopted the latest hair style: long and curling over the shoulders and piled as high as possible at the front.

Laura laughed. 'Listen to you – *old mother Gittings*? She can't be more than thirty.'

'*Thirty*! Flippin' 'eck! That's old isn't it?' Shirley retorted. 'I can't even imagine being thirty, can you?' Shirley applied lipstick to her pouting lips. 'I met this fella last Saturday at the dance,' she confided. 'He's a soldier, stationed quite near here so I reckon I'll be seeing him again. Eddie's his name and he's a bit of all right – lovely brown eyes and wavy hair.' She winked at Laura through the mirror. 'Tall, dark 'n handsome! Heard from your Peter lately, have you?'

'He tries to write every week but they're so busy now that he's been posted.'

Every Friday evening Laura wrote to Peter, trying to make her disappointments and frustrations sound light-hearted and funny. Writing the letters helped in a way, they put things into perspective for her and made her see the funny side of things too. Like Mrs Gittings's husband, Peter hadn't had leave for months and in his last letter he had told her that it was doubtful he would even make it home for Christmas. She missed him so much. Laura knew that he had been sadly disappointed when he was first called up. His ambition had always been to become a fighter pilot and to fly Spitfires, but because of his engineering qualification he had been chosen to train as a flight engineer instead. Six months ago he had been posted to a bomber squadron stationed in Hampshire. Secretly Laura was glad he wasn't a Spitfire pilot. So many brave young men had lost their lives in what Mr Churchill called the Battle of Britain, but hearing about the Germans' frequent attacks on airfields in the south of England lately she wondered now if what he was doing was just as dangerous.

It was dark as Laura walked home. Black-out time was early now and there were no friendly lamplighters any more to light the way for her. She fumbled in her handbag for her torch and switched it on, careful to direct it at the ground. As she walked, she wondered what Mum would have for supper. Meg managed well considering all the shortages and the meagreness of the rations. Money was tight too. The takings at the shop had gone down now that sweets were scarce. Tobacco also was in short supply but the sale of newspapers had doubled. Everyone wanted to read the news nowadays and clustered eagerly round their wireless sets every night at nine o'clock to follow the progress of the war. Most of the shop owners in Jessop Street helped each other out, sending round the word when they had a delivery so that their fellow traders had first pick. Meg was friendly with the owner of Maidley's fish shop, so the Nightingales often had fish for supper when the meat ration had been used up.

So far the terrifying blitz that had been raging relentlessly over London and other major cities had not affected Millborough directly, although the sirens sounded most nights as German bombers flew over on their way to Coventry some fifty miles away. The sight of the great dark hordes that filled the skies and the menacing sound of their throbbing engines filled the residents with dread and many people spent the night in the shelters. Occasionally a damaged bomber, limping home after a raid would jettison its bombs randomly and on one such occasion the town centre had been hit, destroying several buildings and killing two unfortunate fire-watchers.

Harry continued with his ARP work, taking it all very conscientiously. He had attended all the courses and was very proud of his status as chief warden at the local post. Many of the more hapless local inhabitants on his route had good reason to dread his booming call of 'Put that light out!' as he did his nightly rounds.

The shop was just about to close when Laura got home. Vicky was putting on her coat and winding her scarf around her neck as Laura walked in.

'Hello, Laura. Your mum's just gone up to get the supper. She said to ask you to lock up before you go upstairs.' She handed Laura a canvas bag. 'I keep telling her that the day's takings ought to go in the night-safe, but she says it might get bombed and then where would you be.'

Laura took the bag. 'I know. It's not safe keeping so much cash in the flat, but she won't be told.' She looked closely at the other girl. 'You look tired, Vicky. Are you all right?'

Vicky nodded. 'It's just Dad. His leg doesn't get any better.' She paused, looking at her feet. 'Neither does his temper.'

'I'm sorry.' Moved to pity by the other girl's down-trodden expression Laura had a sudden idea. 'Tell you what – we don't open on Mondays at Mrs Griggs's. Why don't I ask Mum if you can have the afternoon off so that you and I can go to the pictures?'

Vicky flushed with pleasure. '*Oh*! I'd love that – but your mum. . . .'

'Leave her to me,' Laura told her. 'I'm sure she won't mind.'

Vicky bit her lip. 'But Dad. . . .'

'You'd be here anyway so he needn't know, need he? Unless you want to tell him of course.'

'I suppose not.'

'Is that a date then? I'll ask Mum tonight.'

'Oh – I don't know.'

'They've got *Rebecca* next week at the Plaza,' Laura tempted.

'Laurence Olivier and Joan Fontaine are lovely in it, so they say.'

Vicky sighed. 'Oh, I'd love to see that.'

'Right then, leave it to me. We'll sort out the details tomorrow.'

Upstairs Meg was busy in the kitchen, clearly in a good mood by the sound of her singing. Harry sat reading the evening paper in front of the fire. He looked up as Laura came in.

'Your mum's got a bit of news,' he said, nodding his head towards the kitchen. 'Good news, as you might guess by the sound of it.'

Laura went through to the kitchen. 'Can I help, Mum?'

Meg took a steaming casserole dish out of the oven. 'It's all done, love,' she said. 'I hope you're hungry. I managed to get a nice piece of liver and some bacon scraps – off ration at the butcher's, so I've made a casserole.'

'Dad says you've got some news – good news.'

Meg put the hot dish down on the table and straightened up, her face flushed. 'I had a letter from Moira,' she said. 'She's coming home.'

'Home? She hasn't given up her training course has she?'

'No, but apparently she's got to the stage where she needs to do some practical work. She asked if she could be assigned to a school here in Millborough and they've got her a place at Snape Street Elementary, starting in January.'

'But this is such a long way from her college.'

'They've tried to get the girls places in the safe areas where the schools are overcrowded with evacuees and you know what it's been like here,' Meg said. 'They've had classes in halls and meeting-rooms, even in the church. And they're so short of teachers with the men away.' She took the plates down from the warming rack above the cooker and began to dish up. 'A great piece of luck, isn't it? Of course, she'll have to go back to college for a few days each month but it's only for another twelve months and then she'll be qualified. It'll be so nice to have her home again, won't it?'

Laura was hardly listening. Her exam had been scheduled at

last for early in the new year and now she would be sharing a room with her sister again just when she needed her own space in which to study. Holier-than-thou Moira who made spiteful fun of the dream that was closest to her heart.

'You don't look very pleased.' Meg was staring at her.

'What? Oh no, I mean *yes*! It's really good news,' Laura said, her heart sinking. Preoccupied as she was with the prospect of Moira's impending return she almost forgot to ask her mother if Vicky could have the afternoon off on Monday. When she remembered and asked towards the end of the meal, Meg looked puzzled.

'An afternoon off – why couldn't she ask me herself? Is it to do with her father?'

'No. I thought it would be nice for her to have a little treat,' Laura explained. 'So I asked her if she'd like to go to the pictures with me.'

Meg bridled. 'Oh, you did, did you? In my time! You might have asked me first.'

'I know. I'm sorry, Mum. It was just that she looked so tired and washed out and I asked her on impulse.'

Meg nodded. 'Poor girl, I don't think she has much of a life of it. Yes, I suppose it's all right. We're never very busy of a Monday.'

Laura and Vicky enjoyed the film enormously; Laura dreamt of playing the Joan Fontaine part whilst Vicky fantasized about meeting a handsome man like Maxim de Winter and being swept off her feet and removed from Artillery Terrace for good. As they came out of the cinema into the darkening street Laura asked Vicky what she would be doing for Christmas. The other girl sighed.

'Nothing really. Dad doesn't really hold with Christmas. He says it's just a way to get folks to spend money.'

Laura looked at her. 'You mean you don't have presents or a special dinner or anything?'

Vicky shook her head. 'When Mum was alive we used to, but not now.'

'What a shame. Well, you—' Laura broke off as a man suddenly loomed up in front of them, a tall thin man wearing a grubby mackintosh.

' 'Ello, Vick. Fancy meetin' you.'

Vicky visibly shrank. 'Sid! Good evening.'

He leered. '*Good evenin'* is it? Oh, *very* formal, ain't we?' He glanced at Laura. 'Who's yer friend then?

'This is Laura – Laura Nightingale.'

'From the shop where you work?'

'That's right.'

'I see, gettin' yer feet under the table, are you?' He took a step closer. 'Yer Dad know you've been to the pictures when you're supposed to be workin', does he?'

Vicky flushed. 'I don't think it's any of your business,' she said.

He laughed. 'Oh, you'd be surprised what me business is.' He reached out to touch her arm. 'I might come round yours to see you tonight, Vick. Be at home, will you? Or are you off gaddin' again.'

Before she could reply he walked off into the gloom, chuckling to himself.

'What a horrible creepy man!' Laura said. 'Who is he?' As she turned to look at Vicky she was shocked to see how badly shaken she was by the exchange.

'His name's Sid Taylor. He's a friend of Dad's. He's the only person who ever comes to see him so I have to put up with him. I dread Friday nights when he comes round. He comes down to the kitchen afterwards and he's always making – remarks.'

'I'd have thought a man of his age would have been called up by now.' Laura said.

'I know. I kept hoping he would be, but so far he hasn't.'

Laura took the other girl's arm. 'Don't let him get you down,' she said. 'He's got no right to intimidate you like that. You should stand up for yourself. Look, let's go and have a cup of tea – my treat.' But Vicky shook her head.

'Thanks, Laura, but I'd better not. I've got to go and get something for Dad's supper before the shops close.' She looked at

Laura with glistening eyes. 'Thanks ever so much for asking me to go to the film with you. I really loved it. It's just a pity that—'

'That that horrible man had to go and spoil it,' Laura finished for her. 'Well, don't let him. All right then, Vicky. Mind how you go. See you tomorrow.'

True to his word Sid came round to Artillery Terrace that evening. Vicky had been jumpy ever since she got home and when she heard a tap on the back door as she was washing up the supper things, her heart jumped into her mouth. For a moment she stood rooted to the spot, praying that whoever it was would go away again, but the tapping came again, more insistently and this time accompanied by Sid's voice hissing through the keyhole.

'Come on, Vick, open up. I know you're in there.'

She put down her tea towel and opened the door a crack. 'What do you want? It's not Friday.'

He chuckled. 'I'd worked that out for meself. It's you I want to talk to, not yer dad.'

'Why? What do you want?'

'Do you want me to yell it out 'ere where all the neighbours can 'ear?' He put his face close to the door. 'Not to mention yer dad. You know 'e's got ears like a bat.'

Reluctantly she opened the door and let him into the kitchen. 'Say what you have to say and go. Dad will be wanting a cup of tea and I have to get on.'

'Cup of tea, eh?' Sid sat himself down at the table. 'That sounds nice. Don't mind if I do.' He looked her up and down in the way she found so repellent. 'Told 'im you'd been to the pictures with your boss's daughter, 'ave you?' Vicky was silent and he chuckled. 'Thought not. So what's it worth for me not to spill the beans?'

She turned to face him. 'It's not a secret. Tell him if you want to.'

'Oh, you reckon 'e won't mind, do you – even when 'e knows you're knockin' about with a girl who's goin' on the stage?'

Vicky felt her cheeks warm. Sid knew as well as she did how bigoted and narrow-minded Dan was about such things. He considered anyone in the world of entertainment no better than immoral. 'Why are you threatening me?' she asked. 'What have I ever done to you?'

He stood up and came towards her. 'Nuthin'. There's a lot you *could* do for me though.'

Vicky stepped back until she could feel the sink pressing against her back. 'I don't know what you mean, and – and I don't *want* to know,' she said breathlessly. 'Anyway, why aren't you in the army?'

If she had meant the remark as a diversion it failed to work. 'Flat feet,' Sid told her coolly. 'That and me asthma. Something chronic me chest is in the winter.' He tapped his chest and coughed by way of demonstration, sending a wave of stale tobacco-laden breath into her face. He took another step towards her and leered into her eyes. 'Not a lot much wrong with *your* chest though, is there, Vick? Got a lovely pair, you 'ave. 'Ow about a little kiss then?'

Vicky felt the bile rise in her throat as one large groping hand reached out to her. Putting both hands against his chest she pushed him as hard as she could. '*Get out!*' she shouted. 'Get out or I'll tell Dad you molested me.'

For a moment he looked shocked as he staggered backwards. 'You don't wanna be nasty to me, Vick,' he said, his eyes narrowing. 'I really like you. Play your cards right and I reckon you 'n me could make a go of things.'

She turned her back on him, her hands grasping the edge of the sink. 'Just *go!*'

'Your dad ain't gonna last much longer you know.' He whispered the words into her ear and she felt him standing close behind her. 'What're you gonna do then, eh, Vick? Where'll you go? Could you afford to stay 'ere on what you earn at Nightingale's? I know the rent's not much but I bet they pay you next to nowt. You're gonna be out on yer uppers when your dad pops 'is clogs. You're gonna need a husband who'll take good care of you.'

'I don't need anybody,' Vicky told him. 'If anything happened to Dad I'd – I'd join one of the services.'

That seemed to take the wind out of his sails for a moment then he laughed. 'The *services*?' he sneered. 'Can't see *you* in the ATS or the WAAFs. They want gels with skills and a bit of savvy. You can't do nuthin'. You're just a stupid little tart. Fit for nowt but a man's bed and it's about time you faced it. You won't get a better offer than mine in a hurry, so think on.'

She went to the door and opened it. 'Clear out, Sid Taylor!' she said, her heart beating fast. 'And don't you ever speak to me like that again.'

As he flung past her he shot her a look of pure venom. 'You'll live to be sorry you said them things to me, Vicky Mason, you mark my words.'

On Monday evenings Laura had a two hour session with Rosa. Soon it would be Christmas and the time for her exam would be almost upon them. She'd waited so long for it and she was so anxious to do well. This one was more demanding than the other three. A piece from Shakespeare involving three characters, one of them male; a modern piece, this time a light comedy by Noël Coward involving two characters, and to finish, whatever sight-reading they gave her. She had learned the lines of both set pieces. Now it was just a question of perfecting the acting.

Rosa's studio was warm and relaxing and she began as always with breathing and voice warming exercises. She was halfway through the Shakespeare when Rosa held up her hand.

'Stop there for a minute and come and sit down.' When Laura was seated she smiled gently. 'What's wrong, darling?' She peered into Laura's eyes. 'You're not yourself tonight. I could tell the moment you began.'

'I knew it would affect my work.' Laura sighed. 'I had some news at the end of last week and I've been worried about it ever since. My sister's coming home from college to do her practical training in Millborough.'

'So why should that be so worrying?'

'With it being so close to the exam it's a disaster. We have to share a room, you see and there'll be nowhere I can rehearse.'

'But she's studying herself. Surely she'll understand and be sympathetic.'

Laura shook her head. 'You don't know Moira. She's always sniping at my ambition to be an actress. She thinks it's silly and frivolous and that I should be doing something sensible, like her.'

'It wouldn't do for us all to be the same, would it?' Rosa smiled. 'Has it occurred to you that she might be just a little bit jealous?'

'Not Moira.' Laura looked at her tutor with desperate eyes. 'If I fail this I don't know what I'll do, Rosa. I've worked so hard for it.'

'I know, darling, and I'm sure you're worrying for nothing. You're going to pass with flying colours. Look, I'll tell you what: why don't you come round here after work each evening? You can have my little box room and rehearse to your heart's content. How's that?'

'Could I really?'

'Of course. It's at the top of the house so you won't disturb anyone. You can rant as much as you like.' She laughed. 'Now – shall we try the Shakespeare again or would you like to have a go at the Noël Coward?'

When the session was over and they were having their customary cup of tea in the kitchen, Laura asked Rosa if she thought she'd ever be able to get a job with a professional company. 'Even if I've got all my RADA qualifications I'd still have to pay a premium to join a repertory company, wouldn't I?'

'I'm afraid so. You'd need to serve your time as a professional before you could get your Equity card.'

Laura sighed despondently. 'It looks as though I'll have to join one of the women's services. I'm fed up with hairdressing and I can't face living at home with Moira again.'

Rosa stroked her chin thoughtfully for a moment, then she looked at Laura. 'Would you consider going into ENSA?' she asked.

'ENSA?' Laura stared at her. 'Do you think they'd have me?'

Rosa laughed. 'I'm sure they'd snap you up with open arms, my darling.'

'Really?' Laura's face was flushed with excitement.

'Wait a minute. Don't get too excited. It's no picnic, you know,' Rosa warned. 'Going abroad to all the danger spots to entertain the troops. You should think about it very carefully and discuss it with your parents. I daresay they'll be against it.' She held up her hand as Laura began to protest. 'You probably wouldn't get to do what you want either,' she said. 'You could be sent out with a concert party or a variety company. You might not even get the chance to do any serious acting at all.'

'But I would get my Equity card at the end of it – yes?'

'Well, yes.'

'Then I'll do it,' Laura said. 'Where do I go? Who do I contact?'

'Hey – not so fast!' Rosa laughed. 'Just go home and test the water. See what your parents feel about it. After all, you're very young. In the meantime I've got one or two contacts and I'll put out some feelers. Are you happy to leave it with me?'

Laura nodded eagerly. 'Of course. Thank you, Rosa. I'll talk to Mum and Dad about it this evening.'

'ENSA? Have you taken leave of your senses, girl?' Harry thundered.

Meg looked startled. 'Why should you go and risk your life, you silly girl? All for the sake of prancing about on a stage?'

'In another year I'll be called up anyway,' Laura pointed out. 'You read the news, Dad. All women between the ages of twenty and thirty. It was in the papers last week. Some will be trained for anti-aircraft crews. There's a war on, Mum We're all in danger.'

'You think I don't know that!' Meg snapped. 'I lived through the last one, didn't I? There's no need to run your head into it though, is there?'

Harry leaned forward. 'Talking of the news, I take it neither of you have heard the latest?' Both Laura and her mother looked at him and he sat back, glad to have their undivided attention at last.

'What do you mean – what's happened, Dad?' Laura asked.

'The Japs have only gone and bombed Pearl Harbor, that's all,' Harry announced.

Meg frowned. 'Where's Pearl Harbor when it's at home?'

'Hawaii. There's a big American naval base there – hundreds killed.' Harry shook his head as both women stared at him uncomprehendingly. 'They've bombed bases in the Philippines too. The Japs have joined forces with the Germans and declared war on us,' he explained. 'And by these bombing raids they've involved the Yanks as well. It's proper world war we're in now and no mistake. And here's you,' he pointed a finger at his daughter, 'here's you calmly talking about joining ENSA and going out there amongst it all! A blood bath – that's what it's going to be. *A bloody blood bath*!'

CHAPTER FIVE

M<small>AISON</small> Griggs grew progressively busy in the weeks preceding Christmas. Ada did a record number of perms for women who were expecting husbands or boyfriends home for the holiday.

'Time you learned to do this,' she told Laura one day. 'We could do double the number of perms if I had someone else competent enough to use the machine.'

'Why not show Shirley?' Laura asked, reluctant to tell her boss that she intended to leave the minute the opportunity presented itself.

Ada pulled a face. 'I hardly think it needs saying, dear.' She lowered her voice. 'That girl's head is full of nothing but dancing and young men these days. I wouldn't dare leave her in charge of anything so risky.'

Earlier that year the newspapers had been full of a story about a woman in the south of England who had been fatally electrocuted by the permanent waving machine and Ada had been extra cautious ever since. Laura realized that it was a compliment to be asked to train to use the machine. Ada must trust her. All the same she was terrified by the mere look of the fearful contraption with its snake-like mass of wires and hot clips.

Moira arrived home the day before Christmas Eve. She looked well and had a new air of optimistic confidence about her that sent Laura's heart plummeting. Over supper on the night she arrived she was full of all she was learning and the new friends she had made.

'I'm looking forward so much to doing some practical teaching work here at Snape Street Elementary.' She turned to look at her sister. 'And how about you? I don't seem to have heard much about your progress lately. Hollywood hasn't discovered you yet then?'

'Laura's going to be learning how to use the perming machine at Mrs Griggs's,' Meg told her proudly.

'*Really?*' Moira turned to her sister with a smirk. 'How super!'

'I've got my exam soon after Christmas,' Laura put in quickly. She knew her mother set far more store on learning to use the perming machine than passing her exam. 'And after that Rosa's going to try and get me an audition with ENSA.'

'*ENSA?*' Moira laughed. 'Oh yes, I've heard of that. Every Night Something Awful. Isn't that what they say it stands for?' She spluttered over the joke, looking at Laura whose cheeks had turned pink. 'Well, the best of British luck. I mean, you're going to need it aren't you!'

'That's what I've told her,' Meg said, completely missing the point. 'Why run headlong into trouble when you could stay at home?'

'Yes, learning to use the perming machine with Mrs Griggs!' Moira finished. 'Exactly! I agree with you, Mum.'

Seething, Laura rose and began to clear the plates. 'I'll start the washing up, shall I, Mum?'

'Need any help?' Moira started to get up but Meg waved her hand. 'No. You sit by the fire and talk to your dad,' she said. 'You've had a long train journey. You must be tired.'

Christmas looked like being an ordeal. Moira's boyfriend, David, was home on leave and she lost no time in pressing home the fact to Laura.

'What a shame that Peter couldn't make it,' she said brushing her new longer hairstyle at the dressing table in the room they shared. 'Still, I daresay they'll make the most of it down there in Hampshire. There'll be dances at the camp with plenty of WAAFs to partner them.' She smiled. 'Theirs is quite the smartest uniform of all the women's services, don't you think? Maybe he won't be all that sorry not to come home to boring old Millborough.'

'You seem happy enough to come home,' Laura countered.

'Ah well, *I'm* furthering my career prospects,' Moira said. 'I've no intention of making any kind of future here.'

Laura bit her tongue and said nothing. She had decided not to let anything upset her before the exam. All her mental energy must be focused on that. Peter had sent her a card with a picture of a Lancaster bomber on it. He enclosed a pretty silver bracelet with a tiny horseshoe charm. In the enclosed letter he wrote that he loved and missed her and that the bracelet was to bring her luck for the coming exam.

Ada closed the salon early on Christmas Eve and Laura went round to see Peter's mother with a card and a small present before she went home. Ethel Radcliffe was a widow. Peter's father had died when he was still at school and she'd had a struggle to keep her only son on at the technical college until he qualified. She worked in the office at Shearing's shoe factory and when Laura called round she had just arrived home.

'Come in, dear. How lovely to see you,' she said. 'I've got the kettle on. The office closed officially at lunchtime today but I've been doing some overtime. We're short-staffed and run off our feet now that Shearing's has got the contract for army boots.' She opened the living-room door. 'I'm sorry it's so chilly in here. When I'm out all day it doesn't seem worth lighting a fire in the mornings.' She picked up the matches from the mantelpiece and lit the gas fire. 'It'll soon warm up. Do sit down dear,' she offered, going through to the kitchen. 'Tea'll only take a jiffy. It's such a pity Peter couldn't get leave. I miss him so much.'

'So do I. What will you be doing tomorrow, Mrs Radcliffe?' Laura asked.

'Oh, don't worry about me. I'm going to my sister's,' Ethel said, coming back with the tea tray. 'She's got her grandchildren coming so it'll be nice to be with them all. Christmas is for kids really, isn't it?'

'Well, as long as you're not going to be on your own.'

Ethel sat down opposite Laura and began to pour the tea. 'It's kind of you to think of me, Laura. I do worry about Peter, of course. He's all I've got. I try not to be an old fuss-pot, as he calls me, but I'm sure you know how I feel.' She unwrapped the box of embroidered hankies that Laura had brought her and exclaimed with delight. 'Oh, how pretty! Thank you, dear. You know, I always tell Peter that he's lucky to have found a steady girl like you. Not that he doesn't know it of course.' She shook her head. 'The way some girls carry on nowadays. Not only the single ones either. Disgraceful I call it.'

To Meg's disappointment Moira spent Christmas afternoon and evening with David's family. It was after eleven when he brought her home and the pair burst in, both of them flushed and bright-eyed.

'We've got something to tell you,' Moira burst out. David put a restraining hand on her arm.

'Wait a minute,' he said. 'I have to be the one to ask.' He turned, solemn faced to Harry and cleared his throat. 'A-hem. Mr Nightingale, I – er – want to ask you for your daughter's hand in marriage.' He gazed from Harry to Meg and back again, scarlet to the tips of his ears. 'Er, um – please.'

Harry rose slowly from his armchair with all the dignity he could muster. 'Well now, this is unexpected,' he began.

'*That* it's not,' Meg interrupted. 'They've been walking out for ages. Come on Father, put the poor boy out of his misery.'

They all laughed and Harry shook his head good-naturedly. 'Well, I don't know, I'm sure! Can't a man give the poor boy a proper answer in his own home?' He smiled. 'Yes, of course you can marry Moira, son – if she'll have you. Good luck to the both of you.'

Moira kissed her mother and father and turned to take David's hand. 'We're getting the ring as soon as the shops open again and we want the wedding to be quite soon. David thinks he might be sent abroad before long.'

Meg looked uncomfortable. 'In that case, don't you think you should wait awhile?' She looked at her elder daughter. 'I mean –

what about your training and getting a job afterwards? I thought they didn't encourage married women.'

'Of course they do, Mum,' Moira said. 'They need all the teachers they can get nowadays. I think things are going to be very different after the war. Anyway, I want to work and start saving up for our home.' She gazed up at David, squeezing his arm. 'We thought it could probably be on David's next leave.'

'Oh. Well, I suppose it's all right then.' Meg looked at her husband. 'Looks as if we're going to have to save up for a wedding.'

Later in their room Laura offered her sister her own congratulations. 'I hope I'm here to see you married,' she said. 'Who knows, I might be halfway round the world by then.'

'I suppose that means you won't be able to be my bridesmaid then,' Moira said.

'Oh! I hadn't thought of that!' Laura reached out a hand to Moira. 'I'd love to be your bridesmaid if you want me to. And I will, if I'm still here.'

'Well, we'll all have to live in hope then, won't we?' Moira said.

In spite of her father's protests that Christmas should be the same as any other day, Vicky had managed to get a nice piece of beef which she roasted carefully so as not to cause too much shrinkage. She cooked sprouts and roasted potatoes to go with it and made a Yorkshire pudding. She was in the middle of the preparations when there came a knock on the back door. She opened it and found to her dismay that Sid Taylor stood on the step.

'What do you want?' she asked sharply. 'I'm busy and Dad was asleep the last time I looked in.'

'Yer dad invited me to dinner,' he said, smiling to reveal his stained and crooked teeth. ' 'E took pity on me seein' as 'ow I live all on me own.'

Sid's mother had died two years before and he had lived in 'digs' ever since with an old lady in Locomotive Street behind the station.

'He never mentioned it to me,' she said.

Sid shrugged. 'Go and ask 'im if you don't believe me.'

Vicky opened the door and reluctantly let him in. He stood sniffing the air appreciatively.

'Smells good,' he remarked. 'I like a woman who can cook. Come to think of it, I ain't 'ad a proper Christmas dinner since me ma passed on.'

As Vicky took the meat out of the oven and basted it, it dawned on her that as Dad would be having his meal upstairs she would have to share hers with Sid. The prospect made her feel sick. As she straightened up he looked at her.

'You got a bit o' colour in yer cheeks today, Vick. Suits you. You're usually so pasty.'

'Thanks,' she said. 'I'm almost ready to dish up so I'll go and see if Dad's awake.' She ran up the stairs and found Dan sitting up in bed. 'Dad, Sid's downstairs,' she said. 'He says you invited him to dinner. Did you?'

Dan nodded. 'Yeah. I thought it'd be company for you.'

'I wish you'd said.'

Dan shrugged. 'Wanted to surprise you,' he said. 'Not often we have company.'

'Dad, you know I can't stand him,' she protested. 'And just lately he's been—' She broke off and Dan looked at her.

'Been *what*? Spit it out girl.'

'He's been – well – over familiar.'

'Oh my gawd!' the old man laughed derisively. 'You sound just like your ma. Why can't you call a spade a spade? Been trying it on a bit, has he? Well, why not? A bit of slap and tickle never hurt no one.'

'I don't like him, Dad. I don't like the way he speaks to me. I never will.'

'Oh leave orf! You don't want to be so damned tight-arsed. Time you was walkin' out anyway. Don't wanna be an old maid, do you?'

Vicky thought this was rich coming from a father who hardly let her out of the house and suspected she was up to no good if she stayed out till after nine. She shook her head. 'I'll bring your dinner up in a minute,' she said. At the door she turned. 'Would you like Sid to have his up here with you?' she asked hopefully.

Dan shook his head. 'What and spoil 'is fun? No, you two young 'uns enjoy yourselves,' he chuckled.

Because she had been unprepared for a third person, Vicky had to eke the food out to make three helpings. Dan would not expect to go short of course and as for her – her appetite had vanished since Sid's arrival. She tried not to look as he sat opposite, stuffing the food into his mouth and smacking his lips noisily, a trickle of gravy running unheeded down his chin. In the absence of Christmas pudding she had made an apple pie and Sid attacked his with gusto, scraping up the last of the custard until she thought he would make a hole in the plate.

While she washed up he went upstairs to sit with Dan for a while and when he came down he stood watching her slyly for a moment.

'Come for a walk, Vick.'

She shook her head. 'No, thank you.'

'Oh come on. A bit o' fresh air'll do you good. I asked yer dad,' he added. 'And 'e says it's all right. He's gonna 'ave a bit of a kip.' Without waiting for any further excuses he fetched her coat from the hall and held it out for her. 'I thought we might go down the canal. Or we could take a turn round the park if you like.'

Vicky chose the park, hoping there would be more people there, walking off their Christmas dinner. To her relief she had guessed right. There were several families with young children, wrapped up warm against the cold, just walking or throwing a stick for the family dog. Sid looked down at her and offered his arm.

'I reckon we make a good lookin' couple, you 'n' me, Vick,' he said.

She ignored the proffered arm and the remark. Sid allowed the rebuff to go without comment. 'That was a really good dinner,' he said. 'You're a good cook.'

'Thank you. I'm glad you enjoyed it.'

'I noticed you didn't eat much though. Why was that then? Not love-sick are you?' He grinned down at her.

'If I'd known Dad had invited you there would have been enough for three,' she told him sharply.

'What, you mean I 'ad your share?' He shook his head. 'That means you're gonna 'ave to let me make it up to you. The pictures p'raps?'

'There's no need, really.'

They walked on in silence for a few minutes, then Sid said, 'You don't 'appen to know anyone who's got a spare room, do you?'

'Not really, no.'

'My landlady, old Mrs Martin, keeps on about going to live with 'er daughter,' he said. 'I reckon it's only a matter of time before she asks me to leave.'

Vicky felt as though a cold hand clutched her heart. 'It should-n't be too hard to find another room,' she said. 'With so many of the men away a lot of women are finding it hard to make ends meet.'

He looked down at her. 'You got that parlour you never use.'

'I suppose we have, but I couldn't manage a lodger as well as Dad and my job,' she told him.

'I think you'd find me very obliging,' he told her. 'Dan likes me. I could give you a 'and with 'im. Artillery Street is nice an' 'andy for Shearing's too.'

She looked at him. 'Shearing's?'

'Yeah, didn't I tell you? They've taken me on as a machine minder. Short of men, they are. So, you see, I'd be able to pay you top whack for the room and board now I'm not on the dole any more.'

Vicky took a deep breath and turned to face him. 'I'm sorry, Sid, but it's out of the question. I doubt if Dad would want anyone else living in the house anyway.'

His smile vanished. 'Well, we'll 'ave to ask 'im then, shall we?'

'Not now,' she said. 'Not today. I think you should go now,

Sid. Dad will be tired and I have to see to his leg when I get back. I'm tired too, so if you don't mind.'

'Don't I even get a cup of tea an' mince pie?'

'Sorry, no. I couldn't get any mincemeat so there aren't any.'

He grabbed her arm and pushed her behind a tree. 'What about a Christmas kiss then?' he said, thrusting his face close to hers. 'Come on, Vick, just to show there's no 'ard feelin's, eh?'

His mouth was wet against her cheek as she turned her face away. Her heart was pounding with revulsion as she pushed him away. 'No! Go away. I want to go home.' She began half walking, half running along the path away from him, feeling the sweat break out on her brow. After a moment she looked over her shoulder to see if he was following but he was still standing by the tree, a smirk on his face.

'See you soon, Vick,' he called out. 'Maybe sooner than you think!'

Reaching the back yard she let herself in and locked the back door. Still breathless, she made sure the blackout was secured and lit the gas. The kitchen fire was almost out and she stirred the embers and put on more coal, drawing up a chair and holding out her freezing hands to the meagre glow. *Oh God, please don't let Sid come and live here*, she prayed. Tears welled up in her eyes as she filled the kettle and settled it on the fire ready for dressing Dan's leg. Was her life always to be like this, she wondered? Would it be nothing but drudgery and worry for the rest of her life?

On the day of Laura's exam she was a bundle of nerves. Mrs Griggs had been reluctant to give her the afternoon off, but she could hardly claim that they were busy. There was always a lull after Christmas and this year business was quieter than usual. As she was leaving at lunchtime, Shirley sidled up to her in the back room and pressed something into her hand. When Laura looked she saw that it was a rabbit's foot.

'Dad give it me,' Shirley explained. 'It's supposed to be lucky. I'll be thinking about you.'

Touched, Laura slipped the gruesome little object into her handbag. 'Thanks, Shirley. I'm sure it'll help.'

Shirley smiled. 'Not that you need any help. I bet you get top marks.'

'I just wish I wasn't so nervous,' Laura confided. 'I feel as though I've got butterflies as big as aeroplanes in my tummy.'

Shirley gave her a quick hug. 'You'll be fine,' she said. 'You're gonna be a big star in no time. I can feel it in me bones.'

As before, the exams were being held in St Mary's church hall and Laura arrived in plenty of time to apply her make-up and get ready. As well as being awarded points for acting, voice production and presentation, she would be judged on make-up, stage presence and business, which was difficult when no stage props were allowed. In the room set aside for dressing, Laura put the finishing touches to her face and sat down to do her deep breathing exercises and go quietly through her lines, trying to remember all the advice that Rosa had given her about creating a 'pool of tranquillity' within herself.

At last the moment came and she was called. She walked shakily down the corridor and through a door to step up on to the stage. Shielding her eyes from the glare of the footlights she announced the pieces she had chosen and the order in which she intended to present them. She had chosen to do the Shakespeare first. Playing three characters all at once, all with different voices and mannerisms was far from easy but with Rosa's expert schooling Laura felt fairly confident that she could make the piece convincing. By contrast the Noël Coward scene needed lightness and wit and Rosa had advised her to present this second. 'Once an audience has laughed at you it's difficult to get them to take you seriously,' she said.

When she came to the end of her second piece, a deep male voice from the auditorium instructed her to pick up the book on the table at the back of the stage where a passage of sight-reading had been marked. She found it and, stepping forward once again, read it through without difficulty. When she had finished, the voice thanked her and invited her to come down and join him.

Relieved that the ordeal was over, Laura stepped down from the stage and walked towards the table in the centre of the room. The examiner was a tall man with kind brown eyes and dark hair streaked with silver. Laura gave a small involuntary gasp as she recognized him as Hugo Ingram, an actor she knew had had a long and distinguished career in theatre and films. He stood up and offered his hand, smiling.

'Miss Nightingale – Laura, come and sit down,' he said in his pleasant low voice. 'I was impressed by your rendition this afternoon, especially with the Shakespeare. I thought you handled the three characters extremely skilfully. Your make-up is clean-cut and attractive and you act with a depth and sincerity far beyond your tender years.' He signed her examination card with a flourish and passed it across the table to her. 'I'm delighted to pass you with distinction, my dear. Congratulations.'

Laura went straight round to Rosa's, hardly able to contain her excitement as she waited for her teacher to answer her door. Rosa had only to look at her shining eyes to know what she had been waiting to hear.

'You've done it,' she said, clasping her hands. 'You've passed?'

'With distinction!' Laura threw her arms around the older woman and hugged her hard. 'It's all down to you, Rosa,' she said, a lump in her throat. 'I'd never have done it without you.'

'Nonsense, silly girl. You have talent. I just recognized it, that's all. Now. . . .' She drew Laura inside. 'You and I will celebrate with a glass of sherry. Pity there's no champagne but amontillado will have to do.'

As they sipped sherry in the basement kitchen, Laura gave Rosa a detailed account of the exam and the remarks that Hugo Ingram had made.

'Praise indeed!' Rose topped up Laura's glass. 'And he doesn't give it for nothing, believe me. I know Hugo of old and he's had many a student in tears before now. You can rest assured that he doesn't flatter.'

'The thing is, where do I go from here?' Laura said.

Rosa paused. 'As a matter of fact I understand that they are auditioning for ENSA next week.' Laura's eyes lit up with excitement but Rosa held up her hand. 'Wait! You'd have to go down to London of course. The headquarters are at Drury Lane.'

'That's all right,' Laura said. 'I can find it.'

'Darling – just wait a minute and listen to me. I want you to go home and sound your parents out first. I've a feeling they might have some objections and I don't want to be accused of persuading you to do something they don't approve of.'

'They won't mind,' Laura said without conviction. 'If they do I'll soon talk them round. When will the audition be? I'll have to ask for time off.'

'You may not have to,' Rosa said. 'You could go on Monday when you're off anyway. But just remember what I said. Make sure you have your parents' permission – and blessing – otherwise I shall feel responsible.'

At Jessop Street Laura went in through the shop where Vicky stood at the counter.

'Laura! How did your exam go?' she asked.

'I passed,' Laura told her proudly. 'With distinction.'

The other girl smiled. 'Oh, well done! You must be so excited.'

'I am. I can't wait to tell Mum and Dad.'

'Your sister's home,' Vicky told her. 'And I think she's had a letter from her fiancé. She's upstairs with your mum and dad now.' She smiled. 'It's all news today, isn't it?'

Upstairs in the flat everyone seemed to be talking at once. Meg's face was flushed and Harry was trying hard to calm his wife and daughter down. The moment Laura came into the room Meg turned to her.

'Guess what! David is coming home the week after next. It's to be embarkation leave because he's off somewhere abroad. Your dad thinks there's probably another invasion plan. Thing is, the wedding will have to be brought forward.'

'I see. Mum,' Laura touched her mother's arm. 'Mum, I passed my exam – with distinction.'

Meg's hands flew to her face. 'I've just thought. How am I to cater for a reception with the rationing and all? And what about your dress, Moira? No time to make you one, even if we could find any suitable material. I wonder if I could alter mine for you? I've still got it.'

'Did anyone hear what I said?' Laura asked.

'I'm sure David's mum will help you out,' Moira suggested.

'Good idea. I'll pop round and see her tomorrow.'

'Good job I put aside those two crates of beer when I got the chance last year,' Harry put in. 'Don't know about champagne. We might have to toast the happy couple with brown ale.'

Moira laughed, her cheeks pink. 'Oh, Dad, what does it matter? David and I are going to be married. That's all that matters to me.'

Harry looked at his younger daughter. 'What was it you were saying just now, love?'

'It doesn't matter,' she said flatly. 'But in case anyone's interested I'm going to audition for ENSA next week – in London.'

All three Nightingales looked at her for a moment, then Moira said, 'Just as long as it doesn't interfere with the wedding, that's all.'

'Hang on a minute!' Harry was on his feet. 'I'm not sure that I'm going to give you my permission to go in for this ENSA thing. You're still under age my girl.'

'It's not a question of permission, Dad. I'm nearly calling-up age anyway. Do you want me directed into the ATS – working with an anti-aircraft crew or something?'

'The war could be over before that happens,' Harry blustered. 'And anyway—'

'You *know* it won't!' Laura interrupted. 'You follow the news closely and you're always saying you can't see any end to it.'

'Oh, why do you always have to spoil everything?' Moira burst out. 'Here's me, excited about getting married and you have to come in and upset everybody! It's just plain jealousy. That's all it is!'

Meg put an arm around Moira's shoulders. 'Nothing's spoilt, love,' she said. 'It'll all get sorted out. You'll see.' She looked pointedly at Laura. 'Come and help me with the supper. We'll talk in the kitchen.'

When the door was safely closed Meg turned to her daughter. 'You know we can't stop you if you want to go off on this mad idea. All I ask is that you have a bit of consideration. I haven't even heard you offer your sister your best wishes yet either.'

'And I haven't heard her offer me hers,' Laura said, her throat tight with tears.

'What for?' Meg asked, looking scandalized.

'For passing my exam – with distinction.'

Shocked, Meg stared at her. 'You should have said.'

'I *did*. At least I tried to! No one was listening though. You were all too wrapped up in Moira's wedding.'

Meg's expression softened. 'I'm sorry, love. Well done. I'm sure you've worked really hard for it. I'm not sure about this ENSA idea though. Is it really what you want?'

'Yes. Don't you see, Mum? It will mean getting some experience, and my Equity card at the end of it.'

Meg sighed. 'I don't know. I can't pretend to understand all that kind of thing. All I know is that it looks as if I'm going to be losing both my girls in one fell swoop.' She turned away and Laura saw her dab at her eyes with a corner of her apron. 'This war is hard on mothers,' she said. 'Very hard.'

CHAPTER SIX

THE train was late. Desperately worried that she would arrive too late for the audition, Laura decided that there was nothing for it but to get a taxi from Euston station. She climbed apprehensively into one of the black cabs with its huge gas bag on top, wobbling like a captive elephant, desperate to escape. Sitting in the back she crossed her fingers that they wouldn't take off into the sky like one of the barrage balloons that hovered all round the city. To Laura's relief they arrived safely at Catherine Street and she alighted from the taxi to stand on the pavement in front of Drury Lane Theatre. For a moment she stood looking up at the regal edifice, awed by the fact that she was actually looking at London's oldest theatre, almost three hundred years old. Here she was, waiting to audition on the very stage where the great Ellen Terry had once performed. She could hardly believe she wasn't dreaming.

Inside, she gave her name to a receptionist and was directed to wait at the back of the stalls where several other artists were waiting their turn. For her audition piece she had decided to do Juliet's soliloquy from Romeo and Juliet, but as she sat listening to the hushed chatter around her she was slightly disturbed by the fact that most of the others waiting to audition were variety artists. When her turn came she climbed the steps onto the stage on shaking legs and began.

'*Farewell, God knows when we shall meet again.*' She reached the end of the piece and looked down into the auditorium. The footlights were unlit and she could plainly see the panel of judges: two men and a middle-aged woman. The woman cleared her throat and looked down at her notes.

'Thank you Miss – er – Nightingale. That was very good, but I have to tell you that auditioning for legitimate actors was earlier this morning. We are now auditioning concert party artists. But thank you for coming and we'll keep a note of your name in case something suitable comes up in the near future.'

As Laura was leaving the stage one of the other judges spoke. 'Just a moment, Miss Nightingale, have you any other talents? Can you sing for instance – dance?'

'I can do a little tap and some ballet,' Laura said.

'A song perhaps. Could you give us a few bars?' He nodded to the pianist in the orchestra pit who began to play 'A Nightingale Sang in Berkeley Square.' The man smiled. 'Very appropriate. I'm sure you know the words?'

Laura swallowed hard and began, in a voice that sounded to her like a mouse squeaking. *'That perfect night, the night we met, there was magic abroad in the air. . . .'* When the song came to an end the three judges were smiling. Laura blushed. Were they laughing at her? She had studied voice production and breath control but so far all her singing had been done safely behind the bathroom door. The man who had spoken before nodded.

'That was very nice. Thank you, Miss Nightingale. Would you perhaps be prepared to accept something other than straight acting?'

Laura shook her head. 'Well, I don't think so. Not really.'

'I see. Well, we'll let you know when we have another repertory tour going out.'

Laura stepped down from the stage with a heavy heart. The whole thing had been a complete fiasco – a waste of time. Now she would have to go home and tell them she had arrived too late and been turned down. She could just imagine the look on Moira's face.

She was putting on her coat at the back of the stalls when a small blonde woman came rushing up to her.

'Miss Nightingale.' She held out her hand. 'I'm Maisie Day.

My hubby and I run the Moonlight Follies. It's a concert party. We liked your audition very much.'

Laura smiled. 'Thank you, that's very kind but I'm not really a singer. It's a pity there's no work suitable for me at the moment. The train was late and—'

'That's why I wanted to talk to you. Our soubrette has just given us notice. Silly girl's gone and signed up for the WRNS.' She shook her head. 'Between you 'n me I think she finds us all a bit over the hill – wants to find herself some chums of her own age.' She winked. 'Not to mention all those sailors! Anyway, she's just announced that she's leaving us and it's left us in a bit of a hole. I was wondering if you'd consider taking her place?'

Laura was taken aback. 'Well, it's not really what I was look-ing for. I'm an actress, you see.'

'I know that, dear, and a very fine one too.' Maisie frowned thoughtfully. 'We do some sketches as well as the musical numbers,' she said. 'So you'd get a chance to act,' she smiled apologetically. 'Well, not what you're used to, of course, but – a bit.' When Laura hesitated she hurried on. 'We're a happy little company. There's Ed, my husband. He's Edward Knight. We call our act "Knight and Day". He and I do songs at the piano. I play, he sings. The finest tenor this side of the Irish channel if I do say so myself. Then there's Arthur. He's a vent act – ventriloquist, you know. He plays the musical saw as well. Don is our com-edian. A proper scream, he is, and we did have Adele, our soubrette, but not any more. We all chip in with the sketches too and we do some group numbers. It's a good show – been very well received. So, what d'you say, dear?'

Laura couldn't help smiling. Maisie reminded her of a robin with her bright eyes and chirpy optimistic manner. It was quite impossible not to like her. 'Well I—'

'Look, if you're not in a hurry why don't you watch our audi-tion? We're on next. Then you'll know what you'd be letting your-self in for. After, you could come and have a drink with us all and we could talk. What d'you say, eh?' She looked so hopeful that to her surprise Laura heard herself agreeing. 'Well, all right then.'

'Oh that's *smashing*!' Maisie clapped her hands. 'Just give us a chance to do our stuff and we'll meet you in the foyer after. OK?'

Watching the Moonlight Follies in action Laura's spirits lifted. First, the whole group did their opening number, 'Happy Days Are Here Again', which they performed with gusto. Then they each did a tiny piece of their own act for the judges. Maisie was a competent pianist and she hadn't exaggerated about Ed's voice. Arthur's dummy, Algernon, was saucy and uncannily lifelike, and Don's jokes had everyone laughing. If Laura hadn't been so desperate for a serious acting job she might almost have agreed to join the Moonlight Follies.

She was waiting in the foyer when Maisie rushed over and took her arm, pulling her over to introduce her to the others. 'Come on troops,' she said when the formalities were over. 'Don't know about you lot but I'm spitting feathers. There's a bar on the corner so what are we waiting for?'

It was warm and cosy in the little bar on the corner of Catherine Street. Maisie found seats for them all and stood rubbing her hands. 'OK, I'm in the chair, what're we all having?'

Ed laughed. 'Hadn't you better see what they've got first?'

As it turned out, all that was on offer was half a pint of bottled beer each. It was lukewarm and rather flat, but the exuberance of the company more than made up for it.

'We passed our audition,' Maisie told Laura. 'We're to be a "D" show. Only the top artists get to be "A"s,' she explained. 'I don't know if you know but the big West End stars are obliged to put in six weeks during the year, entertaining the troops, so they get A and B rating.' She laughed. 'Don't ask me who gets the "C"s.'

Don laughed. 'Chumps and chuckleheads!'

'Well, they've offered us a tour of gun and balloon sites on the north west coast,' Maisie went on. 'So it looks like it'll be a case of winter drawers on, love!' She took a drink of her beer. 'Of course, we accepted. I mean, it's a case of having to. Our best dates have always been end of the pier and the war scuppered that good and proper. I did mention to them before that we were one short,' she added with a twinkle. 'That was why they asked you to sing. I told them we liked you and they said it'd be all right if you wanted to join us. I hope you don't mind, dear?' She smiled encouragingly into Laura's eyes.

'Well, I. . . .' Laura took a sip of her drink, trying hard to find an answer that wouldn't disappoint the endearing Maisie. 'Maybe I could take your address or phone number and let you know? I'd really like to think about it first.'

'Of course you can, duckie.' Maisie rummaged in her handbag for an old envelope and scribbled down a telephone number. 'You can reach us there until the end of the week and if you agree I'll let them know at ENSA and they'll send you the necessary papers. If you do want to take up our offer you'll need a bit of time to rehearse with us and learn the songs. And. . . .' She smiled apologetically. 'Sorry dear, but I'll have to ask you to make up your mind within a couple of days. You see, if the answer's no we'll have to have time to find someone else.'

'Of course. I promise to be in touch one way or the other as soon as I can.' Laura looked at her watch. 'Oh, look at the time. There's a train in fifteen minutes. I'll have to go. Can you tell me where to find the nearest tube station?'

Ed tossed back the last of his drink and stood up. 'No need. We've got the van. We'll take you to the station. It's not far out of our way. Come on.'

The van that the Moonlight Follies toured their company and props in was a rather dilapidated Austin, parked at the back of the theatre. Maisie and Ed invited Laura to climb on to the bench-seat in front with them whilst the others got into the back. Just as they set off the siren sounded. Laura's heart jumped into her mouth and she looked apprehensively at Maisie.

'Oh dear, shouldn't we go to a shelter?'

Maisie shook her head. 'Not if you want to catch that train, duckie.'

'It's better really,' Ed put in. 'It means there'll be less traffic on the road. Hold on to your hats, mates.' As he revved up the van's engine with a roar and moved away from the kerb the Moonlight

Follies began to sing 'Roll Out the Barrel' when suddenly a scream and a loud bang almost bounced the van off the road. They swerved halfway across the road but Ed pulled hard on the wheel.

'*Phew!*' he whistled between his teeth. 'That was close. Sorry, chums.'

As they rattled along Euston Road the raid got under way and more bombs fell. Laura's heart was pounding, but she tried not to show how scared she was. One explosion, uncomfortably close, shook the van and she heard the rumble of falling masonry and the clanging of an ambulance bell. She shuddered, wondering if she would ever see Millborough again. But the Moonlight Follies continued to sing on regardless. Maisie nudged Laura.

'Come on love, join in. It helps stop your teeth from chattering.'

They were now singing 'Silver Wings in the Moonlight' and it made Laura think of Peter. A lump in her throat, she joined in, the other voices giving her confidence until she suddenly realized that they had all stopped singing to listen to her. She stopped abruptly, blushing and Maisie gave her arm a squeeze.

'Sing like that sweetheart and you'll have all the boys falling for you and no mistake!'

At last Ed pulled up the van with a squeal of brakes. 'Right, here we are, madam. Euston Station, safe and sound – well almost. Hope your train's not too delayed.' He reached across to give Laura's hand a squeeze. 'I hope we see you again soon, Laura love. Take care now.'

'Be good!' Don called out from the back. 'Don't do anything I wish I could still do!'

As she got out Laura heard Algernon's squeaky voice call out to her. 'Please join us, lovely Laura. A bit of glamour's just what we need.'

The train was crowded with troops and Laura had to stand for most of the way. In the corridor a young soldier put his kitbag down on the floor and invited her to sit on it. Gratefully, she accepted.

'Live in London, do you?' he asked, offering her a cigarette.

'No, thank goodness. I've been up to audition for ENSA,' she told him.

He grinned. 'Looking at you I might have guessed. Smashing work, they do. It's great to get folks from back home to entertain us. You can't imagine what it means to us.'

Laura felt a little thrill of pride to think that she had it within her power to help the war effort. Maybe she should consider Maisie's offer to join the Moonlight Follies after all.

At Jessop Street Laura climbed the stairs wearily to the flat. In the living-room Moira stood in her slip while Meg was busily running up a seam on her sewing machine, the white satin skirt of her wedding dress fanned out across the table. As Laura came in Meg got up and raised the dress to slip it over Moira's head. Neither of them seemed to notice Laura's arrival. Meg fastened the hooks at the back of the dress and came round to the front to survey her daughter. 'Oh, you look a picture, love,' she said, standing back. 'The hem could do with half an inch off and then I think it'll do. Just go into the bedroom and look in the mirror – see what you think.'

When Moira had gone Meg looked at Laura. 'You're back at last then. I saved some supper for you. It's in the oven. You'd better eat it before it's completely dried up.'

'Thanks, Mum. Where's Dad?'

'At the ARP post,' Meg told her. 'There was a red alert again.'

'There was a raid while I was in London,' Laura said. 'A lot of bombs fell – it was quite frightening.'

Meg was putting the cover on her machine and tidying up. 'Well, you didn't have to go, did you?'

'Aren't you going to ask me how I got on?'

Meg turned to look at her. 'Sorry love, 'course I am. How did it go?'

'I was offered a place in a concert party.'

Moira, who was coming back into the room, burst into a peal of laughter. 'What? dressing up in a pointy hat and pom-poms?'

Laura ignored the jibe. 'They're to tour naval bases on the

north-west coast of England,' she went on.

'Well, at least it's not abroad,' Meg said. 'Are you going to accept the offer?'

Laura sighed. 'I don't know. The train was late so I missed the legitimate actors' audition. I was quite lucky to get this offer. And they're really nice people, Mum. They drove me to the station all through an air raid.'

Meg's face softened. 'You don't have to take the first offer you get, do you love? Go and get your supper out of the oven before it's ruined. You look half-starved.'

Eating her supper Laura listened to Moira going on about her forthcoming wedding. 'The dress is lovely, Mum. You'd never get material of that quality nowadays. Thanks for altering it for me.'

'It's a pleasure, love. I'm just glad I kept it. It's a pity it's not as white as it was. I've kept it wrapped in tissue paper too.'

'Never mind. It looks beautiful – a sort of ivory colour. What kind of flowers do you think would go best with it?'

Laura took her plate into the kitchen and washed it up. Looking at her watch she saw that it was still only eight o'clock and she decided to go and see Rosa who would be waiting eagerly to hear about the audition. On the way she would look in on Peter's mother.

Slipping out of the flat she let herself out through the shop and went along to the little house in Maybury Street. There was a stillness about the house as she knocked on the front door and she wondered if Mrs Radcliffe was out. It was some time before there was any response to her knocking and Laura was about to turn away when she heard the bolt being drawn back and the door opened a crack.

'Who is it?'

'It's only me, Mrs Radcliffe – Laura. I've been to London today and I thought. . . .' The door opened wider and Mrs Radcliffe reached out a hand to Laura.

'Come in, dear. Then I can put the light on.'

When the front door was closed Ethel switched on the light and Laura saw that her eyes were red and her face blotched with tears.

'Mrs Radcliffe! What is it?'

'You'd better come in and sit down.' The older woman led the way into the living-room. 'I'm afraid I've had some bad news.' She reached out a hand to the table to steady herself and Laura went at once to her side.

'Please – tell me.'

'It's Peter.' Ethel sat down with a bump. 'I still can't take it in. The telegram came soon after I got in from work. It's there, on the sideboard. You'd better read it.'

With trembling fingers Laura picked up the slip of paper and the vital words sprang out at her, dancing in front of her eyes: *Regret to inform you – your son, Flight Engineer Peter Alan Radcliffe – missing believed killed.*

As the words danced before her eyes, a thousand thoughts chased through Laura's mind. Peter, his sweet smile and the warmth of his arms, the gentleness of his kisses, never to be known again. Could it be possible? She thought about the air raid she had experienced that afternoon in London and the terror it had stirred in her. She thought about the courage of the people she had been with and how she wished she too could be as brave. Had Peter suffered? Had he been badly injured? Suddenly a suffocating wave of emotion overwhelmed her. As the sobs burst from her Ethel put her arms around her and the two women wept together, their tears mingling.

Laura stayed with Ethel for over an hour. They drank hot tea and talked, about Peter, about the war, recognizing that they were not alone in their loss. So many wives and mothers up and down the country were mourning sons and husbands. They must put on a brave face and carry on. Laura asked if Ethel would like her to stay the night but the older woman refused.

'I'll be all right, my dear,' she said. 'I've got to get used to being alone from now on. Anyway, we mustn't give up hope, after all, it only says "missing". That means they haven't found his – his body.'

Laura nodded. The telegram had stated that Peter's plane had been shot down over Germany and as such she knew it was unlikely that bodies would have been recovered. She shuddered at the thought but didn't voice her fears to Ethel.

'You go home, dear,' Ethel said, getting up. 'Your mother will be wondering where you are. Don't worry about me. I'll be all right.'

Walking down the street Laura felt as though her legs had turned to lead. It was so hard to take in. No more letters from Peter. Not to see him again. No one would ever understand her the way he did. It seemed now that there was nothing to look forward to. She thought of Moira and her forthcoming wedding and knew in that moment that, selfish as it might seem, she would not be able to face it. At the corner of the street was a tele-phone booth. On impulse she slipped inside and fumbled in her bag for her torch. Finding the tattered envelope Maisie had given her she spread it out on top of the coin box and lifted the receiver. It took some time for the operator to put her through but at last she heard the ringing tone at the other end and a click as the receiver was lifted.

'Hello. Maisie Day speaking.'

Laura pressed button A and heard her coins drop into the box. 'Maisie – it's me, Laura Nightingale.'

'*Oh*! Hello duckie. I'm glad you got home all right.'

'I'm fine thanks, Maisie. This is just to say that I'd like to take you up on your offer. I'd love to join the Moonlight Follies.'

Maisie's delight was plain to hear in her voice. 'Oh! That *is* good news. Wait till I tell Ed. I'll get on to it first thing in the morning. Have you got a phone number I can ring?'

Laura gave her the shop's number. 'I'll have to give in my notice at work, but I don't think they'll want more than a week.'

'Right. I'll get in touch with ENSA and get them to send you all the necessary papers then we'll sort out a place where we can pick you up.' She gave a delighted little giggle. 'Oh, I'm *so* pleased you've said yes. I just know we're all going to get along like a house on fire! 'Bye duckie. I'll be in touch.'

' 'Bye, Maisie.'

Laura walked home in a kind of daze. In one short hour her

entire life had turned upside down. Nothing would ever be quite the same again. She had the distinct feeling that this was a turning point in her life – one that she'd always remember.

At home Moira was making herself a cup of cocoa in the kitchen. She looked up as Laura came in. 'Where have you been? Off to see that Rosa I expect. You might have said where you were going. Mum's gone to bed.' She stopped, peering at Laura's pale, tear-stained face. 'Laura! What's the matter?'

'Peter's been killed,' Laura told her. 'I've just been to see his mother. She had the telegram this afternoon. His plane was shot down over Germany. "Missing believed killed", it said, but shot down over Germany – you know what that means.' She sat down at the table and felt her throat tighten again. Too tired and hurt to hold back the tears she let them stream down her cheeks. Moira pushed the mug of cocoa towards her sister, her face shocked.

'Drink that. There's plenty of sugar in it for – for shock,' she said. She laid a hand on her sister's shoulder. 'Oh, Laura, I don't know what to say.'

'I'm leaving as soon as it can be arranged,' Laura told her. 'I've just telephoned to say I'm accepting the offer I had today. I'm sorry I won't be here for your wedding but I can't stay here any longer. Not now.' Her voice broke on a sob and she raised brimming eyes to look at her sister. 'Oh, Moira! How in the world am I going to get through it?'

'Laura. . . .' Tears filled Moira's eyes as she put her arms around her sister and held her close. 'I'm sorry. So, *so* sorry. Please forgive me for being so bitchy.'

'You haven't been – not really. We're just so different. That's all,' Laura said, her voice muffled against her sister's shoulder.

'You must have realized that I've always resented you because you were prettier and more talented than me,' Moira confessed.

Shocked, Laura shook her head. 'That's nonsense.'

'No, it's true. There you were, making a name for yourself in all those plays – everyone admiring you.'

'And there *you* were, passing exams that I couldn't even aspire to and forging ahead with a worthwhile career.'

'If I tell the truth *I* wanted to be the one off to see the world and meet new and exciting people.'

'And *I* wanted to be the one marrying the man I love – having Mum and Dad excited about my wedding.' She looked into Moira's eyes. 'You're my clever sister – the one with the brains.'

'And you're the pretty one – the one with the talent.'

'Oh! *Rubbish*!'

They laughed together tremulously then Moira's face sobered. 'I can't imagine how awful you must feel,' she said. 'Every day I try not to think of losing David, but the dread is always there. I wonder what I'd do. I think it would kill me.' She hugged her sister hard. 'We've been so stupid. It's high time we grew up.'

'Let's make each other a promise,' Laura said. 'No more bickering. Sisters and friends from now on.'

Moira nodded. 'Sisters and friends,' she said.

Dan Watts's leg was getting worse every day. Vicky was at her wits' end. On one occasion she had asked an elderly woman who lived at the end of the street to look in. Phyllis Thorne was the local 'nurse'; she attended all the local births and layings-out and gave advice about everything from pregnancy to whooping cough. She made her own herbal remedies and Vicky told Dan that the woman might have something that would help him with the pain and reluctantly he agreed to let her come.

Phyllis was a large lady and climbing the narrow stairs made her puff and wheeze. In Dan's bedroom Vicky drew back the bedclothes and took the bandage off his leg for her. Leaning forward and breathing heavily, Phyllis took a look at the affected leg.

'You need a doctor to look at that, Mr Watts,' she said. 'It's too far gone for me to deal with.' She glanced sideways at Vicky. 'And if you don't mind me saying so, it's not fair to expect a young girl like Vicky to keep dressing it either. You need full-time care, Mr Watts, and that means hospital if you ask me.'

'Well I'm soddin' well *not* asking you!' Dan roared, red-faced as he pulled the bedclothes up. 'Have you got any medicine to keep the pain away or haven't you?'

'I'm sorry, Mr Watts, but there's nothing I can give you.'

'Well bloody well sling your 'ook then! I never asked you to come and gawp at my leg, woman, an' I don't want your daft opinions neither.'

'Now then, Mr Watts, no call to go upsetting yourself.' Phyllis shook her head at him, infuriating him more than ever.

Raising himself on one elbow he shouted, 'Bugger off, you old bag. And don't bloody well come back!'

Phyllis Thorne had suffered far worse than Dan's insults, as she told an apologetic Vicky downstairs in the kitchen. She was thick-skinned when it came to the frenzied raving of folks in pain.

'That leg is gangrenous,' she said, folding her arms across her ample chest. 'I've seen enough cases of gangrene to know it when I see it. That leg needs to come orf!'

'*Oh!*' Vicky felt the colour drain from her cheeks. 'He'd never agree to that. He won't even see a doctor, let alone go into hospital. As for having an operation. . . .' She shook her head. 'What will happen if he doesn't get treatment?'

Phyllis sucked in her breath pessimistically. 'I'm sorry, love, but I wouldn't give you tuppence for his chances as long as that leg stays on. I'm not even sure it ain't too late already.'

When the woman had gone Vicky made a pot of tea and took Dan a cup, hoping to make him see sense. He was still angry and glared at her as she came into the room.

'What did you want to bring that old cow in here for?' he growled. 'What the 'ell does she know about anything?'

'She didn't mean to frighten you,' Vicky said. 'But she's right in one way, Dad. I do wish you'd let the doctor look at your leg – if – if only to prove her wrong,' she added with a sudden spurt of inspiration.

'*You* can look after it,' Dan said stubbornly. 'You've done all right so far ain't you? I don't need no doctor.' He sipped his tea and looked up at her. 'One thing's sure though. You're gonna have to give up that job.'

Vicky's heart plummeted. 'My job – at Nightingale's? Why?'

'You heard the woman. It was your idea to bring her here. I'm gonna need more lookin' after from now on. Full time care, she said. That means you gotta stop leavin' me on me own all day.'

'But – we need the money,' Vicky said.

'Ah well. . . .' Dan handed her his empty cup. 'There's a remedy for that.'

'What remedy?'

'We got the chance to take in a lodger, as you well know,' Dan said. 'Sid's lookin' for a place. He's workin' and he could afford to pay a good rent. If we take him in you could give up your job and concentrate on lookin' after your dad like a dutiful daughter should.'

Vicky felt her heart freeze. 'Dad, please – don't make me do that. You know I don't like Sid. I love my job and—'

'Shut up!' Dan bellowed. *'Don't like*? Self, self, *self*! That's all you think about. Don't you think you got a duty to the father what's fed and clothed you all these years? If I say Sid can come, then he can. This is my house and what I say goes. He'd have moved in weeks ago if you hadn't been so mardy with him. He's a considerate fella. He told me himself that he wouldn't come unless you was willin'. So you'd better get on and make yourself agreeable to him.'

'But, Dad. . . .'

'Just do it! The likes of you can't afford likes and dislikes, so get on with it.'

On Friday evening Sid arrived on the dot. Vicky let him in and he went straight upstairs to Dan. When he came down Vicky was in the scullery, preparing the evening meal. He stood leaning on the door jamb regarding her for a moment, his arms folded and a smirk on his face.

'Yer dad says you got something you want to say to me,' he said at last.

Vicky steeled herself. 'He wants me to give up my job,' she said.

'Well, you could afford to if I came 'ere. Most girls'd jump at the chance to stay at home all day.'

'But I don't want to give up my job,' Vicky said. 'I like it. The Nightingales are – they're like my own family.'

Sid snorted. 'Huh! That your idea or theirs?' he taunted. 'I reckon shop girls are ten-a-penny. They'd soon replace you.'

'Mrs Nightingale is always saying I'm the best assistant she's ever had,' Vicky protested. 'She says she could leave me in charge without a moment's worry – she even trusts me to cash up the day's takings.'

'Ah, that so, is it? Sid looked thoughtful. 'So, I'm to tell yer dad that you don't want me 'ere then, am I?'

Vicky shrugged. 'He says it's his house and what he says goes. I'm not giving up my job though.'

'Oh well, that's between you 'n 'im,' Sid said. 'I'll move me stuff in tomorra then, shall I?'

Vicky pressed her lips together. Dad might have won the battle over Sid moving in but she wasn't going to give up her job. No one would make her do that. 'I suppose so,' she said. 'As long as you know it's against my better judgement.'

Sid beamed triumphantly. 'Seems to me no one gives a flying fig for yer *better judgement*,' he sniped. He stepped forward and closed his hand around her upper arm, giving it a squeeze that made her wince. 'Never mind, Vick. Once I'm settled in an' you 'n me 'ave got to know each other better I reckon you'll find I'm a likeable fella. You might even end up quite fond of me.'

Vicky gritted her teeth. 'Never in a million years,' she said under her breath.

The parlour had been Vicky's mother's pride and joy. As well as her piano and the rug with the pansies on it that she had pegged herself, there was a chintz-covered three-piece suite and an aspidistra on a stand in the window. On the mantelpiece were her precious Staffordshire china dogs and the little chiming clock that had been hers as a girl – now never wound up because the chiming disturbed Dan. Vicky stood in the doorway surveying it all, hating the thought of Sid touching and using the things her mother had cherished. She wrapped the ornaments and the clock up in newspaper and put them away in a box at the back of the kitchen cupboard. Now she moved one of the armchairs and the plant stand through to the kitchen to make room for the truckle bed with its rolled-up mattress which she had brought down from the attic. She had also found a small table up there and she added an upright chair in the hope that Sid would eat his meals in his room, freeing her from the prospect of having to share hers with him. She didn't hold out much hope of his agreeing to this but to her surprise he made no comment when she took his evening meal through to him on the first evening.

'That looks very tempting,' he remarked, rubbing his hands. 'Thanks, Vick.'

Closing the door on him she heaved a sigh of relief and went to fetch Dan's supper tray from the kitchen.

CHAPTER SEVEN

MAISIE and Ed Knight were based in Burnt Oak, near Edgware, where they rented a little semi-detached house as their permanent address. It was there, at 15 Deans Drive, that Laura was invited to occupy their spare room whilst rehearsing for the ENSA tour with the Moonlight Follies.

They had just two weeks before they began their tour and there was a lot to do. Along with the others Laura collected her ENSA uniform, a smart coffee-brown jacket and skirt which suited her very well. She quickly learned the Moonlight Follies' songs, which, being current popular ones were familiar to her anyway. Maisie taught her the simple steps of the dances and Ed took her through the sketches, the scripts of which he had written himself. The costumes that had originally been made for the absent Adele needed a little alteration, but Maisie got out her sewing machine and accomplished these without any problems.

Each day the other members of the team would arrive and they would go through their programme in the Knights' front room which was bare of furniture except for Maisie's piano. Laura was impressed by the professionalism everyone put into the little show, the only exception being Don, who was a law unto himself. When he arrived the proceedings had a way of turning into a fiasco. Not only did he write his own material but he made a joke of everyone else's performance as well. At first Laura found this rather off-putting until at last Ed took him aside and reminded him that she was still new to the business and unsure of herself.

After that the comedian apologized to her.

'Sorry, love,' he said with a smile. 'I don't mean anything. Truth is I think you're doing marvellously.' He grinned. 'You'll get used to me. I can't help making a gag out of everything. It's just my way.'

But no one was ever serious for long and most days were filled with good-humoured banter and laughter. As the two-week rehearsal period drew to a close Laura found herself looking forward excitedly to the coming tour.

Leaving home had been something of an ordeal. Harry had been full of grave-faced advice about everything from borrowing money (*Never a borrower or a lender be*), to making sure she never let anyone down. Meg was of a more practical frame of mimd: 'I know it's nearly spring but it's always cold up North so don't forget to pack your woolly vests and plenty of warm knickers to keep the cold out of your kidneys,' she warned. 'And take that jar of Vick from the bathroom cabinet in case you get one of your chests.' Laura hadn't had 'one of her chests' since she was six but she didn't argue. They were not going to let her leave home without all the good advice and warnings they could think of. It was their way of letting her know they loved her. And she knew she was going to miss her parents as much as they would miss her.

As for Moira, since the night that the barriers had come down between them they had made up for lost time, talking far into the night after the light was out, catching up on all the things they had never discussed with each other before. Moira promised to send her a wedding photograph and a piece of cake and at Laura's request she also promised to go and see Mrs Radcliffe now and again to make sure she was all right. Laura in her turn promised to write regularly.

A day never went by without Laura thinking of Peter. It was so hard to believe that someone as alive and vibrant as he had been could be dead. Sometimes she toyed with the notion that there might have been a mistake, that he wasn't dead after all. But deep inside, she knew that mistakes like that were not made – not in wartime. If his plane had crashed over Germany with all its crew on board there was very little hope of any of them still being alive.

As well as the uniform, ENSA had provided the Moonlight Follies with a more reliable vehicle than the little Austin van they referred to as 'Kitty'. Ed spent the time not taken up with rehearsals draining the sump and radiator and taking the wheels off. Now the battered little van was stowed away on four piles of bricks in the garage at Deans Drive.

They christened the new van 'Winnie' after Mr Churchill. She was camouflaged like an army vehicle and had a powerful engine and moderately comfortable seats in the back. There was also storage space for the hampers containing their costumes and props.

So it was at 4 a.m. on a wet morning in early May that the Moonlight Follies set off, Ed at the wheel of the new van; their luggage and costume baskets were stowed away on the back, for the long drive to the north-west and, for Laura, it was the beginning of the adventure. They were all to stay at an ENSA hostel in Ulverston, where they finally arrived, hungry and travel-weary at seven o'clock that evening. The hostel was basic but clean and warm and the meal, for which they were more than ready, was hot and plentiful.

Next morning they set off armed with a map for Millington where they were to do a lunchtime concert at a munitions factory.

'It'll only be a potted version of the show,' Maisie had explained to Laura the previous evening. 'We only have forty-five minutes – their lunch break in other words – so we take out the sketches and just do the musical numbers, plus Arthur and Algernon. Don will act as compère and introduce us all.'

Ed found the factory without too much trouble in spite of the fact that all the signposts had been taken down. To their surprise the factory boasted an entertainments manager who welcomed them warmly and took them along to one of the offices which had been set aside for a dressing-room. Sandwiches and tea had been provided for their lunch and a screen set up for the ladies' privacy.

'Talk about prudish!' Maisie laughed as she peeled off her uniform and climbed into her costume for the opening number. 'Anyone who can't stand a tantalizing glimpse of my corsets had better look the other way!'

Laura on the other hand took advantage of the screen to change. She was nervous as the Moonlight Follies took to the stage for the opening number, but she needn't have worried. The canteen was packed and their appearance received a reception that almost raised the roof. The audience roared with laughter at Don's jokes and Algernon's squeaky cheekiness. They loved Ed's songs at the piano and joined in the chorus of 'There'll Always Be an England' with patriotic gusto. When Don introduced her, Laura was surprised to hear him announce her as 'Laura, the Berkeley Square nightingale'. When she sang 'The White Cliffs of Dover' and did her graceful little dance they called for an encore.

The forty-five minutes flew and almost before she knew it the Moonlight Follies' first performance was over. For Laura the ice had been broken. And as she changed back into her street clothes in the makeshift dressing-room she felt a warm glow that had nothing to do with the electric fire provided by the factory. She had loved every minute. At last she was a professional performer.

That evening they travelled to Barrow-in-Furness to perform their show at the shipyard. The venue was in a huge shed, draughty and cold, with a makeshift platform at one end. The 'dressing-rooms' consisted of a curtained-off area behind the stage. At first it looked less than promising, but someone had provided an electric fire and quantities of hot tea. Once again they received a rousing reception, especially Laura whose appearance was greeted with loud whistles of approval. When she came off the stage blushing and slightly indignant that they hadn't listened to her number, Maisie laughed.

'That's something you're going to have to get used to, love,' she said. 'These lads haven't seen a pretty girl like you since they left home. You're a sight for sore eyes for them all and no mistake. They don't give a damn whether you can sing or not. It's that luscious pair of pins they're looking at!'

In the weeks that followed, the Moonlight Follies played for sailors at naval bases and soldiers at gun sites and army camps up and down the north-west coast. Spring turned into summer and Meg's foreboding about the weather in the 'frozen north' turned out to be wrong. Laura found the summer weather and the beautiful Cumbrian scenery breathtaking and wrote home to tell her parents so.

Occasionally they would play right through an air raid and Laura grew used to the sound of bombs exploding and losing half their audience as they rushed off to their various duties. Sometimes the electricity would fail and they would finish the show by the light of Tilley lamps kept for such emergencies.

Sometimes Maisie would take it into her head that they were getting stale and she would choose some new numbers, rehearsing them when and wherever they could find a piano. Don's act was never stale. He was always coming up with new jokes and Arthur did his best to vary Algernon's material as much as he could. But wherever they went and whatever they did the reception was always the same. Sometimes a supper would be laid on for them and they would meet some of the boys they had entertained. They always wanted to know where they came from and seemed hungry for news from home, however trivial.

Laura wrote home as often as she could. At the end of May she had received a letter from Moira along with a photograph of herself and David on their wedding day. The pair of them looked so happy that it brought a lump to Laura's throat. Sadly the piece of cake that accompanied it was crushed beyond recognition. In her letter Moira said David had only managed to get a forty-eight hour pass and that he was now on his way to an unknown destination overseas. She was still living with Mum and Dad in the flat above the shop apart from the few days each month that she spent at college. She was looking forward to taking her final exams and returning home for good at the end of the summer to take up the teaching post she had been offered at Snape Street Elementary School.

I know it's not very adventurous, she wrote. *And in a way I wish I could do something more exciting, like you. But I feel that with David in so much danger one of us has to be safe. When he comes home we plan to get a place of our own and I'll be saving up as hard as I can for when that day comes.*

Laura later heard that David was in the desert, fighting with the Eighth Army in El Alamein. She read the letter with sadness, hoping that he would be safe and wishing that she could look forward to Peter coming home safe and sound. She dropped the occasional postcard to his mother and wrote regularly to Rosa, trying to make her letters interesting and entertaining. She knew that Rosa was disappointed that she had joined a concert party. She had hoped for something better for her star student. In her replies she constantly urged Laura to apply for a place with one of ENSA's touring repertory companies and promised to contact anyone she thought might help. But Laura was in no hurry. For the present she was happy where she was. She enjoyed performing for the boys and was growing fonder of her colleagues every day.

Back home in Millborough life went on as usual. Meg and Harry were happy to have Moira at home with them. Harry spent almost every evening at the ARP post as air raids became more frequent during that summer. Since the thousand-bomber raid on Cologne in May Hitler seemed determined to bomb every cathedral city in the country. They became known as the 'Baedeker Raids'. Harry was incensed. How dare that evil little man ruin England's precious heritage as though it was a pack of cheap cards? Harry might not be young enough or fit enough to go and fight. But while he had breath in his body, he told Meg, he would do everything he could to defend his country! For her part, Meg was preoccupied about the sweet rationing, brought into force in July. More paperwork for her and more cutting out of those fiddly little coupons, though she hoped it would mean an end to the shortages and constant queues whenever the shop had a delivery.

Vicky found life hard work since Sid had moved in. Shopping

and cooking for one extra was an effort, not to mention the extra washing and ironing. On Monday mornings she would get up at dawn to light the copper in the wash house so as to get finished and pegged out before it was time to go to work. Sid's laundry added to the load of Dan's endless sheets and pyjamas, and the sight of his grey vests and underpants and tattered pyjamas, filled her with revulsion. Always by Monday evenings she was dead on her feet.

Dan's leg wasn't getting any better either. When the siren sounded he always refused to be helped to the shelter, which meant that she couldn't go either. Some nights he was delirious and woke her with his ravings. She would go in to him, trying to reduce his temperature with cold water and a flannel, which he would push roughly away, his thin arms flailing like windmill sails. But in the morning he always insisted that she must have dreamed it and that he had slept like a baby. In spite of Sid's initial offers to help with Dan he never seemed to hear either the siren or Dan's cries, apparently sleeping soundly on his narrow bed in the front parlour, the door firmly closed. Often while she was cooking the evening meal he would come into the kitchen and stand silently behind her. Vicky hated it. His silent presence unnerved her and gave her the creeps.

'Isn't there something you'd like to do?' she asked him one evening.

He smirked. 'Oh yes, there is – but you wouldn't let me, would you? Don't wanna get my face slapped.'

'I *meant* don't you want to look at the evening paper?' she said, averting her scarlet face.

'Oh, I know what you meant, Vick,' he said coming up behind her and touching the back of her neck in a way that made her flesh crawl. 'Trouble is with you, you're too tired to flirt after workin' all day in that shop. Why don't you pack it in?'

She shook off his hand and moved away. 'I've told you before. I like it there. I don't want to give it up.'

'Yer dad's gettin' really bad,' he said. 'He could really do with 'avin' you at 'ome with 'im.'

She rounded on him. 'Don't you tell me what I should be doing for Dad,' she said. 'When you moved in you said you'd help with him. After all, he is your friend. When did you last get up in the night to help me with him?'

'Woa!' He held up his hands in mock surprise. 'Easy, tiger!' He grinned. 'Proper little spitfire, ain't you? Reason I don't come up is I know it'd be more 'n my life's worth to venture up them stairs after lights-out. I reckon you'd scream blue murder if I was to get a butcher's of you in yer nightie.'

Too disgusted to reply, Vicky turned back to the meal she was preparing. 'I often wish I could get Dad to the shelter when the siren goes. You could carry him.'

'Carry him! That's a laugh. Can you imagine yer dad lettin' anyone carry 'im if 'e didn't want 'em to?'

Vicky shrugged. She had to agree that it wouldn't be easy.

'Me room could do with a good clean,' he ventured.

Vicky turned to look at him. 'When you first moved in it was on the understanding that you did your own cleaning,' she told him. 'How do you think I can manage to wash, iron and cook, look after Dad – *and* clean your room?'

'It's like I said – you could if you didn't work at that shop,' he pressed. 'I could even pay you a bit more if that's what you're after.'

'I'm not *after* anything. And I do work at the shop so that's that.' She dished up the meal and passed him his plate. 'Are you going to have this in your room or will you take it up and have it with Dad?'

He smiled maddeningly. 'Is that a hint that you don't want me company? You're cruel, Vicky Watts. That's what you are. A cold-'earted little tease.' When she didn't reply he shrugged. 'OK, I get it. I'll eat it on me tod in me room.' In the doorway he turned. 'One o' these days you're gonna be sorry you turned down a good catch like me.'

It was a week later when Meg Nightingale was cashing up near to closing time that the shop bell tinkled.

'We're closing in a. . . .' The words froze on Vicky's lips as she looked up to see Sid standing at the counter. 'What do you want? Why aren't you at work?'

He started back, looking round in mock surprise as though he thought she was addressing someone behind him. 'What *me*? I thought you might like me to walk you home. I knock off at five, remember, and it's twenty-five past – OK?'

'We don't close till half past,' Vicky reminded him.

Meg glanced at her. 'You can go now if you like, dear.'

'No, it's all right. We haven't finished cashing up,' Vicky said firmly.

Sid took up his position by the door. 'That's OK. I'll wait.'

There was little she could do and Vicky held the bag while Meg slipped the rest of the loose change into it and tied the top. Meg glanced at Sid, sensing and misinterpreting the atmosphere.

'I'll take the coupons upstairs and check them,' she said. 'Why don't you get your coat and go home. You can lock up as you go as usual, can't you dear?'

'Of course.'

Meg took the Oxo tin she collected the sweet coupons in and went through the door to the stairs. 'Goodnight then, Vicky love. See you in the morning,' she said, casting a curious look in Sid's direction as she went.

Vicky slipped through into the lobby to put on her coat then came back into the shop. Glancing at the counter she asked, 'Where's the bag?'

Sid looked puzzled. 'Bag. What bag?'

'The bag – with the day's takings. Mrs Nightingale usually leaves me to put it—' She broke off, looking at Sid. 'Where is it?'

He shrugged. 'D'you mean that brown leather bag with the string round the top?'

'Yes.'

'The old gel took it with 'er when she went upstairs.'

'But she – I usually. . . .' Vicky bit back the words. She had almost given away the fact that the takings were always put in a secret hiding place until closing time. Clearly Meg hadn't wanted

Sid to see. 'Oh, I see.' She opened the door and stood aside for him to pass through then she followed, locking the door behind her. Sid looked as she slipped the key into her bag.

'They trust you with a key, do they?' Sid sneered. 'A bit fool-'ardy ain't it?'

'What do you mean?'

'Never trust no one, that's my motto,' he said. 'It's the only way you don't get let down.'

To her surprise Sid kept out of the way all that evening. He had a wireless in his room and sometimes he listened to the news and the variety programmes. Occasionally he went to the pub on the corner for an hour. Vicky didn't care what he was doing as long as he was out from under her feet. She had a huge pile of ironing to do and for once Dan wasn't too demanding. It was when she went into work the following morning that the trouble began. Meg was waiting for her, a worried look on her face.

'What did you do with the takings last night, Vicky?'

Vicky shook her head. 'Nothing. You took them upstairs with you.'

'Me? Course I didn't.' Meg frowned. 'You know I never do that. I always leave you to put the bag in the cupboard under the counter.'

'Yes, but last night was different. You—' Vicky broke off. 'You mean – you mean they're missing?'

'I've searched high and low. The money's gone, bag and all.'

'But who could have taken it? I locked up when I left.' Vicky stared at her employer. 'Mrs Nightingale – you don't think that *I* took it?'

'*No!*' Meg coloured. 'No, of course not. It's just that – I mean who else could have taken it?'

'Then you *do* think it was me?' Vicky's eyes filled with tears. 'I'd never steal from you or anyone else, Mrs Nightingale.'

Meg reached out a hand to her. 'Vicky, love. I know you find it hard to make ends meet. If you needed anything I wish you'd said.'

'It wouldn't matter how hard up I was, I'd never steal.' Vicky fumbled for her handkerchief, unable to keep the tears at bay. 'I'd better go. You won't want to employ someone you think is a thief.'

'Vicky, look. We can sort this out. If the bag were to be found again then nothing more would be said. And if you need a rise then I'm sure we can. . . .'

'*If I put it back*, you mean?' Vicky shook her head in disbelief. Meg clearly didn't believe her. It was like her worst nightmare. 'I'll go now, Mrs Nightingale. I didn't take the money and I can't stay where I'm not trusted.' She was putting on her coat as she spoke.

Meg remained silent, her face pink with awkwardness. She watched helplessly as Vicky went out through the door and walked away down the street. She didn't want to believe that the girl was a thief. Vicky Watts was the best assistant she'd ever had and she didn't know what she would do without her. But a whole day's takings meant a lot, especially in these hard times, and really, what was there to think? She was the last person to handle the bag.

At home Vicky let herself into the house. All was quiet and she went through to the kitchen and gave way to the tears she had been holding back all the way home. That Mrs Nightingale could have thought her capable of stealing was unbearable. When the tears abated she went upstairs to check her father and found him asleep. She crept downstairs so as not to wake him and it was as she was taking off her coat that a sudden thought struck her.

Silently she went through to the hall and let herself into the parlour. Sid had left the room in turmoil, his bed unmade and clothing strewn about. She looked around, unsure of where to begin looking and loath to touch any of his things. Her search – under the bed, in the fireside cupboard, down the sides and back of the armchair – revealed nothing. Then, just as she was about to give up she noticed that there was a fresh fall of soot in the empty fireplace. Pushing up her sleeve she knelt down and reached up into the chimney and there, sure enough, on a ledge a little way up, was the bag. Shaking the loose soot from it she opened it. At a glance, the takings seemed to be intact and there, at the bottom of the bag, was her key to the shop. Sid must have taken the bag last night while she was putting on her coat, knowing that she would be accused of stealing and lose her job. The problem was, even now that she had found it, how could she prove that Sid was the culprit? After mulling the problem over for a while and failing to come to a conclusion she decided to put the bag back where she had found it and say nothing for the moment.

That night Vicky was wakened by the now-familiar wail of the sirens. She got up and checked on Dan, but as usual he refused to be disturbed even though they could already hear the drone of the planes and the occasional thud of a distant explosion.

'If my number's on it then it won't matter where I am,' he grunted, turning over in bed. 'Still, now you're up, I'll have a cup of tea.'

Vicky wondered about *her* number but she said nothing as she went back to her room and dressed. As the kettle was coming to the boil downstairs in the kitchen; Sid suddenly appeared in the doorway.

'Makin' tea? Just the job.' He rubbed his hands and sat down at the kitchen table. Vicky noticed with revulsion that he still wore his ragged pyjamas with a sweater over the top.

'You never wake as a rule,' she remarked. 'What got you up tonight?'

'Somethin' goin' on out in the street woke me up,' he said. 'A lot of them busy-body wardens millin' about blowing whistles and bawlin'. Bloody little Hitlers, they are.'

The next moment there was a loud banging on the street door and a voice shouted. 'Open up! ARP!'

Vicky opened the door and found herself looking into the face of Harry Nightingale.

'Oh, it's you, Vicky,' he said. 'I'm afraid we've got an unexploded bomb at the end of the street. We're gonna have to evacuate everyone till the UXB boys get here to deal with it.'

'Oh, but I can't—'

'I'm sorry, love, but orders is orders. Just get your coat and go to St Mary's Hall on Villiers Street,' he went on. The WVS ladies are there so there'll be tea and something to eat.'

'But there's Dad,' Vicky said. 'He's bedridden. I can't leave him.'

'Oh, of course, so he is. Right, leave it to me. I'll get the ambulance chaps on to it.'

Vicky went back into the kitchen where Sid was still drinking his tea. 'You'd better get dressed,' she told him. 'Seems there's an unexploded bomb at the end of the street and we have to evacuate to St Mary's Hall.'

Sid didn't need telling twice. It took him only minutes to throw on some clothes and he was out of the door and heading down the street without a thought for Vicky or her father.

The ambulance drew up outside a few minutes later and two burly men in the familiar navy blue uniform knocked on the door. Vicky followed them upstairs and began to explain to Dan that they had to leave. However, the ambulance men had him out of bed and wrapped in a blanket before she had time to finish. Dan made surprisingly little fuss, only groaning a little when they lifted him from the bed and carried him down the narrow stairs between them.

'Shall I come with him?' Vicky asked, but the driver shook his head.

'Sorry, love, we've already got two more casualties on board. No room for relatives. We'll be taking him to St Freda's though. You can visit in the morning and see how he is.'

She stood helplessly in the road as the ambulance drew away. Poor Dad. It was the first time he'd left his room in over a year. He must be frightened. Seeing him so submissive was even more upsetting to her than if he'd shouted and railed. He'd looked so frail and pathetic in the arms of the two brawny ambulance men.

'You all right, love?' It was Harry who spoke, touching her shoulder.

Vicky turned to him, a lump in her throat. 'Yes, thank you, Mr Nightingale. Will the bomb go off, do you think?'

He shook his head. 'I'm sure it'll be all right. Those UXB blokes know what they're doing. Right as rain in a couple of hours, I shouldn't wonder. Lucky it didn't go off. It would've razed the street to the ground if it had.'

Vicky shuddered and Harry squeezed her shoulder. 'Don't you worry, love. You'll be moving back in by breakfast like as not.'

'I hope you're right.' She pulled her coat around her. 'I'd better go then. Did you say St Mary's Hall?'

Harry pushed his tin hat to the back of his head and looked down at her. The girl looked so small and forlorn. 'Listen love, why don't you go along to the shop? Our Moira's in Wales at the moment. We can put you up for a few nights.'

Vicky shook her head. 'Oh, no thank you. I couldn't.'

'Come on, Vicky love. I know there's been a bit of a misunderstanding but the missus is really upset about what happened. I know she'd welcome a way to make it up to you.'

'Well. . . .'

'Anyway, with your dad in hospital you can't really come back here and live for the moment, can you?' Harry went on, 'Not on your own with that lodger fella. Wouldn't look right, would it?'

Vicky hadn't thought about Sid, but now that her attention was drawn to the fact that they'd be sharing the house alone together she shrank from the thought.

'I suppose not.'

Harry took her arm. 'Look, there's nothing else I can do here at the moment so I'll walk you round to Jessop Street.'

When Harry walked in with Vicky and explained about the bomb and her father's removal to hospital Meg immediately began to bustle round putting the kettle on. 'I'll make up the bed and put a hot water bottle in,' she said. 'Sit down, love. You look done in and you must be dying for a cuppa.'

Harry went back to his duties and Vicky joined Meg in the kitchen, trying awkwardly to apologize for her sudden arrival. 'I really didn't want to put you out,' she said. 'I could easily have gone to St Mary's Hall with the others,' she said. 'But Mr Nightingale insisted.'

'I should just hope so too.' Meg poured two cups of tea and sat down opposite her at the table. 'I'd never have forgiven him if he hadn't.' She reached out a hand to Vicky. 'I'm so sorry about the takings and everything. I never meant to accuse you. Harry and I feel really bad about it. I know you're as honest as the day's long and you'd never—'

'I know who took the bag,' Vicky interrupted. 'I know where it is at this moment. But I've no way of proving that it wasn't me.'

'You don't have to,' Meg said firmly. 'Was it that lodger of yours?' When Vicky didn't reply she shook her head. 'I might've known. Never did like the look of him – shifty eyes.'

'He didn't want the money. He did it to make me lose my job,' Vicky told her. 'He and Dad have both been on to me to give in my notice for ages and he must have seen it as a good way of forcing my hand. I had my suspicions and I searched his room this morning after I left here. He's hidden it up the chimney.'

'Well I never!' Meg looked thoughtful. 'I can see that you must find it hard, looking after two men and a house and working here as well. I'd understand if you wanted to leave.'

'But I *don't*!' Vicky said. 'You and Mr Nightingale are so kind. You're like – like family to me. I love working here. The thought of being shut up in the house all day with only Dad. . . .' She paused, her eyes brimming and her throat too tight for words. Meg squeezed her hand.

'There now, love, don't take on. Look, I said if the bag were to be found nothing would be said. When Harry gets back why don't you give him your key and tell him where to look?'

Vicky bit her lip. 'But when Sid finds it gone he'll say—'

'He can hardly *say* anything, can he?' Meg was smiling. 'Does he know you left your job?'

'No, there hasn't been time to mention it.'

'It'll be a mystery to him then, won't it?' Meg began to chuckle. 'I'd like to be a fly on the wall when he fmds the money gone.'

By morning the bomb had been defused and the residents of Artillery Terrace were given the all-clear to return to their homes.

Harry Nightingale had paid a visit to Artillery Street the previous night with Vicky's key and found the takings bag exactly where she told him, on the ledge in the parlour chimney. He had agreed with his wife that it was wisest to say nothing at all about the discovery.

'Give a bloke enough rope and he's sure to hang himself,' he remarked, tapping the side of his nose. 'But between you 'n me, Meg, this wasn't all I found.'

Meg looked at him. 'What do you mean? What did you find?'

'There was another bag of money up that chimney besides our takings,' he told her. 'That fella's up to no good, you mark my words.'

Meg agreed but after some consideration they decided to say nothing to Vicky about Harry's discovery.

'The poor girl's got enough on her plate without piling any more on top of it,' she said.

Meg gave Vicky time off to visit Dan in St Freda's the following afternoon. Visiting time was from two till three-thirty and Meg gave her some sweets to take in for him.

When she arrived she was directed to the men's surgical ward and found Dan looking shrunken and pale in the end bed. He was restless and irritable.

'Thought you'd forgotten all about me,' he complained. 'Out of sight, out of mind!'

'I came as soon as I could, Dad. They don't allow visitors till the afternoon.' She gave him the bag of sweets. He opened it and peered inside.

'Toffees! You know I can't eat toffees,' he grunted. 'Get stuck all over me plate, they do.'

'Dad! They're from Mrs Nightingale. She gave up part of her sweet ration so that I could bring them to you.'

'More fool 'er then!' Dan screwed up the bag and tossed it at her. 'Eat 'em yourself if you want.'

'How do you feel?' she asked him.

'Terrible! Leg's givin' me gyp. Them clumsy blokes 'eavin' me about like a sack of spuds didn't 'elp!' He looked at her. 'Where's Sid?'

'At work I should think. The street was evacuated to St Mary's Hall last night so I haven't seen him today.'

'Is it safe now?'

'Yes. We've been given the all-clear.'

'You'll be goin' 'ome tonight then?'

'No, Dad. The Nightingales are putting me up for a few days, just till you get home. I can't be there with Sid on my own, can I?'

'Can't see why. What do them Nightingales wanna go pokin' their noses in for anyway?' He glared at her. 'You gotta go 'ome tonight. It's Friday.'

Vicky shook her head. 'I know it is, Dad. What's that got to do with it?'

'You gotta see that Sid. . . .' He stopped, plucking at the bed clothes and looking agitated. 'He – he—'

'He always spends some time with you on a Friday evening. Is that what you're trying to say?'

Dan nodded. 'Yeah. I – I need to see 'im.'

'All right. I'll ask him to come in and see you this evening at visiting time.' This seemed to pacify the old man for a moment until Vicky asked, 'So – are you all right, apart from your leg?'

'No, I'm bloody well not all right,' he barked. 'You wanna taste the muck they call food in 'ere! Never seen nuthin' like it! I thought your cookin' was bad enough! Tryin' to polish us off if you ask me!'

A nurse hovered at the end of the bed. 'Time for your medicine, Mr Watts.'

Dan pulled a face. 'Told you they was tryin' to poison me!'

The nurse gave Vicky a sympathetic smile. 'The sister would like a word with you,' she said quietly. 'She's in her office now if you'd like to slip along.'

Vicky tapped on the half-open door of the office in the corridor and a pleasant voice called to her to come in. The ward sister looked up from her desk and Vicky was surprised to see quite a young face under the flowing triangular cap.

'The nurse said you wanted to speak to me,' Vicky said. 'I'm Daniel Watts's daughter.'

'Ah, yes.' The sister swung round in her chair. 'Sit down, Miss Watts. Thank you for coming. Obviously you know that your father's leg is badly ulcerated and infected.'

'I've been doing my best to keep it clean and dressed,' Vicky said. 'He refuses to see a doctor.'

Sister nodded. 'I gathered that. You must have had a very difficult time with him. I imagine that he hasn't been the easiest of patients. However, the doctor has now examined his leg and confirmed my suspicions that gangrene has begun to set in.'

'Oh!' Vicky bit her lip. 'I was afraid it might have. I'm sorry.'

'The last thing you should do is blame yourself,' the sister said. 'If it hadn't been for your care it could have been a lot worse by now.' She took a deep breath. 'The trouble is that the prognosis isn't good. There is only one course of action, I'm afraid. The leg will have to be amputated if the gangrene is to be prevented from spreading. That is why he's here in a surgical ward. And it needs to be done as soon as possible.' She looked at Vicky, her head on one side. 'You will already have guessed that he refuses to sign the consent form.'

Vicky swallowed hard. 'I'm not sure that I can persuade him to change his mind.'

'Will you at least try?'

'Of course I will.'

'We're very busy here at St Freda's,' she went on. 'If he won't agree to the operation all we can do is to send him home and I'm sure you know what that means.' She looked at Vicky. 'I should warn you now that things will get very difficult if he refuses the operation – for you as well as for him. The pain will be excruciating and the nursing intensive, and as his condition worsens I doubt whether you could manage him yourself. You're very young and it really isn't fair on you.'

'But what else could I do?'

The sister sighed. 'Apart from a private nursing home your

only alternative would be St Edmund's.'

Both of them knew that the hospital now known as St Edmund's had been the old workhouse and although the care was adequate it was still considered a dreaded last resort by most of the old folk.

The sister opened a drawer and took out a form. 'I'll give you this. Take my pen and see what you can do before you leave.'

Back in the ward Dan looked drowsy after his medication. Vicky sat down beside him, her heart beating fast. 'Dad,' she ventured. 'Dad, the sister says you need an operation. If you don't have it your leg will get much worse.'

'Shove off,' Dan muttered. 'I'm not gonna be cut about just so some 'am-fisted old quack can practise on me. An' *you* – all *you* care about is—'

'*Dad*! Don't you want to be free of the pain? Can't you see that all I care about is you?' Her voice was strong and positive and she felt a small stab of surprise at the power she suddenly knew she possessed. 'You *have* to have this done, Dad,' she went on. 'If you refuse – I can't keep taking care of you at home. You'll end up having to go to—'

'The workhouse!' His pale eyes opened wide, staring at his usually submissive daughter with shock. 'That's what you're sayin' ain't it? You'd really send your own dad to the work'ouse!'

'It's not called that any more, but *yes*, Dad,' she said firmly. 'I'd have no choice. We couldn't afford a private nursing home. I've tried to help you, but there's nothing more I can do for you. The doctors and nurses in here want to help you and they can. Now it's time you helped yourself.' She put the consent form in front of him. 'Sign it, Dad. I meant what I said.'

For a moment he continued to stare at her as though he was seeing her for the first time, then very slowly he pulled himself upright in the bed. Taking the pen she held out to him he scrawled his name at the bottom of the form then threw the pen down.

'There! Satisfied, are you?' Tears filled his eyes and began to trickle down his cheeks. 'Fine daughter *you* turned out to be!' He turned away from her. 'Bugger off then,' he muttered. 'And don't forget to tell Sid to come. I might not be 'ere tomorrow.'

Vicky tapped on the door of the sister's office and handed in the form. The sister looked at it and smiled.

'Well done,' she said. 'It's the right decision. We'll be operating first thing tomorrow.'

At the end of the corridor, once out of sight of everyone, Vicky leaned against the wall and allowed the tears to fall. If anything happened to Dan it would be her fault. All her life she'd put up with his unfairness and his bullying, but seeing him so defeated, so frail and weak, gave her no sense of vengeance or triumph. All she could feel for him was pity and, inexplicably, guilt.

CHAPTER EIGHT

As summer turned to autumn and then winter the ENSA tour of the Moonlight Follies drew towards its close. They had gone up as far as Scapa Flow and the Isle of Orkney then all the way back down again. Laura had asked if they would need new material for the return visit but Maisie shook her head.

'Most of the lads who were there last time will have moved on by now,' she said sadly.

The tour was to close at the end of December and Laura was looking forward to going home. She followed the news with interest and was heartened by the fact that the Eighth Army seemed to be winning in the desert. It would clearly please Moira who wrote of the letters she had received from David. They were heavily censored of course, and it was typical that he said very little about the dangers he faced daily, complaining only about the food, the heat and the flies.

Victory in the desert would make up for the disastrous attempt at a landing at Dieppe where so many brave young men had been lost. It would be so good for the morale at home which seemed to have reached an all-time low in this winter of 1943.

The Moonlight Follies continued to sing and dance their way up and down the north-west coast, playing their part in cheering the boys, especially over the Christmas period. Sometimes they enjoyed comfortable accommodation in private lodgings. At other times they stayed in hostels where the rooms were cold and the food less than basic, but Laura learned to be what Maisie called a 'trouper'; taking the rough with the smooth and enjoying the support and camaraderie of her fellow entertainers.

Maisie had been delighted very early in their acquaintance to learn that Laura was a trained hairdresser and her skills were soon put to good use, cutting the men's hair as well as caring for her own and Maisie's. One Sunday evening when Laura was giving her a shampoo and set she became talkative on a more intimate subject than usual.

'I hope you're going to stay with us, Laura,' she said. 'You know, you've become like a daughter to Ed and me since you joined us.'

Laura was touched. 'I've been very happy with the Follies,' she said.

Maisie looked up at her through the spotted dressing table mirror. 'But you still want to go off somewhere and play Juliet and Rosalind, don't you?'

Laura laughed. 'Plenty of time for that,' she said. 'Anyway, I'll have to wait for the opportunity.'

Maisie was silent for a while. 'You know, we had a daughter once, Ed and me,' she said quietly. 'It was a long time ago.'

Laura was surprised. 'Did you? Where is she, at boarding school?'

Maisie shook her head. 'We lost her when she was four. Diphtheria. Nothing anyone could do. All over in two days, it was. It broke our hearts. It still doesn't seem quite real, you know. Sometimes I have to remind myself that she was ever with us at all.'

'Oh, Maisie. I'm so sorry. And you never – never thought of. . . .'

'Having more kids?' Maisie shook her head. 'No child could ever replace our little Molly. Anyway, it seems it wasn't to be. It was like we had just the one chance and we messed it up.'

'It wasn't your fault,' Laura said.

Maisie shook her head. 'We were away such a lot. We had to leave her with my mum. I used to blame myself. If I'd given up the business and stayed with her there might have been something I could have done. But we had such plans, you see. We wanted to work hard and save up for her future. Little did we know she wouldn't have one.' She looked up at Laura. 'Sometimes when I look at you I kid myself that she might have looked a bit like you.' She blushed and shook her head. 'I hope that doesn't upset you.'

'No, no. It's a great compliment.'

'She would have been about your age now, you see.'

Laura put her arms around the older woman and gave her a hug. 'Maybe I could be your honorary daughter,' she said.

Maisie laughed shakily. 'Bless you, love, you're that already. The way you've taken to us and our barmy ways is nothing short of amazing. And there'll always be a welcome for you at 15 Deans Drive when we're at home, even when you're starring at The Old Vic. That's if you're not too grand for us by then.'

'I'll never be that,' Laura said. 'Never in a million years.'

Maisie was silent for a moment as Laura took the pins out of her hair and began to brush it. Then she said, 'That young chap of yours – what's his name – Peter?'

'Peter, yes.'

'He's only missing, you know. Never give up hope, sweetheart.'

Laura shook her head. 'His plane was shot down over Germany. All the crew went down with it. We have to face facts. I asked one of the boys at the RAF camp we visited a few weeks ago,' she said. 'He said that a plane that had been hit would almost certainly catch fire before it hit the ground or immediately after. There'd be. . . .' She swallowed hard. 'There'd be no one – nothing left to identify. That's why. . . .'

'Don't!' Maisie squeezed her hand. 'You mustn't dwell on it. Who was cruel enough to tell you this? Whoever he was he should be ashamed of himself!'

'He didn't know – I never told him why I wanted to know. These boys get quite hardened to the facts. Death is something they face every day.'

'All the same.' Maisie searched her face, her eyes concerned.

'You must try not to think about it, love. It can't do any good.'

Laura nodded. 'I know. I keep telling myself that there are so many others worse off than me. Young wives with children to bring up; mothers like Peter's who have no one else. I try to think of the good times we had.'

Maisie reached up to pat her cheek. 'That's the ticket, love. And there'll be someone else for you some day. Oh, I know you don't believe it now but there will be. Just you wait and see.'

When Laura got off the train at Millborough Central and walked through the town things looked somehow strange and unfamiliar. There had been some bomb damage, not much, but enough to distort the appearance of the landscape. Some shop windows were boarded up. Most shop and house windows were still crisscrossed with black sticky tape to prevent flying glass, and ugly blast walls stood sentinel outside many front doors. Moira had written that a crippled German bomber had crashed in the market square one Sunday night and miraculously had done hardly any damage.

It was Friday afternoon and people seemed to be going about their business normally. When Laura turned the corner into Jessop Street she was relieved to see that most things looked much the same as before. There had been a light fall of snow and the taped windows with their mock-leaded appearance gave the place quite a Dickensian look, especially Nightingale's shop with its bowed shop front. Laura's heart lifted. It was good to be home. When she opened the shop door Vicky gave a little squeal of delight.

'Oh! Welcome home, Laura!' Coming round the counter she stood smiling shyly. 'Don't you look smart in your uniform? Your mum and dad will be so pleased to see you. They've been waiting all day. I'll just give them a shout.' She opened the door behind the counter and called up the stairs. A moment later Meg and Harry were there, smiling their welcome.

'I didn't know when to expect you,' Meg said. 'I've had the kettle on and off since dinner time.'

'I came as far as London with the ENSA van,' Laura told her. 'I had to get the train from there and you know how unreliable they are.'

'Never mind. Get that coat off and come up and get warm,' Meg fussed. 'What a pity our Moira can't be home. This is her last term at college. She takes her finals in a couple of months and after that they've offered her a job at Snape Street Elementary so she'll be home for good.'

Laura laughed. 'I know, Mum. She wrote and told me.'

Harry gently pushed his wife out of the way so as to give his daughter a hug. 'Welcome home, lass. How long have you got?'

Meg bridled. 'Give the girl a chance to get in the door before you start asking her when she's going back!'

After Laura had unpacked and changed out of her uniform into civvies she went down to the shop to see Vicky.

'How are you, Vicky? And how is your father?' she asked. 'Mum wrote and told me about the unexploded bomb in your street and how you'd stayed here while your father was in hospital.'

Vicky nodded. 'It was so kind of them to put me up. Dad's much better, thank you, though you wouldn't think so to hear him grumble. I expect you heard that they took his leg off.'

'Yes, Mum said. It's awful to think of losing a limb.'

'Not for Dad though,' Vicky pointed out. 'It had given him so much pain. In a way it was a blessing in disguise, that unexploded bomb. But for that Dad would never have gone to hospital and seen a doctor. They told me he wouldn't have lived much longer without the amputation.'

'So can he get about now? It must be good for him not to be bedridden any more.'

'Well. . . .' Vicky sighed. 'They wanted to fit him with an artificial leg but he won't have it. He wouldn't let the district nurse come in and dress his wound for him when he first came home either.'

'So you had to do it?' Laura enquired.

Vicky nodded. 'Yes. It's healed nicely now though. He does get up and let me help him downstairs most days, but he just sits in the chair most of the time.'

'That's a pity.' Laura looked at the other girl, noticing for the first time how pale and tired she looked. 'What about that horrible man – Sid, was it? I hope he's stopped bothering you by now.'

'He lives with us now, I'm afraid,' Vicky told her.

'*Lives* with you?' Laura was appalled.

'Yes. That was why your mum asked me to stay here while Dad was in hospital. Sid's landlady asked him to leave as she was going to live with her daughter and Dad seemed set on offering him our parlour.' She sighed. 'He works at Shearing's and of course his rent does help. I have to admit that, but. . . .'

'But you hate having him round you all the time?'

Vicky gave a little shudder. 'He gives me the creeps. He's even suggested that we should get married.'

Laura's jaw dropped. 'Oh, you're *joking*! What did you say?'

'What do you think? I seem to spend most of my time avoiding him,' Vicky told her.

'Mum told me about the time he took the shop takings to get you the sack,' Laura told her. 'Of all the dirty tricks. Why don't you tell him to leave?'

Vicky sighed. 'It's Dad. He seems to like Sid – can't see any wrong in him. Sometimes it's almost as though Sid has – I don't know *hypnotized* him. Even when I told him about Sid's, you know, pestering me he just laughed. Said I was being too fussy.'

Laura felt desperately sorry for Vicky. She couldn't imagine living that kind of life, waiting on two such unpleasant men as Dan Watts and Sid Taylor. 'Tell you what,' she said. 'While I'm home you and I will have another trip to the pictures. Would you like that?'

Vicky's eyes lit up. 'Oh, I *would*. Thanks, Laura. That would be lovely – something to look forward to.' She glanced at the door to the stairs and lowered her voice. 'Your mum and dad seem to be happier with you acting for a living nowadays, don't they?'

Laura smiled. 'I think they're gradually coming to terms with it,' she said. 'Though I sometimes wonder if they'll want me to carry on once the war's over.'

Vicky bit her lip. 'I was ever so sorry to hear about your friend, Peter Radcliffe.'

Laura nodded. 'I know.' Anxious to change the subject she pointed to a pile of evening papers that had just been delivered. 'Right then. Shall we have a look and see what's on?'

Next morning Laura ran into Ethel Radcliffe as the older woman was coming home from her Saturday morning shift at Shearing's. She seemed in good spirits and was pleased to see her.

'You will come home with me and have a cup of tea, won't you?' she invited.

As they drank tea together in Ethel's neat little living-room Laura couldn't help looking at the framed photograph of Peter in his ATC uniform that stood on the mantelpiece. Ethel caught her looking at it.

'He looked so handsome, didn't he?' she said. 'That was taken when he got his wings just after his first solo flight. He was so disappointed not to be allowed to be a pilot in the RAF,' she went on. 'I've never understood why they turned him down. You'd have thought they'd need all the pilots they could get, wouldn't you?' Her eyes filled with tears, which she hastily dabbed away. 'Take no notice of me, dear,' she said. 'It all comes over me now and again.' She put the photograph back on the mantelpiece and tucked her handkerchief back into her sleeve. 'Have you got a photo of him?' she asked.

'No, not even a snapshot,' Laura told her. 'I wish I had.'

'Oh, then I must find you one.' Ethel got up and took a large biscuit tin out of the sideboard cupboard. 'I've got them all in here, right from when he was a baby. Just look through them and take what you want. Goodness knows there are plenty of them. I keep promising myself to stick them all into an album.'

Laura looked through the snapshots and felt a lump fill her throat. It was all here; a complete record of Peter's life, right from birth. There were snaps of him as a chuckling baby in his pram, others as an awkward, knobbly-kneed schoolboy in short trousers and a school blazer. There was one of him as a gauche teenager proudly astride his new bike, and another in his first grown-up suit, his hair slicked down with brilliantine and his hands stiffly at his sides. Then she found it. It had been taken at a day out at the seaside that she'd almost forgotten. Looking at it brought the day vividly back: the salty scent of the sea, the warm sand between their toes. There they were, standing at the water's edge, two barefoot teenagers laughing into the sunlight and holding hands. She recalled with sudden poignancy that Peter had kissed her on the way home in the bus. It had been their first kiss. Tears tightened her throat and she swallowed hard. Over the past couple of years she'd neglected Peter in favour of her acting classes. He'd asked her out so many times but all too often she'd been too busy. At the time she had thought he would always be there. Now he was gone for ever and she wished so much that she could turn back the clock.

'May I have this one, Ethel?' she asked. 'We're both in it.'

'Of course you can, dear.' Ethel watched as Laura put the snap away in her handbag. 'I haven't given up, you know,' she said quietly. 'The telegram only said "missing" after all. I'll never give up hope.'

Laura couldn't reply. Instead she crossed the room and gave the older woman a hug. 'I think you're so brave,' she said, hiding her face against Ethel's shoulder.

'That's the one small part that mothers like me can play in this war,' Ethel said softly. 'We can't give up and give in. That's for cowards.'

When she left Ethel, Laura went on to visit Rosa. Her old drama teacher was overjoyed to see her.

'Now, let me look at you,' she said, holding Laura at arms' length as they stood in the studio. 'Mmm.' She frowned, her head on one side. 'A little too thin, I think.'

Laura laughed. 'Mum's cooking will soon put that right,' she said. 'The food isn't always up to much in the digs.'

'So – sit down and tell me all about it,' Rosa requested. 'I know from your letters where you've been but I want to hear what you've been up to.'

Laura told her how she had met one or two celebrities on her travels with the Follies. 'Ivor Novello was in Orkney when we were there,' she said. 'I saw him playing and singing the songs from *Glamorous Night*. I only got the briefest glimpse of him but I did get his autograph afterwards. The boys loved him. He'd written some new songs especially for them. Then George Formby was appearing at the Kirkby RAF camp with his famous ukulele. He had special material too.' She grinned. 'Some of it a bit saucy.'

Rosa looked wistful. 'I hope you're not getting into bad habits.'

Laura bridled. 'What kind of bad habits?'

'It's all very well, darling, doing a bit of a song and dance but I don't want you to forget that you're an actress,' Rosa said. 'I don't want you wasting your talent.'

'I'll never do that,' Laura told her. 'If I could only get the chance I'd join a legit company tomorrow.'

'Ah – well, I might just be able to help there,' Rosa said. Seeing that she had Laura's attention she went on. 'I had a letter from a friend a couple of days ago. She knows Hugo Ingram and apparently he's working with ENSA now. Not acting but as a producer/organizer. 'He's getting a company together and they're taking out a tour of *The Corn is Green*. It's Emlyn Williams's latest play and very good; some say his best yet. Now. . . .' She held up a conspiratorial finger. 'If by some happy coincidence you happened to apply now, you might just get an audition for it. Hugo was impressed by you at your exam, remember, and if you were to remind him. . . .'

'Oh, Rosa!' Laura felt excitement tighten her stomach muscles. 'Do you really think I'd be in with a chance?'

'I certainly do. I've read the play and there's a part in it that's just made for you.' Rosa looked at her watch. 'Why don't you telephone now? You can use my phone.'

Laura got through to ENSA headquarters and could hardly

believe her luck when Hugo Ingram happened to be in the building. As she waited for him to come to the phone her heart was beating fast, and when she heard his voice on the other end of a crackling line her mouth went so dry that she was afraid she wouldn't be able to speak.

'Hello, Miss Nightingale?'

She took a deep breath. 'Yes. I wonder if you remember me, Mr Ingram. You were my examiner here in Millborough recently when I took my LR.'

'I certainly do remember you. It's Laura, isn't it? What can I do for you?'

'Well. . . .' She looked at Rosa who nodded encouragingly. 'I heard on the grapevine that you were auditioning for a new tour.'

'Really? On the grapevine, eh? Well in this case the grapevine was reliably informed. It so happens that I'm auditioning next week. But only ENSA members.'

'I am already a member of ENSA actually,' Laura told him. 'I've been touring with the Moonlight Follies but what I really want is to further my acting experience.'

'The Moonlight Follies, eh?' Hugo could hardly keep the amusement out of his voice. 'That sounds like fun. What made you join up with them?'

'It's a long story,' Laura told him. 'When I came up for my ENSA audition the train was late and I missed my session. But the Follies were short of a soubrette and they asked me to join them. It was. . . .' She swallowed, anxious not to sound disloyal to her friends the Knights. 'As you say – great fun and at the time it was better than nothing.'

'I see. But now you're planning to leave them in the lurch?'

'Oh no! We've just finished our tour and they understand that if I were to get a chance of a part in a play, I'd take it. They've always known that.'

'And you think that I can help?'

Laura bit her lip and looked at Rosa. 'Well, I'd like to audition for you and as you say you're auditioning next week. . . .'

She heard Hugo chuckle softly at the other end of the line. 'Well, now. let me see.' There was a pause and then, 'Can you come up to Drury Lane on Thursday? The play is Emlyn Williams's *The Corn is Green*. I can't promise anything of course, but you're welcome to join the other hopefuls.'

'Oh yes, of course I can come.'

'Good. I'll put you down for the afternoon session,' he said. 'Maybe you can find a train that's running reliably this time. Otherwise goodness knows what you'll end up doing – touring with an acrobatic troupe perhaps!' He chuckled. 'I look forward to meeting you again, Laura. Goodbye.'

'Goodbye.' Laura put the receiver down and jumped up to hug Rosa. 'I've got it,' she said. 'I've got an audition!'

Rosa held up a warning hand. 'An *audition*, darling. That doesn't mean you've got the part. Don't count your chickens.'

'I'll get it, Rosa. I just *know* I will,' Laura said.

'I hope you're right and I know it won't be for the want of trying. I'll lend you my copy of the play and you can read it before you go.' She smiled and patted her shoulder. 'I'll keep my fingers crossed for you. We'll see, my darling. We'll see.' She reached for her stick. 'Meantime come down to the kitchen and we'll celebrate modestly with a cup of tea. I managed to get some Garibaldi biscuits yesterday, so you're in luck!'

Meg was happy to give Vicky the afternoon off on Monday so that she could go to the cinema with Laura.

'The poor girl never gets a break,' she said. 'Stuck in that miserable little house with her awful father and that Sid Taylor. I wouldn't trust that man as far as I could throw him.'

'Vicky told me he asked her to marry him,' Laura confided. Meg looked shocked.

'Oh my dear Lord!' she said. 'I hope she told him where to go.'

Laura smiled. 'I get the feeling that Vicky is learning to stand up for herself a bit more these days,' she said.

'Well, not before time,' Meg said. 'Seems to me it's her only hope of not getting walked all over!'

They went to the matinée at the Plaza. The film that was show-ing was *Mrs Miniver* with Greer Garson. Sitting there in the dark as the opening titles appeared on the screen the two girls were each busy with her own thoughts.

Laura's mind was on the coming audition. She had read the script that Rosa had lent her and loved it. The role of Bessie was just the kind of part she longed for. Every time she thought about it her stomach turned over with excitement and apprehension. She just *had* to get that part. She'd be so disappointed if she didn't. She had telephoned Maisie to warn her that there was a chance she wouldn't be with them for their next tour. The older woman had been disappointed but not surprised.

'I'll be keeping my fingers crossed for you,' she said. 'Part of me hopes you won't get it of course. I'd be a hypocrite if I said anything else, but I do know how much you want this, sweet-heart, so I'll put my own feelings aside for once.'

'I just hope the trains are running on time,' Laura said.

'Well, why don't you come up on Wednesday and stay with us overnight?' Maisie suggested. 'We'd love to have you and that way you'd be sure to get up to The Lane in good time.'

'Oh, Maisie! How kind. Yes, I'd love that.'

Vicky was thinking about the fuss that Dan had made about her outing the previous evening.

'It's all right for you, gaddin' about enjoyin' yerself,' he complained. 'No thought for yer dad, sittin' 'ere all on me own. 'Ardly able to move and 'avin' to get me own tea.'

'It's only this once, Dad,' she'd argued. 'I never go out, you know that. It's just for a couple of hours. I'll be home in plenty of time to get your tea.'

'Oh, go on then. Can't expect no consideration from you, can I? You've always been an ungrateful child.'

It was more or less what she had expected. What she hadn't expected was the incident that had occurred this lunchtime which was deeply worrying.

Meg had let her go early so that she could make Dan some lunch and have time to get ready for the early afternoon showing at the cinema. She let herself in and went straight upstairs to take off her coat. At the top of the stairs she was surprised to hear someone moving about in her father's room. Knowing that she had helped him downstairs that morning before she went to work she was puzzled. He never attempted to get back up the stairs without her help. She opened the door.

'Dad! How did you—' She stopped, the words freezing in her throat. Sid was standing at the chest of drawers. All three drawers were open, their contents spilling out on to the floor. Vicky's mouth dropped open. 'What on earth do you think you're doing?'

Sid straightened up. His colour deepened but his expression was defiant. 'I lent yer dad a book,' he said. 'I didn't want to bother askin' for it back so I thought I'd just come up and get it.'

It was only then that she noticed other disturbances in the room. The bed was rumpled and the door of the bedside cabinet hung open. 'Why are you here?' she asked, looking round her. 'You never come home in the middle of the day.'

'I – I had a couple of hours off to – go on an errand,' he stammered.

'So you thought you'd come and get your book back?'

'That's right.'

'So – have you found it?'

Sid was making a clumsy attempt at tidying the chest, picking up items of clothing and stuffing them back into the drawers. 'No.'

Vicky began to fold her father's things and put them in order. 'It's funny,' she said. 'But I can't remember seeing either you or Dad with a book.' She straightened up and looked at him. 'What book was it? What was it called?'

He shrugged. 'Oh, just a book – about Shearing's – in the old days when he used to work there.'

'Well, I'll ask him where it is for you, shall I?'

'No! Don't bother 'im with it. It don't matter.' Sid turned and began to walk away.

He had reached the doorway when she said, 'It's risky you

know – looking for books in other people's bedrooms. If it were to happen again I might take you for a burglar and send for the police.'

Sid spun round, his dark eyes gleaming with malevolence. 'Think you're clever, Vicky Watts, don't you? Talkin' in riddles and makin' threats. I wouldn't make an enemy out of me if I was you. One of these days you're gonna go down on your knees and beg me to 'ave pity on you.'

Vicky's heart missed a beat but she kept her head. 'Get out,' she said, as firmly as her pounding heart would let her. 'This is Dad's room and you have no right to be here. If I were to tell him—'

In one stride he was across the room and pinning her to the wall. She let out a cry of alarm as one large hand fastened tightly round her neck. His face almost touching hers, he hissed, 'Don't you threaten me, you little cow! I've been good to yer dad. I'm the only friend 'e's got and 'e 'owes me.' For a moment his eyes burned into hers and she knew a moment of real fear. Then suddenly he slackened his grip. 'You'll say nothing to yer dad about this,' he said. 'If I was forced to leave 'ere I'd make sure yer dad knew it was your doing, and you know 'e'd never let you forget that, don't you?' When she made no reply he tightened his grip on her throat again. 'Did you hear what I said?'

Her mouth too dry for words she nodded and he let her go. As she rubbed her bruised neck he said, 'I don't wanna do you no 'arm, Vick. The trouble is I've got this temper an' sometimes it gets the better of me. It'd pay you not to push me too far.' He narrowed his eyes derisively. 'Oh, don't play the drama queen! I never 'urt you so don't make out I did.'

She stared at him, her heart full of loathing. 'This time I'll say nothing to Dad,' she said. 'But if I ever catch you in his room again, I'm warning you – I will.'

He smiled, his lip curling. '*Ooh*! I can see I'm gonna 'ave to be careful,' he mocked. 'Let me give you a bit of advice, Vick. If I was you I'd be a bit nicer to me. You'd find it'd pay you in the end. Right, I'll be off now. There's no 'arm, eh? No need for Dan to know I was ever 'ere. Ta-ra, Vick. See you later.'

Sitting in her cinema seat Vicky relived the scene and shuddered inwardly. If she had suspected it before she was now convinced that Sid had some kind of hold over her father. She wished there was someone she could confide in, someone who could help, but there was no one. She tried hard to push the disturbing images out of her mind and enjoy the film.

It was already dusk when they came out of the cinema. There was a bitingly cold wind and the heavy grey skies threatened rain. Laura put up her collar and shivered.

'If it wasn't for the wartime double summertime it would already be blackout time by now,' she remarked. 'Though I do hate the dark mornings.' She peered at Vicky's sombre face and asked, 'Are you all right? Didn't you enjoy the film?'

Vicky managed a smile. 'Oh yes, it was lovely. Sad though.'

Laura tucked a hand through the other girl's arm. 'Tell you what, let's go up to the cinema café. My treat.'

'Oh no, I couldn't. . . .'

'Yes, you could.' Laura insisted. 'You've got plenty of time and we haven't really had time to have a chat.'

Vicky allowed herself to be escorted back into the cinema and up the stairs to the balcony café where Laura ordered a pot of tea and toasted teacakes. She told Vicky about the audition she was to attend later that week but as she was talking she noticed once more the distracted look on the other girl's face. Laying her hand on Vicky's arm she asked, 'There something bothering you, isn't there? Do you want to talk about it? I'm not prying, Vicky, and I can promise you it'll go no further. Is it to do with your father?'

'No.' Vicky smiled gratefully. 'It's something that happened this dinnertime.' She told Laura what had passed between herself and Sid. 'It's obvious he's looking for something,' she concluded. 'Though I can't think what. Dad and I are as poor as church mice. All Dad's got is his watch and he always keeps that on.'

'Well, Sid obviously thinks he's got more,' Laura said. 'Or perhaps it's not cash he's after. Either way I think you should tell your father, no matter what Sid made you promise. You can't let

117

him get away with violence and threats. In your own home too! It's disgraceful.'

Vicky nodded. 'Maybe you're right. Surely Dad wouldn't stand up for him if he knew what he'd done.' She took a bite of her teacake. 'Let's talk about something else. Wasn't Greer Garson lovely? I loved the bit where she found the German parachutist, didn't you? She was so brave.'

Outside the Plaza half an hour later the two girls parted company. Laura was concerned for Vicky's predicament, but she didn't really see what she could do to help. Before long her thoughts had returned to what was never far from her mind – the impending audition and her longing for that part.

Vicky tried to think only of the film she had enjoyed, but as she drew nearer to Artillery Terrace she dreaded the atmosphere at home. Dad and his constant complaining, Sid and his nastiness and devious ways. His sheer presence in the house disturbed and alarmed her now. Laura had been kind and sympathetic, but she had her own life to live and anyway, what could she or anyone else do to help? If only there were someone she could turn to, someone who could resolve her problems and make a difference. At that moment she felt more alone than ever before.

CHAPTER NINE

As the time drew near for Laura's audition she became more and more nervous. She travelled up to London on the Wednesday afternoon to stay with the Knights and stayed up late with Maisie and Ed, drinking coffee and talking about the future. The Moonlight Follies had been booked for an overseas tour and they were excited about it. They were to go to Egypt and Maisie couldn't wait to see Cairo and the Pyramids. As soon as they had heard that Laura might not be rejoining them they had begun telephoning around for a replacement. As luck would have it they had traced a young woman they had worked with a couple of summers before the war in Bournemouth. It happened that she was about to sign up for ENSA work anyway and she was only too glad to accept their offer.

'She's coming up to see us next week,' Maisie said. 'We always got on well with her before so it should work out OK.' She smiled. 'Sally's quite a bit older than you, Laura, and she won't be as good as our Berkeley Nightingale.'

'I'm sure she'll be better,' Laura said. 'I was never much of a singer.'

'Nonsense,' Ed insisted. 'You put those songs over with heart and sincerity and the lads loved you.'

On Thursday morning Maisie offered to accompany Laura up to Drury Lane. 'That's if you'd like some company,' she said. 'But don't worry, I won't come to the theatre with you,' she added quickly. 'I'll find a café somewhere near and wait for you there with a nice cuppa to celebrate.'

'If there's anything to celebrate,' Laura warned. 'It's not cut and dried.'

'They'd be barmy not to snap you up,' Maisie said stoutly.

They parted company on the corner of Catherine Street and when Laura said goodbye to Maisie and watched her disappear into a nearby café she felt suddenly apprehensive. Suppose she didn't get the part? Why should she anyway? There were bound to be other actresses more experienced than she was. Hugo had said that everyone at the audition would be hand-picked. Maybe she was wasting her own and everyone else's time.

She walked up to the theatre and went inside. Seated halfway back in the stalls were several people both male and female whom she took to be the committee. On the empty stage an older woman was auditioning, speaking a passage that Laura recognized from the play. She stood quietly at the back and it was as the woman finished that Hugo Ingram looked round and saw her. He stood up and beckoned to her.

'Come and sit down, Laura,' he said with a smile. 'There are one or two others to audition before you so you've got time to catch your breath.' He indicated the back row of the stalls and sat down beside her as a woman with a clipboard called out another name and a middle-aged man got up from the front row and took the stage.

'We're hoping to cast today,' he whispered. 'So there'll be no time to play around. If you want the part you'll have to make up your mind quickly.'

'Oh, I want the part,' Laura told him.

He turned to her, one eyebrow raised. 'What part? How do you know what I'll be offering you – if you're successful?'

She coloured. 'Oh! Well, there's really only the one, isn't there? I mean I wouldn't be suitable for—'

He patted her arm, laughing. 'I'm teasing you. You want to play Bessie, of course you do, who wouldn't? Well, as you'll see, I'm auditioning two other actresses for the part, so we'll just have to wait and see, won't we?'

At this news Laura felt more nervous than ever. And when she heard the other two actresses go through their paces she was even more worried. They were both very good and clearly far more experienced than she was. On the other hand, both of them were older than she was; one of them at least ten years older and the part called for an actress who could play a young schoolgirl in act one.

At last it was her turn. Her name was called and she stood up, her heart beating wildly. She had chosen the scene where Bessie returns to Wales from London, no longer a child, but a young woman, dressed in all her finery. She knew the scene by heart, having studied it from Rosa's copy of the script. The moment she began her nerves calmed. She was Bessie, the rebellious teenager. Brassy and bold, displaying her brand new adult image with buoyancy and scorn. When she had finished there was a moment's hush. She peered out into the auditorium and heard Hugo say. 'Thank you, Miss Nightingale. That will be all.'

She had been the last to audition and when she resumed her seat Hugo got up and walked up on to the stage.

'Thank you, ladies and gentlemen. That concludes the auditions for today. As some of you will already know, this tour is scheduled to go out in the first week of February which gives us only two weeks of rehearsal, so there is no time to waste. The play will tour the north and east of England first and later we might get an overseas tour, probably to the Middle East, depending on the course the war takes. My colleagues and I will meet in a few minutes' time to consider the casting. If you have a train to catch perhaps you will leave your details with my secretary, but I would appreciate it if you could stay. We hope to take no more than an hour, so can we please meet again here at . . .' He looked at his watch, 'say half past five?'

As Laura joined Maisie in the cafe a few minutes later the older woman looked up expectantly.

'How did it go?'

Laura sat down with a sigh. 'I've no idea. They're having a casting meeting and they want us all back there at half past five.'

Maisie called a waitress over and ordered a fresh pot of tea. 'Never mind, lovie,' she said. 'I know it's nerve-racking but the time will soon pass,' she said. 'Do you think you did well? You must have some idea.'

'I haven't.' Laura shrugged. 'There were two other girls auditioning for the same part, much more experienced than me. I'm pretty sure one of them will get it.'

'You can't be sure. Let's just wait and see.' A waitress brought the tea and Maisie began to pour, shaking her head as a thin, pale stream trickled into the cup. 'Oh my gawd!' She took the lid off the pot and stirred it vigorously. 'I reckon they *count* the flippin' leaves in this place,' she grumbled. 'It's too damned weak to crawl out of the pot.' She passed Laura a cup. 'Drink it anyway. I expect you're spitting feathers.'

'Thanks, I am.' Laura sipped the tea and tried to relax.

At twenty-five past five they began the walk back up the street to the theatre, Laura's stomach quaking with apprehension. Inside the auditorium the band of hopefuls were already assembled and at exactly half past Hugo walked out on to the stage, a sheet of paper in his hands.

'Thank you for your patience, ladies and gentlemen,' he said. 'Now that my colleagues and I have had time to deliberate, we have reached our decision. Your director on this tour will be Max Higham who will also play the leading part of Morgan Evans. The rest of the cast is as follows. . . .'

Laura waited with bated breath as the cast list was read out. First the older principal members of the cast then the supporting extras. The female juvenile lead came last of all. Hugo raised his eyes and looked down into the auditorium. 'We had three contenders for the part of Bessie Watty and, my first choice is Laura Nightingale.' His eyes searched her out in her front-row seat. 'Are you happy to accept the part, Laura?'

Maisie nudged Laura hard in the ribs. '*There*! What did I tell you?' she hissed. 'Go on – tell him yes!'

Laura rose shakily to her feet. 'Oh yes, I'd love to play it. Thank you, Mr Ingram.' Out of the corner of her eye she saw the other two actresses looking at her and sat down again quickly.

Hugo was speaking again but Laura could hardly take in what he was saying. 'Thank you all, ladies and gentlemen. If the cast members would like to stay behind for a few minutes I'll give everyone a rehearsal schedule and an itinerary.'

Half an hour later Laura and Maisie were on their way back to Burnt Oak on the train, Laura almost speechless and numb with disbelief.

'I still can't believe I got it!' she said, shaking her head incredulously. 'I *did* get it, didn't I, Maisie? I'm not dreaming?'

Maisie laughed. 'No, love, you're not dreaming. You deserve that part and you're going to be a big hit in it. Just wait till we tell Ed.' She looked at Laura with twinkling eyes. 'And did you get a gander at that Max Higham? Talk about a helluva hunk of man!'

'Is he? I didn't notice,' Laura said.

Maisie chuckled. 'Oh you will, my love,' she said under her breath 'You will all right!'

After the day that Vicky caught Sid in Dan's bedroom she felt that he was watching her all the time, always looking over her shoulder, and the feeling of intimidation grew as the weeks went by. He offered to help her father upstairs to bed each night, something which Dan accepted happily. But it seemed to Vicky that he spent far more time upstairs with her father than was necessary.

It was one day during her lunch break when Vicky had slipped home to make Dan a snack that she discovered that it was Sid who had persuaded him not to accept the artificial leg.

'If you let them fit you with a new leg you could get out of the house,' she remarked as she poured him a cup of tea. 'It's almost spring now and the fresh air would do you good.'

'Don't want no wooden leg,' Dan grumbled, sinking his teeth into the cheese sandwich she had made him. 'It would'a cost me a fortune and Sid reckons that if you let 'em screw a wooden leg on they have to keep cuttin' another bit of your leg off every few months.'

Vicky was shocked. 'What does Sid know about it?' she asked. 'That might have been true years ago but not any more. And it wouldn't be a *wooden* leg either. They use some other, lighter material now – aluminium or something.'

'It's not worth it at my age,' Dan said, pouring his tea into the saucer and slurping it noisily. 'I ain't got no plans to go nowhere anyway.'

Vicky knew she was fighting a losing battle so she did not pursue the matter. She did wonder why Sid was so anxious for Dan not to be mobile though. It made no sense to her. 'Well, when it gets warmer why don't you let me put your chair out in the yard?' she suggested. 'Then you can get some sun on your face. You're so pale.'

'Oh yeah? An' what 'appens if it starts rainin'?' Dan said. 'I s'pose I just sits there and gets soaked, do I?'

Vicky gave up. Dan could easily get around on his crutches. He wasn't completely helpless. He just chose to have her waiting on him hand and foot. 'I've got to get back to the shop now, Dad,' she said. 'Is there anything else you want before I go?'

'No. Never you mind me,' Dan moaned. 'Just you get off back to them Nightingales. You think more o' them than you do of yer old invalid dad.'

It was a couple of days later that Vicky met Phyllis Thorne on her way home. The older woman had two heavy bags of shopping and Vicky offered to carry one for her.

'Oh, thanks love,' the old woman wheezed. 'I don't know what things is coming to. Time was when the shops was glad to deliver groceries. Now they expect you to lug it all home yourself.'

'It's the petrol shortage,' Vicky offered.

'Used to be a young lad on a bike.'

Vicky smiled. 'They've all been called up I expect. Either that or they're doing war work.'

Phyllis nodded. 'I shouldn't grumble, should I?' she said. 'We've had it easy here in Millborough, not like them poor devils in the big cities.' She glanced at Vicky. 'By the way, how's your dad? I heard he'd had his leg off. Best thing that could have happened if you ask me.'

'He's been much better since he had the operation,' Vicky agreed. 'You were right, gangrene had begun to set in.'

Phyllis nodded. 'Thought so. Seen enough if it in me time not to make a mistake.'

'He won't have an artificial leg fitted though,' Vicky told her. 'So he still doesn't get about much.'

'That's a pity. Still, I daresay it would have cost him quite a bit. And what with the rents being put up . . .'

'They've gone up?' Vicky looked at her in surprise. 'Dad didn't say anything.' Every week Dan gave her an envelope addressed to a building society to post at the same time as she picked up his pension. He told her it was the rent money and she never questioned it. Surely if the rents had been put up she would have heard about it. She couldn't imagine him letting something like that go without complaint.

'Almost doubled,' Phyllis said, sucking in her breath. 'How they expect the likes of me to fork out that much each week I don't know. Soon won't be able to afford to keep body and soul together!' They had reached the end of Artillery Street now and Phyllis took the bag from Vicky. 'Thanks for giving me a hand with the shopping, Vicky,' she said, fumbling in her handbag for her key. 'You're a good Samaritan.' She looked up with a wry smile. 'Can't say the same for your dad. You must get it from your poor mum.'

Dan was sitting in his chair by the range when she got in. He looked up as she opened the door. 'You're late,' he said. 'Thought you was never comin'!'

'I helped Mrs Thorne carry her shopping home,' she explained. 'We were talking and she told me the rents had gone up. You never said anything.'

Dan drew in his breath sharply. 'Gone up?'

'She said they've almost doubled,' she said. 'I was surprised you hadn't mentioned it.'

'None o' yer business,' her father snapped. 'Or old mother

Thorne's either, for that matter.'

'It is if she's expected to pay it.' She looked at Dan. He'd gone very red in the face. 'What did we pay before anyway?'

'Never you mind,' Dan said. 'Like I said, it's none o' yer business. Anyway, What does that old bat wanna go shoutin' 'er mouth off for?'

'She only mentioned it. She seemed to think I already knew.'

'Maybe it's only some of the rents that've gone up,' Dan said. 'So ours hasn't then?'

'I'd've said so if it had, wouldn't I?' Dan was looking away from her into the fire. When she did not reply he turned to her, his usually pale face scarlet with anger. 'Well! Are you gonna stand there all night, chewin' the fat? Or are you gonna get me me tea. I'm famished!'

Later that night when Dan was ready to go to bed Vicky tapped on Sid's door as usual. 'Dad's ready to go up now,' she called.

The door opened immediately almost as though Sid had been standing on the other side waiting for her. 'OK, I'm coming.'

As Vicky washed up in the kitchen she heard the familiar thumps and moans as Sid helped her father to negotiate the narrow stairway. Once upstairs the bedroom door closed, but a few minutes later Vicky heard her father's raised voice. She dried her hands and crept to the bottom of the stairs. Dan was shouting. She could catch only snatches of the conversation. 'How long – what do you think you're doing? Where's the. . . ?' Sid's replies were low and controlled and she could hear none of what he said. Then there was silence and she crept back to the kitchen in case Sid came out on to the landing and caught her listening.

He joined her in the kitchen a few minutes later. She did not look round but felt his presence as he stood in the doorway behind her.

'Yer dad's a bit grumpy tonight,' he said. 'I think his leg's playin' 'im up.'

Vicky turned to look at him. 'If only he'd let them fit him with an artificial leg he'd be able to get around. He's bored, sitting at home all day.'

Sid shrugged. 'Up to 'im, ain't it? If he don't want one. . . .'

'You put him off with all your horror stories,' she accused.

He affected surprise. '*Me*? I ain't said nuthin'. Anyway, d'you think yer dad'd take any notice of me if I did?'

It was on the tip of her tongue to tell him she thought he had a great deal of influence over Dan but she stopped herself in time. It wouldn't do to let him think he had power over them. Instead she shrugged. 'Maybe when the summer comes he'll think again,' she said.

He took a couple of steps closer. 'Yer dad worries about you, you know,' he said in the quiet voice she had come to hate.

'About me? I don't think so.'

'Oh, he does. He worries about what might 'appen to you when he's gone. I keep tellin' him he needn't – that I'll always take care of you.'

'I don't need anyone to take care of me,' Vicky told him. 'I've been taking care of myself for years now – Dad too.'

'Ah, but you couldn't afford the rent of this 'ouse on yer own, could you? You'd need a 'usband, Vick. Every young girl needs a lovin' 'usband to look after 'er.' He reached out and grasped her shoulders. 'Them Nightingales forgave you for pinchin' their takin's, but if you was to do it again. . . .'

'I didn't take the money. They know I didn't.'

Sid smiled. 'Come off it, Vick. Who else could've done it?'

'I think we both know the answer to that.'

His eyebrows shot up. 'I dunno what you're talkin' about.'

'I think you do. I know you took it, Sid. And I know why. I know where you hid it too.'

His eyes narrowed and too late she realized she'd said too much. A stab of fear shot through her as he reached out and grabbed her shoulders, his fingers biting into her flesh. 'I always knew it must 'ave been you. You sly little bitch What did you do with it, eh?'

Vicky took a deep breath to keep her voice even. 'The Nightingales got it back,' she told him. 'Which is why I got my job back.'

He stared at her for a moment, then his fingers on her shoulders slackened. 'OK, we'll let it go this time,' he said. 'But if you ever try anything like that again. . . .'

'If *I* try it again!' Vicky thrust his hands away from her. 'Don't you threaten me, Sid Taylor. If my dad knew half the things you'd said to me he'd make you leave this house.'

'He can't make me leave,' Sid sneered. 'And neither can you, so just button yer lip, and while we're at it, you'd better treat me with respect from now on. If you played yer cards right you could be sittin' pretty.'

'As Mrs Sid Taylor?' she said. 'I'd rather die!'

He was really angry now. Flecks of spittle appeared at the corners of his mouth and his eyes were malevolent black slits. 'I'll make you sorry you said that, Vick Watts. I've got you just like that!' He clicked his fingers under her nose. 'One o' these days – not too far off either, you're gonna get the shock of yer life. I'm gonna make you sorry you was ever born.'

Vicky was late for work the following morning. It was something that had never happened before and as the minutes ticked by Meg began to worry. When Vicky did eventually arrive she looked distressed.

'I'm so sorry, Mrs Nightingale,' she said breathlessly as she almost fell in through the shop door. 'I didn't sleep very well last night and I didn't hear the alarm. I – I—'

'My dear girl!' Meg came round the counter and took her arm. 'Never mind all that. Just come and sit down a minute. You look exhausted.'

The kind words were too much for Vicky and to her horror she burst into tears. 'Oh – I'm sorry.' She clasped a hand over her mouth, feeling in her pocket for a handkerchief. 'Don't take any notice of me. I don't know what's the matter with me this morning.'

'Just you go upstairs,' Meg said firmly. 'Tell Harry I want him to mind the shop for me for a bit. Take off your coat and put the kettle on. I'll be up in a minute.'

Harry looked concerned when he saw the girl's tearstained

face, but he asked no questions, going downstairs to relieve his wife as she had asked. A moment later Meg joined Vicky in the kitchen.

'Now,' she said, closing the door. 'Tell me all about it. You know it'll go no further and it's obvious you need someone to talk to.' She poured two large mugs of tea and passed one across the table. 'Drink that up while it's hot. I've put plenty of sugar in it.'

Vicky took a long draught of the tea and felt it begin to calm her ragged nerves. 'I'm so worried,' she said. 'Something's going on between my dad and Sid but I can't find out what. Sid found out that I found the money he took from the shop. I let it slip and he was angry. He's begun to threaten me.'

Meg's face went pink with anger. '*Threaten* you! I think you should go to the police.'

'I can't do that. I've got no proof. It would be his word against mine, and Dad would be furious.'

'Does your father know he's been threatening you?'

Vicky shook her head. 'It's no good. He wouldn't listen. Sid keeps asking me to marry him. He says that if anything happened to Dad I'd be homeless, but that if I married him I'd be all right.'

'And you've told your father this?'

'Yes, but he doesn't see why I don't want to do as Sid says.'

'What's the matter with the man?' Meg said. 'How can he want his daughter to marry a man like that? I think it's outrageous!'

'I dread going home at night,' Vicky confessed. 'I hate Sid, but he seems to have the upper hand. I found out that it was him who persuaded Dad not to have the artificial leg fitted. He'll never leave and I don't know what to do about it.'

'Well I think it's time you had a good talk to your father,' Meg said. 'You must tell him very firmly how you feel and how this awful man is threatening you.' Suddenly she stopped short as she remembered something. 'Vicky – that night, the night you all had to move out because of the bomb, Harry went back to your house to get the takings from the chimney, remember?'

'Yes of course.'

'Well, he told me afterwards that there was other money hidden in the chimney besides ours. Did you know anything about that?'

Vicky looked mystified. 'No. As far as I knew there was only the one bag.'

'So he must have hidden it there later. That man is up to no good if you ask me and it's high time someone looked into what's going on.'

Meg persuaded Vicky to take half an hour extra for her lunch break so that she could talk to her father. As she walked home to Artillery Street her heart was thudding. She was far from convinced that Dan would listen to her or even believe her when she told him of Sid's threats but she knew Meg was right. She had to try.

As she let herself in she could hear the rumble of voices coming from the living-room and she realized with dismay that Sid was there. As she opened the door he looked up with a smile.

'Aah, if it isn't our little angel,' he said. 'Come to make us a bite to eat, eh, Vick?'

'What are you doing home?' she asked as she took off her coat. 'I thought you usually ate in the works' canteen.'

'We all like a change sometimes. Don't we?' Sid said. 'Anyway, I thought your time was 'alf twelve.'

'Mrs Nightingale asked me to take my break earlier today,' Vicky said. 'Lunch is only some soup and a sandwich.'

Sid rubbed his hands. 'Made with your own fair 'ands it'll taste like nectar o' the gods, eh, Dan?'

Dan made no reply and Vicky looked at her father. He looked pale and drawn and she noticed that his hands shook as he quickly removed an envelope from the table and slipped it into his pocket.

'Are you all right, Dad?'

Dan nodded. 'Could do with a cuppa tea,' he mumbled.

As Vicky made the sandwiches and heated the soup in the kitchen she wondered what fresh mischief Sid was up to. She carried the tray through to the living-room and sat on the other side of the table to eat her own. Dan hardly touched his, but Sid made short work of the soup, slurping it greedily and consuming the sandwich in record time. As he swallowed the last remnants he rose from his chair.

'Right. Gotta get back now.' He looked at Dan. 'Gimme that letter. I'll post it for you.'

Dan shook his head. 'No. It'll take you out of your way. Vicky can do it on her way back to work.'

Sid looked slightly taken aback. 'It's no trouble,' he said. 'Give it 'ere. I'll see to it.'

But Dan was stubborn. 'I told you. Vicky can do it,' he said. 'Get back to work before you get the sack.'

Sid stood for a moment, looking from one to the other then he turned towards the door. 'All right, suit yerself.'

When Vicky heard the street door slam she looked at her father. 'Is it something important, Dad?' she asked.

'No.' Dan pulled the envelope out of his pocket and tore it in half, throwing the pieces into the hearth. 'I think I've been hasty. It's something I need to think about.'

Vicky touched his hand. She knew instinctively that this was not the time to talk to him about Sid. He was clearly upset about something. 'Dad, are you all right?' she asked. 'Is your leg hurting you? Are you feeling poorly?'

He shook his head, snatching his hand away. 'I'm all right. Don't fuss, girl.' He shifted uneasily in his chair. 'Just help me out to the yard, will you? I need the lav.'

Vicky helped him outside and when he was gone she picked up the torn remains of the letter from the hearth and put the pieces into her handbag. When Dan returned she settled him in his chair again and went back to work.

Meg was waiting for her. 'Well, how did you get on?'

'Sid was there,' Vicky told her. 'So I didn't get the chance to talk to Dad.'

'Pity. I hope you don't mind dear, but I talked to Harry,' Meg told her. 'I told him about that Sid Taylor and he agrees with me that you've got to put a stop to whatever's going on.'

'Easier said than done,' Vicky said. She opened her bag and took out the torn pieces she had rescued from the hearth. 'Dad had written a letter,' she told Meg. 'I'm sure it's something Sid talked him into doing. He wouldn't let him post it and after Sid had gone he said he needed to think about it. Then he tore it up. I rescued the pieces.' She spread them out on the counter, discarding the pieces of envelope and fitting the rest together. Meg gasped as she looked over her shoulder.

'It's a will!' she said. 'Look. . . .' She read, her finger moving along the lines *I, Daniel John Watts of 13 Artillery Street, being of sound mind do bequeath all that I own, estate, property and moneys to Sidney Arthur Taylor of the above address.* It was dated and signed *D. Watts* in a shaky hand and witnessed beneath, *S. Taylor.*

Vicky stared at it for a long moment, her heart almost stopping in her breast.

'He's talked Dad into leaving everything to him,' she said. 'But I don't understand. Dad has nothing but his pension and that will stop when he dies. Other than that there's just the few sticks of furniture we own. Why is he doing this?'

CHAPTER TEN

THE tour of *The Corn is Green* began in Suffolk. Laura had hoped that she would manage to get home for a weekend at the end of the rehearsal period but the company had hit one or two snags so that in the end there was no time off for anyone before they hit the road.

Rehearsals had gone well on the whole, except that Madge Frazer, who was playing the leading female role became ill and had to drop out halfway through. A new actress had to be found and rehearsed in the part of Miss Moffat which held up proceedings by several days.

Laura took to Kate Mayfield on sight. She was about fifty and had been in the business since she was in her teens. She reminded Laura a lot of Rosa with her no-nonsense approach and her professional outlook. She learned the extensive part in record time and was word-perfect by the dress rehearsal. Max Higham, who was directing and playing the male lead, could not fault her work, although the two of them were not the best of friends, having disagreed on some aspects of his direction.

'Who does she think she is?' he complained exasperatedly at the end of one particularly stormy rehearsal. 'Ellen bloody Terry! She should know by now that the director has the last word.'

Laura kept out of the argument. She had heard Kate complain that Max was still 'wet behind the ears' and had a lot to learn about his craft before ordering professionals like her about!

Their vehicle was larger than the one requisitioned for the

Moonlight Follies. Packed with props, scenery and actors, it trundled its way east to play RAF stations throughout Suffolk. At the end of the first month it was clear that the play was a success. Audiences were loudly appreciative and Laura was applauded on every exit. She loved playing the part of Bessie, the rebellious daughter of a Salvation Army single mother. Max, who was playing the young Welsh miner-turned-student was brilliant in her eyes. His accent was perfect and he played the part with just the right amount of surly truculence. Maisie had been right, he was certainly handsome with his dark good looks and brooding brown eyes. She thought he was a good director too although she had little to compare him with. In the dramatic scene where she had to seduce him she had been nervous, but he had put her at her ease, encouraging her to take the initiative until eventually their performance had become highly charged with sexual tension, bringing loud whistles from their audiences – something which drove Max mad with irritation.

'Don't they get the significance of it?' he complained.

Kate laughed. 'What? A bunch of sex-hungry young servicemen? You've got to be joking. All they're thinking is, lucky swine!'

As spring got under way and the play settled down, Laura was able to relax. She had a letter from Maisie, written on the day before their embarkation. They were to sail on a troop ship, which meant they would start working immediately, giving shows on board for the soldiers being shipped out to Egypt. The letter was full of news and funny anecdotes. Maisie wrote that she hoped that none of them would be seasick, remarking that the furthest she had ever been on a boat was across the Thames on the Woolwich Ferry. She wrote enthusiastically about the new numbers they were trying out and said that Ed had written two new sketches. As Laura folded the letter and put it away in her handbag she felt quite nostalgic for the Moonlight Follies and her friends the Knights. However, she got along well with her new fellow cast members and a bond was gradually developing between herself and Max. She was learning so much from him:

all important timing and how to woo an audience; how to analyse the playwright's lines in order to get the most meaning out of them; how to relax into a part without ever letting your guard slip and always being ready for emergencies, such as a fellow actor fudging his lines.

The third week of the tour was spent at Martlesham, not far from the coast, and on one free Sunday evening Max invited Laura to go into Felixstowe with him for a drink. It was a mellow spring evening and they walked along the seafront in the fading light. The beach, now closed to the public, was deserted. Solid concrete blocks guarded the promenade. Barbed wire entanglements scarred the golden sands and, out to sea, beach defences rose out of the water like a row of crossed swords, defending the coast from the invader. Laura shivered.

'Do you think it will ever happen?' she asked. 'Will Hitler invade, do you think?'

Max dropped an arm casually across her shoulders. 'Never! In the beginning I was afraid he might, but since the Yanks have come in with us I think he's realized his limitations. If you ask me the war won't last more than another twelve months.'

'Do you really think so?' She looked up at him with shining eyes. 'I do hope you're right!'

He laughed softly. 'That was heartfelt. Someone special you're waiting for?'

She shook her head. 'Not now, no.'

They turned into the warmth of the Cavendish Hotel and found seats in the lounge bar. Max returned from the bar with two half-pint glasses of beer. 'I'm afraid this is all they have, but I did get the last two packets of crisps. I hope you like them.' He handed her a packet and she smiled.

'I love them. It's ages since I saw any.'

He regarded her as she opened the packet and popped one into her mouth.

'You know, it's funny but I don't really know the first thing about you, do I?' he said.

She shrugged. 'There's no reason why you should, is there? As

135

long as I do my job, it doesn't matter.'

He pursed his lips. 'I don't agree. I think a good director should know as much as possible about his actors. Where do you come from?'

'A little town in the Midlands. You've probably never heard of it. It's called Millborough.'

'You're wrong. I have heard of it,' he said. 'They make shoes or something.'

'That's right.'

'So.' He looked at her. 'Brothers, sisters?'

'One sister,' she said. 'Moira – married to David who's fighting in the desert. Mum and Dad own and run a newsagent's shop.'

'Did you go to drama school?'

'No. I had part-time lessons from a retired actress called Rosa Seymour. After I left school I worked in a hairdresser's to pay for them. Mum and Dad didn't see the sense in paying for me to go to RADA. They thought – and probably still do – that acting isn't a proper job.' She took a sip of her drink.

'But you were determined.'

She nodded. 'I took all the exams: bronze, silver and gold medals, and then my LR.'

'Wow! I'm impressed.'

'So was Dad. It showed him that if all else fails I can always teach,' she said. 'That's the kind of qualification he understands.'

'What does your sister do?'

'She's a teacher. I used to get fed up with having her held up as the perfect example. We used to fall out a lot because of it. But since . . .' She paused, remembering that it was Peter's death that finally drew them closer. 'Since the war – and her marriage – we've got along better.'

'Maybe because you don't see as much of each other now, eh?'

Laura shrugged. 'Something like that.' She took a sip of her beer and looked at him. 'What about you? Shouldn't an actress know a bit about her director? Not to mention her leading man?'

He laughed. 'I walked right into that, didn't I? Not a lot to tell.

RADA then a couple of years in rep where I got the chance to direct a bit. A bit-part in a West End play and then came the war and ENSA.'

'Parents? Brothers and sisters?' She looked at him, her head on one side. 'You wanted to know about mine.'

He laughed. 'So I did. Parents both dead, I'm afraid. And I was an only child.' He affected a woebegone expression. 'So I'm just a poor orphan.'

'I'm so sorry for you.'

He leaned his head closer. 'How sorry?' he whispered.

Laura laughed. 'So sorry that I'm going to buy you a drink.' She stood up. 'Do you want another beer? Providing the towels haven't gone up.'

Later they walked back along the seafront before returning to the hostel. A new moon had risen and Laura did not object when Max's arm crept round her waist. They walked in silence for a while then he said, 'Your Rosa Whatsaname did a very good job on you, Laura. You're a very accomplished actress.'

'Thank you.'

'Bessie's seduction scene is very convincing.'

'Well, you're a very good director.'

'While we're playing it I could almost convince myself that you mean it,' he said.

She turned to look at him. 'Maybe I do – at the time. Isn't that what acting is all about?'

He stood still, turning her round to face him. 'And when we're not acting?'

She caught her breath. The way he was looking at her was making her heart quicken. 'H-how do you mean?'

'I mean like this.' He drew her into the shadow of a beach shelter and kissed her. One soft kiss at first then harder as he pulled her close. When at last he released her she was trembling and breathless. He looked down at her, one eyebrow raised. 'Oh dear. Are you about to slap my face and tell me to go to hell?'

'Is that the reaction you usually get?'

He laughed. 'Not at all. It's just that you look – what shall I say? – less than impressed.'

'I'm not sure it was a good idea, that's all.'

'Are you saying you didn't want me to kiss you?'

'No. I'm not saying I wanted you to either. It was just – just. . . .'

'Inevitable? It had to happen, didn't it, Laura? All those love scenes. It's been like trying to keep the lid on a boiling pot. Many a night I've wished the audience would just melt away.' He leaned back to smile into her eyes. 'And did you think I hadn't noticed you becoming more and more responsive?'

She pulled away from him, her cheeks burning. 'No!'

'So, it was all acting, was it? Don't pretend, Laura.' He caught her shoulders and drew her close again. 'I've played love scenes with a good many actresses. With most of them I couldn't wait to get off-stage. With you it's different. There's something – a spark – no, a flame between us. Don't tell me you haven't felt it too.'

When he kissed her again she gave up trying to pretend and surrendered to the powerful attraction he had developed for her since they first began acting together. At last she said, 'The others mustn't know about this, Max. It's so – so unprofessional.'

He laughed. 'And so *normal*, my darling!' He kissed the tip of her nose. 'All right. I'm certainly not going to tell anyone, but you know of course that it's only a matter of time before they realize what's going on. That's if they haven't already. You can't keep this kind of thing quiet for long. Apart from anything else I'm going to have one hell of a problem keeping my hands off you after tonight.'

'But for now – please.'

'All right, if you say so – for now.' He kissed her again and all her fears were forgotten at the intoxicating thrill of his tongue exploring her mouth; the sensation of his hands under her coat, exploring her body, touching her in ways that seemed to melt her very soul and send her senses soaring.

'Dad! Dad, are you awake? I need to talk to you.'

Dan Watts opened his eyes and looked at his daughter. 'Wotcha want?' he mumbled. 'Can't I have a quiet kip without you yellin' in me ear?'

'Dad, I've brought you a cup of tea. Let me help you sit up. I need to speak to you. It's important.' Vicky took the torn pieces of paper out of her pocket. 'Dad – I know I shouldn't but I looked at the letter you tore up.'

He was instantly wide awake. 'You did *what*? None o' yer bloody business! What you wanna do that for?'

'It's a good job I did. What's going on, Dad? I think you owe me an explanation. Sid made you do this, didn't he? Why though, doesn't he know that you've got nothing to leave?'

The anger seemed to melt from Dan's face. He looked suddenly old and frail. He took the cup from her and took a gulp from it. 'It's nothing for you to worry about,' he told her. 'Just a misunderstanding, that's all.'

'Dad.' Vicky leaned closer. 'Dad, Sid is making my life a misery and I suspect yours too. Can't we ask him to leave?'

'No!' The familiar stubborn expression that Vicky knew so well was replaced now with one of disquiet. 'He – he does jobs for me. Makes himself useful.'

'There's nothing he does for you that I can't do,' Vicky insisted. 'And I want you to think again about having a new leg fitted. You could learn to walk again; have a normal life.'

'Will you shut up about the bloody wooden leg?' Dan was his old truculent self again. 'Anyway, what d'you mean about Sid makin' yer life a misery?'

'He's always making suggestive remarks – asking me to marry him.'

Dan snorted. 'Most gels'd be flattered to have a bloke beggin' 'em to marry,' he said. 'Who do you think you are – Lady Muck?'

'I hate him, Dad. You know I do. He threatens me too, he's always hinting that he could make me homeless if I don't do as he says.'

Dan looked thoughtful for a moment then he said, 'All right. I'll have a word with him – get him to lay off you. But just don't get on the wrong side of him, d'you hear?'

'Why, Dad? Why are you so scared of him? Why can't we just ask him to leave?'

Dan slid down in his chair again, his head sinking on to his chest. 'Maybe it's time you were told things, gel,' he said. 'You never knew yer grandma and grandpa, did you?'

'Your parents?'

'No, yer mum's.'

'No. But what do they have to do with anything?'

'Your grandpa died soon after you was born and when your mum was ill your grandma—'

The door opened suddenly and Sid stood in the doorway, his face like thunder. 'What's goin' on?' he demanded. 'What's she doin' 'ome at this time o' day?'

'We could ask the same of you.' Vicky said. 'Mrs Nightingale sent me on an errand and I looked in to make sure Dad was all right – not that it's any of your business.'

Sid's face darkened. 'I went off sick,' he said. 'Comin' down with the flu, I shouldn't wonder. Comin' to somethin' when a fella can't come 'ome ill without bein' cross-questioned.'

Vicky looked at her father. He nodded at her. 'You get off back to work,' he said with a warning look. 'I'm all right now.'

She rose and went out into the hall, dismayed to sense Sid following behind her. As she reached for the front door his hand shot out and grasped her wrist. 'You post that letter for yer dad?'

She shook his hand off. 'No. Dad decided he didn't want me to post it after all.' She met his eyes. 'I know what was in it. What do you think you're doing, Sid? Did you think Dad was rich or something? Do you think we'd live in a house like this if he was?'

For the first time ever she saw Sid's face change colour. 'Wasn't my idea,' he muttered. 'If you ask me yer dad's goin' a bit funny in the 'ead. One thing I do know though. He worries about you and what'll 'appen to you when he's gone.'

'So that's why he willed everything to you, is it?'

'Yeah, because he knows I'll always look after you, Vick. You ought to know that by now.'

'All I know is that I can't bear to have you anywhere near me,' Vicky said. 'I wish you'd leave us alone. I – I want you to find somewhere else to live.' Her voice shook and she could feel the blood draining from her cheeks. Her stomach was churning so much she thought she might be sick. None of this escaped Sid's notice. He knew he had the upper hand and was quick to take full advantage of the fact.

'Ooh! Quite the little spitfire, ain't you, Vick?' He took a step nearer her and grabbed her coat collar, pulling her close. 'You're gonna eat them words!' he hissed, spraying her face with spittle. 'Let me tell you this: you an' yer dad'll do as I say. I'm not goin' nowhere an' what's more, I'm gonna *have* you, Vick – one way or another I'm 'avin' you. So make up your mind to get to like me or it might not be very nice for you.'

All the way back to the shop Vicky's mind was full of Sid's thinly-veiled threat, her blood chilling at the thought. Clearly he had some kind of hold over her father. But what? And why did that hold extend to her?

As spring turned to early summer the company toured on: north to Norfolk and then Lincolnshire, playing at airfields and army camps. The play continued to be successful. Laura was ecstatically happy. Not only was she playing a part she loved but day by day she was falling more and more in love. At first she had been flattered by Max's attentions, telling herself that she could handle a flirtation and enjoy it. It all added to the authenticity of the play and the fun of touring. But as the weeks went by she found it harder and harder to resist Max's seductive magnetism and at last he succeeded in persuading her to take their affair a step further. After that she was lost, fmding herself wanting to be near him all the time. Often she thought about Peter and felt she was being disloyal to his memory. But she had to acknowledge that she had never felt such exhilaration, suffered the same aching longing for him as she did for Max. This, she told herself, must be what love was like – real, true, passionate love. Most nights she shared Max's bed and his practised lovemaking took her to heights she had never dared to imagine, enslaving her ever more to him. She was aware by now that the rest of the company were conscious of what was going on. No one said anything but she caught the occasional meaningful look pass between them. She didn't care. Let the whole world know, she told herself. As long as she could be with Max, nothing else mattered.

One evening after the performance the cast was invited to the officers' mess for a drink and Laura found herself sitting next to Kate. The older actress kept looking at her and eventually Laura laughingly asked, 'Have I got a smut on my nose?'

Kate shook her head. 'I've been trying to make up my mind whether to speak or not,' she said.

'About what?'

'You and Max.'

Laura felt her colour rise. 'What about me and Max?'

'It's none of my business.'

'Go on, you might as well say what's on your mind,' Laura urged.

Kate leaned forward. 'Darling, it's so blatantly obvious that you're head over heels in love with him,' she said. 'You wear your heart on your sleeve so. I'm terribly afraid he'll hurt you.'

Laura laughed. 'Is that all? I don't think he will, but if he does I'll have to cope with it, won't I?'

Kate patted her hand. 'Just be careful, my love,' she said softly. 'You're so young and so vulnerable. It hurts me just to see the sheer naked adoration in your eyes when you look at him.'

'Don't worry about me,' Laura said. 'I'm tougher than I look.'

'I hope you're right.'

The exchange hadn't escaped Max's notice and later, when they were walking back to the hostel together he asked Laura what the older woman had said.

'She thinks I wear my heart on my sleeve,' Laura laughed. 'And that you'll hurt me.'

His brow darkened. 'Interfering old cow!' he said. 'Why can't she mind her own bloody business?'

'I'm sure she didn't mean to interfere,' Laura said. 'Kate is a lovely person. She's just concerned, that's all.'

'I see. It sounds as though you think she has something to be concerned about?' He was clearly angry and Laura was a little shocked.

'There's no need to be so annoyed about it.'

'That woman has had it in for me from the first day,' he said. 'You're going to have to make up your mind, Laura.'

Her eyes widened. 'About what?'

'About where your loyalty lies. If you're going to believe every spiteful little jibe—'

'There haven't *been* any spiteful jibes,' Laura interrupted. 'And there's nothing for me to believe or disbelieve.'

'Is this your way of telling me you want to cool things?'

Laura was shocked. 'No! Max, what's the matter? You asked me what Kate said and I told you. That's the end of it.'

He took her hand and pulled her roughly to him. 'I thought you loved me.'

'I do.'

'Then listen to *me*, not to some jealous, frustrated old has-been!' He kissed her hard then took her hand and began to run. 'Let's get back. I want you – and I want you now!'

That night his lovemaking was powerful, almost brutal in its intensity. When at last it was over Laura found herself shaken and bewildered. His passion had always excited her but tonight his near violence had surprised and shocked her. He had fallen into an exhausted sleep almost immediately afterwards, while she lay awake, aching and confused, wondering how he could be so sadistic if he really loved her. It had been as though he had taken pleasure in hurting her.

It was a week later that the news came. HMS *Southark* had been sunk by a U-boat in the Atlantic. No survivors, the report in the paper said. That meant everyone, including the Moonlight Follies. Laura wept uncontrollably.

Max was sympathetic at first but when she continued to be upset he grew impatient. 'Oh, come on, Laura. It's wartime. This kind of thing happens all the time.'

'But they were my friends,' Laura sobbed. 'They were lovely people and they were good to me. I'm sorry, Max, but I don't think I can go on tonight.'

'Oh yes you *can*!' His face darkened. 'Pull yourself together. You can't let everyone down. I won't let you!'

'Maisie was looking forward to seeing Egypt so much.' She dabbed at her eyes. 'We were so close. She told me once that I was like a daughter to them.'

'But you weren't their daughter, Laura. They were just some people you worked with. Your real parents are still alive. Maybe you should be thankful for that.'

She took a deep breath, realizing that the more upset she became the angrier he was getting. 'I'm all right now,' she told him. 'I won't let anyone down, don't worry. I just need some time on my own.'

He shrugged. 'Oh, well, don't mind me!' He stormed out of the room, leaving her bereft. Why couldn't he understand how she felt? How could he be so hard and unsympathetic? It wasn't just the loss of her friends that she found so harrowing. The news had brought back the horror and disbelief of Peter's death. The sadness overwhelmed her and she knew that no one else could possibly understand the depth of her feelings. It was something she was going to have to suffer and come to terms with alone.

That evening she understood the true meaning of what it was to be a trouper. Remembering everything that Maisie had taught her about putting aside your own sorrows, she threw herself into her performance. On her final exit the applause was louder than ever before, but back in the dressing-room the sadness overtook her again and she dissolved into tears. Kate put her arms around her.

'Just let it all out darling,' she said, stroking her hair. 'I know how much losing your friends hurts but it will fade with time, I promise. It's just so new and raw at the moment.'

'It isn't just that,' Laura said. 'I had a boyfriend in the RAF. His plane was shot down over Germany.'

Kate rocked her gently. 'I thought there was more to it,' she said softly.

Laura looked at her. 'Have you lost someone too?'

Kate nodded. 'Not in the war. It was a long time ago. My husband – in a car accident. We'd only been married a year. So I know what you're going through.'

That night Max made love to her gently and lovingly. Holding her close he kissed her hair. 'You do understand, don't you darling?' he said. 'I had to be tough with you this morning. I couldn't afford to be too sympathetic. You'd have gone to pieces.'

'I know.' She nestled against him. The evening's performance together with the day's emotion had drained her and she felt exhausted.

'Only another few weeks before this tour is over and we go abroad ourselves,' he reminded her.

'How long will the overseas tour last?'

'Two months.' He tipped his head back to look at her. 'Why? You're not afraid of going overseas, are you?'

She shook her head. 'Not for myself, no.' She looked at him. 'Max, there'll be some leave before we go, won't there?'

'Of course.'

'Will you come home with me?' she asked him.

'Home? What do you mean?'

'To Millborough. To meet my parents and Moira.'

He frowned. 'Why should I do that?'

She smiled. 'They'll want to meet you. I thought you'd want to meet them too. After all, we are—'

His eyes widened. '*Going steady?*' He threw back his head and laughed. 'I don't believe you! My darling girl, how very provincial. Will they entertain me with cucumber sandwiches do you think – in the parlour?'

Humiliated, Laura turned away from him. 'Don't make fun of them!'

He was still laughing. 'Oh come on. You must admit that kind of thing went out with crinolines and bonnets.'

145

'Not in Millborough, it didn't.'

The smile faded from his face. 'Are you telling me that you take every man you sleep with home to meet your Ma and Pa?'

She turned to stare at him. '*Every man I sleep with*? There's only been you, Max. That's why it means so much to me.'

'Oh dear, we're getting very intense, aren't we?' Max got out of bed and pulled on his dressing-gown. 'Don't you think you're taking all this a tad too seriously?'

Laura stared at him. It was as though he'd slapped her hard in the face. 'Seriously? How else am I to take it?' she asked him. 'We – we're together, aren't we? I thought. . . .'

He sat down on the edge of the bed and took her chin in his hand. 'You thought it was for ever? Is that what you were going to say?'

'Well – it is.' She swallowed hard. 'Isn't it?'

He shook his head at her. 'Oh *please*! Be realistic, sweetheart. You know what tours are like. It would be impossible to get through one without a diversion of some sort.'

'A diversion? Is that all I've been?'

'No. I admit it's been a bit more than that. You're very sweet and we've had some good times, but all good things have to end, don't they?'

Laura said nothing. Inside her heart felt like a block of ice. 'Max, I can't believe that you really see what we've had as some kind of game. To me it's been much more than that.' She reached across and took his hand. 'Max – the reason I asked how long the overseas tour would be was because I'm pregnant. We're going to have a baby.'

He stared at her disbelievingly. 'You can't be!'

'But I am.'

'Are you sure?'

'As sure as I can be.'

His brow darkened. 'You little fool! How could you let it happen?'

'How could *I*? It takes two, Max.'

'Well, you can't have it.'

146

She tried to swallow the lump in her throat that threatened to choke her. This wasn't how she'd imagined it at all. '*Can't?* I don't know what you mean.'

'You'll have to get rid of it. Don't worry, there's always some old biddy who'll oblige. I'll ask around.'

'No. I won't!' She was appalled. 'It's dangerous.'

'Not necessarily.'

Try as she might she could not stop the tears that welled up in her eyes and spilled down her cheeks. 'Why can't I have it? The tour would be over long before.... Please, Max. Don't be so angry. It'll be all right. We can get married, can't we?'

'Of course we can't get married!' He was pacing the room and now he turned look at her with something like scorn in his eyes. 'I've already got a wife and family, you stupid girl!'

'No!' she gasped. 'Why didn't you didn't say?'

'You didn't ask.'

'You should have told me. It isn't fair!'

'Well, I didn't.' He ran an exasperated hand through his hair. 'For God's sake, Laura, I thought you knew the score. I never expected you to take things this seriously.'

She felt stunned. She kept hoping that she'd wake up in a minute and find it was all a bad dream. 'What shall we do?' she asked in a small voice.

'You've dismissed my suggestion so I don't know what you intend to do,' he told her brutally. 'But I've got a tour to organize. You'll have to leave the company, of course. You can't go abroad with us now. I'll have to wire for a replacement as soon as possible. They're not going to be too pleased about it either. I'll have to tell them that you've got family problems at home.'

'But what about *me?*' Laura stared at him. It was like the worst nightmare she had ever had. The acting part she loved; the tour she had looked forward to so much; Max, the man she had loved and trusted, her whole career.... It was all over. Smashed. How could she go home like this? Max might sneer but in Millborough unmarried mothers brought shame and disgrace on their families. She couldn't put her parents through that.

147

'I can't go home,' she said bleakly.

'That's up to you. There's still the other option.'

'Butchery? Don't you care what happens to me?' she lashed out. 'You said you loved me.'

'Oh, for God's sake, Laura, stop snivelling and face up to reality. It needn't be a disaster as long as you pull yourself together. We had a nice time and now it's over. Get used to it.'

It was just after 2 a.m. when Laura heard the soft but persistent tapping on her door. She was out of bed immediately, hurrying to open the door, sure that it was Max, coming to apologize and tell her he would stand by her, that everything would be all right. But to her disappointment it was Kate who stood outside in the corridor in her dressing gown. The older woman looked concerned.

'Darling, are you all right? I'm just next door and I heard you crying. You sounded so distraught. What's wrong?'

'I'm fine, thanks.' Laura made to close the door again but Kate pushed it open and came inside. 'You're far from fine,' she said. 'What's happened? Is it Max? Have you had a row?'

'It's worse than that. I'm leaving the company.' Laura turned away as the tears began again.

'Leaving?' Kate was incredulous. 'You mean he's sacked you?'

'No. There's a problem at home – my family. It's disappointing but it can't be helped.'

Kate took her arm and pulled her around, peering into her eyes. 'I'm sorry, love, but I'm not buying that. What's gone wrong? Tell me.' She held Laura's eyes until she lowered her gaze. 'Darling,' Kate whispered. 'You're not pregnant, are you?'

Laura nodded miserably.

'And I assume he doesn't want to know. Am I right?'

'He's already married,' Laura told her. 'He never said. Apparently I wasn't supposed to take it seriously because it was only a – a diversion.'

'The bastard!' Kate said under her breath She pulled Laura close and held her. 'How far gone are you, darling?' she asked gently.

'I'm not sure. About two months, think.' Laura looked up. 'I don't know what to do, Kate. I can't possibly go home. I'll have to get a job of some sort and – and—' She broke off her throat too tight for words.

'Sit down.' Kate drew her over to the bed and sat down beside her. 'Listen darling. I have a sister in Norfolk. Her name is Peggy Scott and she has a little boarding house on the coast. It's a safe area and she was billeted with evacuees at first, but most of them have gone home now and the summer visitors have started to come back. I'm know she'd put you up and I'm sure she could do with some help. At least it would help you to sort yourself out.' She looked. into Laura's eyes. 'What do you say, shall I ring her?'

Laura nodded. 'Thank you, Kate. It would be a great help until – until. . . .'

'I was coming to that,' Kate put in. 'Have you thought about what you'll do when the baby comes?' When Laura shook her head she said, 'Maybe you should consider adoption.'

'I don't think I'd have any choice.'

Kate slipped an arm around her shoulders and gave her a squeeze. 'Plenty of time to think about that. I'll make that call to Peggy first thing tomorrow and we'll take it from there.' She put a finger under Laura's chin. 'Cheer up, darling. We'll get you through this one way or another.'

CHAPTER ELEVEN

Vɪᴄᴋʏ had tried several times to talk to her father again but he had refused to be drawn. What had he been about to tell her about her grandparents?i And why had Sid been so anxious for him to make a will? She tried on numerous occasions to bring up the subject with Dan when they were alone together, but he stubbornly refused to talk about it, insisting that he had said nothing about her grandparents and that she was mistaken. Then one evening in late spring when she was walking home from work something happened to make her even more suspicious of Sid.

She met Phyllis Thorne on the corner of Artillery Street and the old woman fell into step beside her. 'I wonder at you givin' house room to that Sid Taylor,' she remarked. Vicky did not reply and she added, 'Sly sort of a feller, if you ask me. D'you know 'e's got the cheek of the devil when 'e comes round for the rent of a Friday night. 'E won't be kept at the door. Oh no! Always insists on comin' in and expects me to make 'im a cup of tea! Says the landlord wants 'im to report on 'ow well the place is bein' kept. Damned nerve if you ask me!'

Vicky turned to look at her. 'Sid collects your rent?' she said. 'How long has that been going on?'

Phyllis looked surprised. 'Ooh, a long time – years. But 'e must collect yours an' all, don't 'e?' Vicky shrugged noncommittally and Phyllis said, 'I suppose yer dad gives it 'im. Maybe 'e knocks it off Sid's lodgin' money.'

'You're probably right.'

Phyllis had reached her house and Vicky said goodnight and walked on, her mind busy with what she had just learned. It was some time ago that Phyllis had told her about the rents going up. If Sid was the rent collector was he swindling the landlord? Was that where the other money had come from that Harry had found hidden in the chimney? This time she was determined that her father would answer her questions.

He was dozing in his chair as usual when she got in and as soon as Vicky took off her coat she began. 'Does Sid collect our rent, Dad?'

His eyes snapped open and he looked at her. 'O' course he don't. What makes you ask?'

'Mrs Thorne has just told me that Sid collects the rents in Artillery Street.'

Dan snorted. 'That nosy old bat again! What's it got to do with her?'

'She just mentioned it. I expect she thought I knew.' She pulled up a chair and sat close to him. 'Dad, it seems to me that there's a lot I don't know. I think it's time you told me, don't you?'

Dan looked flustered. 'You might make me a cuppa tea before you start givin' me the third degree. I'm fair parched.'

'In a minute, Dad. Listen, Sid will be in soon. There are things I don't understand and it's time you explained them to me. I think you owe me an explanation, don't you?' He shifted uneasily in his chair, trying to divert her attention by complaining about cramp in his good leg. Vicky ignored it. 'Some time ago you were going to tell me something about my grandparents. What was it?'

'I told you. It were nuthin'.'

'You're not being straight with me, Dad. I want to know.'

'Make me a cuppa tea then.'

'Afterwards. Tell me first.' She knew that there was no time to lose. Once Sid put in an appearance, Dan would shut up like a clam again.

He groaned. 'Oh, all *right*. When yer grandma died she left Artillery Street to yer mum.'

Vicky's mouth dropped open. 'She owned Artillery Street? You mean all of the houses in it?'

'Yeah. It belonged to yer granddad so it was left to her. When she died yer mum came into it.'

'Did Mum ever know?'

'No. She was too ill herself at the time. She died soon after.'

'So then *you* inherited it?'

'Yeah. Now can I have me tea?'

But Vicky was still trying to take in the implications of what she had just heard. 'So all the houses in this street belong to you?' she said slowly. 'And you employ Sid to collect the rents?'

'Oh, all right then – yes.'

'So it was *you* who put the rents up?'

Dan grew red in the face. 'Mind yer own business. If they went up then o' course it were me. Stands to reason, don't it?'

But Vicky did not believe him. Sid had been cheating, creaming off the extra money for himself and for some reason Dan was protecting him. As she stood in the kitchen, waiting for the kettle to boil she thought about it. It was hard to take in the fact that her father owned the whole of Artillery Street. All these years he had deprived her of so much. She could have had a high-school education. Her mother would have wanted that. All this time he'd enjoyed a generous income from the rents and kept the money for himself. But what had he done with it? He certainly hadn't put it in the bank. Was that what Sid had been looking for that day when she caught him in Dan's room? So much was now becoming clear. It was like pieces of a puzzle falling suddenly into place. Sid knew that she would eventually inherit Dan's property and that was why he was so keen to marry her. When it looked as though she would not be persuaded he'd talked Dan into making a will leaving everything to him. What would be his next move, she wondered? And how on earth were they to loosen his vice-like hold on them?

She took Dan his tea and sat down beside him again. 'Dad, I have good reason to believe Sid is cheating you,' she said. 'We have to get rid of him.'

Dan shook his head. 'No! He's all right.'

'But Dad, he's charging people more rent and keeping the extra for himself.'

'You don't know that! You can't prove it.'

'Dad – he stole the day's takings from Nightingale's shop a while back and threw the blame on me. Later I found it hidden up the chimney in his room. There was more money there too and I believe now that it was the rent money. Surely you're not going to let him get away with that?'

'It's not true. I don't believe it.' Dan's mouth was set in a stubborn line. Vicky tried again. 'I even found him in your room a few weeks ago, searching through your belongings for something. He threatened me when I said I'd tell you, grabbed me round the throat. He's capable of violence.' Dan's face remained mulish. 'Dad, look, I can collect the rents for you if that's what's worrying you,' she said. 'What Sid is doing is against the law. We have enough evidence to report him to the police.'

This brought an instant reaction from Dan. Hot colour flooded his cheeks. 'Will you leave off, girl!' he snapped. 'Just keep yer nose out of me business. It ain't nuthin' to do with you!'

Vicky gave up. Getting to her feet she went into the kitchen to start the evening meal, but she was far from happy. There was more to this, much more and somehow she had to find out what was going on before Sid had complete control.

Peggy Scott was a widow. She had run the little boarding-house in Balmford-on-Sea since 1930, soon after her husband Frank had died. Perched on the cliff-top overlooking the sea, Marine View had nine bedrooms and every summer throughout the thirties the same families had come to stay for their summer holidays. The war put a stop to all that. In the autumn of 1939 the house had been requisitioned for evacuees and Peggy had cared for fifteen lonely and bewildered children for the next three years until, one by one, they all went home.

Peggy was used to looking after confused young people and

when her sister Kate had telephoned with an urgent request for her to help out a young fellow actress, she had been only too glad to agree. Apart from the commercial travellers which were now the mainstay of her business, she still had the occasional summer booking. But she usually had rooms to spare and, as her sister had guessed, she could always do with help around the house. Kate had told her a little of Laura's background and on the evening that she arrived Peggy could see by the girl's pale face how traumatized she was.

'You must be Laura,' she said, opening the door. 'Come inside and welcome, dear. You must be starving hungry.'

She took Laura's case from her and led the way up two flights of stairs to a bedroom on the second floor, overlooking the sea. 'It isn't one of my best rooms but I think you'll be comfy here,' she said, smoothing the blue candlewick bedspread. The sun shines right in that window first thing in the mornings. Bathroom's on the next floor down and there's always plenty of hot water. Would you like a bath?'

Laura nodded gratefully. 'Oh yes please. That would be lovely.'

'Help yourself then. You'll find towels in the airing cupboard on the landing. Just come down to the kitchen when you're finished and I'll make you something to eat.'

Laura felt better after her bath and downstairs in the sunny kitchen she found Peggy bustling about preparing a meal. She wasn't at all like her sister. In contrast to the elegant Kate, Peggy was round and dumpy with twinkling blue eyes and fading auburn hair scraped back into a tight bun. She looked up as Laura came in.

'Sit you down, my love. I hope you like egg and chips. It was all I could rustle up. I knew you'd be hungry. No restaurant cars on the trains any more.'

Laura was hungry and Peggy watched with satisfaction as she tucked into the food. She asked no questions and Laura wondered just what the arrangement was to be between them. As they shared a pot of tea she said, 'Kate said you need help in the house.'

'I certainly wouldn't say no.' Peggy smiled.

'I'm happy to do anything you want,' Laura said. 'I can't afford to pay much rent at the moment, but I'm hoping to find a job here.'

Peggy waved her hand. 'Don't go worrying your head over that. Just settle yourself in first.'

I've done some hairdressing,' Laura said. 'But I'd be happy to take anything.'

Peggy smiled. 'You'll have to go and have a look around the town in the morning.' She smiled. 'It won't take you long. There's really only the one street.'

When Laura had eaten, Peggy showed her round the rest of the house. On the ground floor there was a large lounge overlooking the sea and a homely dining-room as well as Peggy's private sitting-room-cum-office. Downstairs in the basement was a large kitchen and pantry with steps leading up to a small garden at the back of the house. There were four bedrooms and a bathroom on the first floor and another five on the second. The whole house was comfortable and well furnished and had a welcoming atmosphere. Laura felt she was lucky to be here.

Lying in bed later than night she listened to the soothing sound of the sea below. The thump of each wave and the rattle of the shingle as it ebbed rhythmically back eased away her tension. The past three weeks had been an ordeal and she wanted to put the painful memory behind her. She had had to endure watching her replacement rehearsing, directed by Max, all charm and charisma. She felt far from well, rising each morning to crippling nausea that wrung every ounce of strength from her. Max had treated her like a stranger, barely speaking to her. At first it had hurt unbearably, but in the end all she wanted was to leave, to put their affair where it belonged, in the past, though she knew that the child she carried meant that a fresh start was out of the question. She had written home, explaining that she was moving to the south-east coast. Somehow she was going to have to think of a feasible explanation of why she was not going overseas, but for the moment all she could think of was finding a job and making enough money to live on.

Exploring the little town the following morning Laura found two hairdressers'. The larger of the two was on the corner of the high street. Laura went in and asked to speak to the owner. A stout middle-aged woman appeared a few minutes later and looked her up and down. 'Yes?'

Laura felt slightly intimidated by the woman's cold eyes. 'I was wondering if you had any vacancies?' she ventured.

'Vacancies for what?'

'Hairdressers. I used to work for a hairdresser in Millborough, in the Midlands.'

The woman raised an eyebrow. 'So, you'll have a reference?'

'Well, no, but I could probably get one.'

'Why did you leave?'

'Well, I've been touring with ENSA, but I had to leave for – for health reasons.'

'Oh, I *see*. ENSA, you say?' The woman sucked in her breath and folded her arms, eyeing Laura as though she were some kind of insect. It was all too clear what she was thinking. 'Well, I'm afraid I have no vacancies for that type of person,' she said. 'And if you left for *health reasons* then you're likely to be unreliable, aren't you?' She turned to walk away. 'Good morning.'

Laura crept out of the shop feeling sick and humiliated. The other hairdresser was further up the street but she could not summon up the courage to go in and face another embarrassment. The woman's crushing put-down was more than enough for one morning. She looked around the shops, went down to look at the pier and the sea front and then climbed the steep cliff road to Marine View again.

Peggy was vacuuming in the hall. She switched off the machine and looked up expectantly. 'Hello, love. Any luck?'

Laura shook her head. 'I enquired at the salon on the corner of the high street but the trouble is I don't have any references. The owner seemed suspicious of me.'

Peggy shook her head. 'Hetty Morrison! I should have warned you about her. You're better off not working there. She never keeps her staff for long. Didn't you try at A Cut Above?' Laura shook her head and Peggy went on. 'Mary Newton, the owner of that one, is a friend of mine. I'll give her a ring if you like.'

Laura sighed. 'I wonder if I'm doing the right thing, Mrs Scott.'

Peggy looked at the girl's dejected face and said, 'Come on down to the kitchen and I'll make you a cup of coffee. Perhaps we should have a talk.'

Over the coffee Laura told Peggy that she was pregnant. 'It's only fair that you should know,' she said. 'So you see, I'm not going to be able to work anywhere permanently. And as soon as employers know about it they're not going to want to employ me at all, are they?'

Kate had already told her sister about Laura's predicament, so it came as no surprise. She smiled. 'You might find a sympathetic employer,' she said. 'They're not all like Hetty. Just leave it with me and I'll ask around.' She looked at Laura. 'Have you decided what to do, dear, about the baby, I mean?'

Laura shook her head. 'Adoption seems the only option. I'm trying not to think about it for the moment.'

'What about your parents? Are you going to tell them?'

'No.'

'Maybe they'd be more understanding than you think.'

'No. I don't want them to be ashamed of me. I've already lost so much. I can't risk losing my family too.'

Peggy patted her hand. 'I'm sure that wouldn't be the case, but you're welcome to stay here for as long as you want. I've got a few bookings for the summer and if you'd like to give me a hand around the place we can come to an understanding about rent.'

Thanks to Peggy's recommendation Laura found work at A Cut Above. It seemed she'd come at an opportune moment. One of the stylists, an older woman, was about to retire and the owner was about to advertise for a replacement. It was a small salon, employing two hairdressers as well as the owner and the atmosphere was pleasant and relaxed. She found the work hard, on her feet for eight hours every day and then helping Peggy with the guests in the evenings. At the end of the first month she wondered how she would keep it up. Although the morning sickness had abated, she felt washed out and exhausted most of the time. Some evenings, after helping Peggy to serve dinner to the guests, washing up afterwards then laying the tables ready for breakfast, it was all she could do to climb the two flights of stairs to her room and fall into bed. But one Saturday in mid July an unexpected event occurred that was to change everything for Laura.

She was taking an early lunch break. As it was a beautiful summer day she decided to take her sandwiches down to the seafront. The local schools had just broken up for the summer holidays and excited children filled the street, many of them, like her, heading for the seafront.

As she walked on to the promenade she spotted them – planes, about a dozen of them, flying quite low, small black specks growing bigger by the second as they sped towards the coastline. Some warning instinct told her immediately what was about to happen. She looked helplessly around her at the happy children skipping along, oblivious to the impending danger and knew she had to do something. Desperately cupping a hand to her mouth she called out as loudly as she could, 'TAKE COVER! GERMAN PLANES!' But to her horror no one seemed to take any notice. A moment later the planes were on them, swooping low, their engines roaring and their bulk blocking out the sun. She heard the staccato rattle of machine-gun bullets as the attack began. There were two children immediately in front of her and she threw herself on them, pushing them to the ground and covering them with her own body. All around her she heard the screams of terrified children and the cries of the injured. It had taken seconds only and suddenly the planes were gone, rapidly gaining height, banking and flying out to sea again, leaving a trail of devastation in their wake.

Laura lay still, frozen with horror, aware of a burning pain in her back and her left arm. Then someone was bending over her, gently persuading her to release the children beneath her. They were pulled out, crying and distressed, but unhurt. Laura heard someone say, 'For God's sake don't let her move. *She's been hit.*' And it was only then that she saw the blood pulsing from her arm to form a pool on the ground.

What happened after that was a blur of pain and shock. Someone stayed with her until the ambulances came, talking to her, asking her name and address, ripping off a scarf to staunch the blood from her arm. All around was chaos, then someone put a mask over her face and she drifted away. She had no idea how much time passed as she drifted in and out of consciousness, her memory existed only in snatches. White-coated figures, bright lights, muffled voices, pain, and yet more pain. When at last she regained consciousness fully it was to bright sunlight and Peggy's smiling face.

'Hello love. Welcome back. How do you feel?'

Laura frowned. Her arm was bandaged and in a sling. Her mouth was dry and when she spoke her voice sounded hoarse and strange to her. 'Peggy, how long have I been here?' she asked. 'Am I badly hurt?'

Peggy took her hand and squeezed it. 'It's three days since you came in. You took two bullets love,' she said gently. 'They've operated to remove them. One was in your arm; luckily that was only a flesh wound and it's going to be fine.'

'And the other?' Laura's memory was slowly returning. She tried to move her legs and found that she couldn't. Panic filled her chest and she looked up at Peggy with wide, frightened eyes. 'The other. It was my back, wasn't it? What's wrong with my back, Peggy? I can't move my legs!'

'It's all right,' the older woman soothed. 'Yes, the other bullet hit you in the back and it nicked your spine. But it hasn't done as much damage as they feared.'

'But I can't feel my legs,' Laura said, tears trickling down her cheeks. 'Am I paralysed?'

'No, no! The feeling will come back,' Peggy told her. 'The damage is only temporary – till you heal. The doctors say you'll get full mobility back again. It will just take time. You're going to have to be patient.' She smiled and stroked Laura's hair back from her brow. 'Do you realize that you're a heroine?'

'Heroine? Me?' Laura shook her head. 'How?'

'You saved the lives of two children,' Peggy said. 'Their mother has been in a couple of times to see you, but you weren't allowed visitors. She wants to thank you. The local paper did a piece on you too.'

Children? Yes, Laura remembered them. Her hand went suddenly to her stomach and she felt a chilling dread. 'The baby?' she whispered.

Peggy's eyes clouded with concern. 'I'm so sorry, love. The shock and your injuries caused you to miscarry.' As the tears slipped slowly down Laura's cheeks she held her hand tightly. 'Don't cry, dear. Do you want me to telephone your mum and dad?'

Laura shook her head. 'No! Please, Peggy. Don't do that.'

'All right, love. Just as you say. But I think they should know that you're in hospital. It's at times like this that you need your family.'

'I know, but not yet. Please, Peggy.'

'All right.' Peggy looked at her thoughtfully. 'You know, it might not seem like it at the moment, but sometimes these things happen for the best. Fate often has a way of taking a hand.' She put on a cheery smile. 'I've got a surprise,' she said as she opened her handbag. 'A letter from Kate. It arrived this morning and she enclosed one for you.' She produced the envelope. 'I'll go now and let you get some rest.'

When Peggy had gone Laura opened Kate's letter. It had been written as the company had been about to leave for their overseas tour. Kate wrote of how much she was looking forward to it. The destination was Tripoli, which the British had taken from the Italians in January. Kate said that she hoped to get a glimpse of General Montgomery.

It would be great to see the famous Monty and get his autograph. Maybe he'll come and see our show. By the way, your replacement, Mary Landsmore, is nothing like as good as you in the part of Bessie.

I hope you'll soon be able to make a new start and I do hope that our paths will cross again sometime. You really are a splendid little actress and I could kill Max for messing everything up for you. I'm glad to hear that Peggy is taking good care of you.

Look after yourself, darling. Keep your chin up.

Love Kate.

Laura lay back against the pillows when she had finished reading the letter, tears of weakness slipping down her cheeks and an aching lump in her throat. It hurt so much not to be going with the tour and now, in spite of Peggy's reassurances, she was afraid she might never walk again. What could she have done to deserve punishment like this?

Vicky was becoming increasingly worried about leaving her father on his own and he would not hear of asking Sid to leave. It seemed to Vicky that her father was actually afraid of him and she knew she had to find out why before something bad happened. She decided to confide in the Nightingales. Harry and Meg had been so kind to her and she knew she could trust them.

Harry was in a good mood; 1943 looked like being the turning point for the war. In January the Germans had surrendered in Stalingrad and the allies had taken Palermo. To his delight the RAF had begun to bomb Berlin to blazes, determined to wreck Germany's industry and in May the papers had been full of the daring Dambusters raid. Mr Churchill had even announced that church bells would be allowed to ring again. Things were definitely looking up. He and Meg listened to Vicky's concerns with grave faces.

'Seems to me that Sid Taylor's up to no good,' Harry said. 'Preying on a crippled old man and a young girl. It's despicable, that's what it is. Despicable!'

'But what can I do about it, Mr Nightingale?' Vicky pleaded. 'Dad won't hear of going to the police. It's as though Sid has some kind of control over him.'

Harry looked thoughtful. 'You say that your dad owns the whole of Artillery Street?' He shook his head. 'If you're not careful you could lose what should be yours by right. That Taylor might get your dad to sign it all away and then where would you be?'

Vicky felt her blood run cold. 'So, you think I should take matters into my own hands?'

Harry sighed. 'Seems to me you've got three options: go to the police, tackle Taylor yourself – though I don't recommend that,' he added hastily. 'He sounds like a nasty piece of work.'

'And the third?' Vicky asked.

'See a solicitor.'

'I couldn't afford the fee and, anyway, I've got no proof,' Vicky said. 'It would be my word against his. And when it came to it, Dad would probably back Sid up.'

'Why don't you go round and have a word with him, Harry?' Meg suggested to her husband.

'Oh no!' Vicky shook her head. 'Dad would be rude to you. He'd tell you to mind your own business and I don't want you to be upset.' She had already decided that there was nothing for it but to deal with if herself, though she didn't say so.

'Sorry we couldn't be more help, love,' Harry said.

'But you have,' Vicky said. 'You've made me see it more clearly. I think I know what I have to do.'

That evening she was listening carefully for Sid's arrival and when she heard the front door close she went into the hall and followed him into the parlour, closing the door behind her so that her father couldn't hear. Her heart was beating like a drum but she tried hard to keep her voice strong.

'Sid, I want a word with you.'

'In me room, with the door closed?' he sneered. 'Blimey, aren't *you* the brave one?'

She came straight to the point. 'I now know that Dad owns all the houses in this street and that you've been collecting the rents,' she told him. 'I also know that you've been overcharging and keeping the extra rent money for yourself.'

He threw back his head defiantly. 'I see, and you're threatening to tell yer dad, are you?'

'No. I've already told him!'

'Oh? And what did he have to say about it?'

Vicky moistened her dry lips. 'He seems afraid of you,' she said boldly. 'And I want to know why. Have you stooped so low that you'd threaten a crippled old man with violence?'

'I don't 'ave to!' His eyes narrowed. 'But as we're all for tellin' the truth p'raps there's somethin' you should know.'

'What's that?' Vicky was sure that whatever it was it wouldn't be pleasant. But she wasn't prepared for what he was about to say.

'Your dad don't own Artillery Street,' he told her. '*You* do!'

Stunned, she stared at him. 'What are you saying?'

'Your grandma left the street to yer mum, but it was in the will that if she died first then it was to go to you. Yer dad's always known it weren't rightly 'is.'

Vicky's head was spinning. 'But – I was only a child when Mum died.'

'Right. So 'e 'ad to look after yer interests till you came of age. But 'e never let on even then. I expect he was afraid you'd go off and leave 'im with no one to look after 'im.'

She stared at him. 'How do you know all this?'

'Told me once. It was when we used to work together, one night when 'e'd 'ad one too many.' He grinned. 'I daresay 'e's lived to regret it since.'

'And all this time you've been threatening to tell me – blackmailing him?'

'Oh, now there's gratitude for you!' he said. 'I've done me best for you and yer dad. I even asked you to marry me, didn't I, Vick? I mean, you're no oil paintin' so I was doin' you a favour. I've done everythin' I could to 'elp Dan, too. Not that it's been appreciated by either of you.'

'I want you to leave,' she said.

'I see.' He folded his arms. 'And 'ow are you gonna make me?'

'I could go to the police, or a solicitor.'

'Not without involving yer dad you couldn't. Want 'im taken to court for deception, do you?' Seeing the uncertainty on her face he took a step towards her and put his hands on her shoulders. 'Listen, Vick. I been collectin' the rents for years now. Your dad must have thousands stashed away. God knows where it is but it 'as to be somewhere in this 'ouse. You 'n' me could be sittin' pretty if. . . .'

'Take your hands off me!' She pushed him away. 'I don't know what you're about to suggest and I don't want to know. I want you out of this house.'

'Come off it. You know you ain't got a leg to stand on. Face it, Vick. He's a bad-tempered old bugger. He's 'orrible to you. You don't owe 'im nuthin, so why don't you leave? Thanks to me you know now that you're an independent woman. You could give up that tupp'ny-ha'penny job at Nightingale's and live like a lady on the rents. What's to stop you now that you know?'

'He's still my father and he needs me.'

'A father who's been doin' you out of what's yours for years.'

'I'd still rather be with him than with you!'

His eyes darkened and she backed away as he took a step towards her. Then Dan's voice called out stridently from the hall: '*Vicky*! Where are you? I could be lyin' dead and cold for all you bleedin' care!'

Vicky held her breath as Sid continued to stare at her. His hand shot out and she flinched but he reached past her to fling the door open. 'Go on,' he jeered. 'Go and skivvy for 'im. That's all you're any bloody good for.'

Dan stood in the hall, leaning on his crutches, a petulant expression on his face. When he saw her coming out of the parlour he frowned. 'What are you doin' in there?' Not waiting for her reply he went on. 'I want Sid to help me upstairs.'

'But you haven't had your tea yet, Dad.'

'I know. I'll have it upstairs. I don't feel too good.'

'Why – what's wrong?'

Sid pushed past her. 'Let 'im go up to bed if that's what he wants,' he said. 'Come on, Dan, I'll 'elp you.' He turned to Vicky. 'Go on, do as you're told. Go and get the tea.'

Vicky stood in the living-room trying to take in what Sid had told her. Mum had left her legacy to her. *She* was the owner of all the property in the street and Dad had kept it from her all these years. He had subjected her to near poverty, made her nurse and wait on him when all the time she was an independent woman in her own right. How could she ever forgive him? But now that she was in possession of this knowledge, Sid had no more ammunition with which to blackmail Dad, so, was he about to relinquish his hold over them? Was he giving up? She doubted it. Suddenly she heard raised voices from upstairs. Dan was shouting at Sid.

'You *told* her?

She went into the hall.

'It was only right she knew,' she heard Sid reply.

'I know what you're up to,' Dan shouted. 'You want to get 'er to marry you so's you can get yer 'ands on the lot, then you'll stick me away in some filthy 'ome!'

'She won't marry me,' Sid returned. 'She 'ates the sight of me. Why don't we just let 'er go, Dan? Tell 'er to get out. We'll be all right, you 'n me. I'll look after you. Let the dozy little cow sling 'er 'ook.'

'Let *you* look after me?' Dan screamed, beside himself with rage. 'You think I'd let *you* take care of me? You'd 'ave me shut up 'ere like a prisoner. I reckon what she said about you is right. You been doing me down for years. Well I ain't 'avin' it no more!'

'Why, you ungrateful old. . . .'

There was the sound of a scuffle. Vicky looked up to see her father come out on to the landing. He turned and jabbed at Sid with one of his crutches. 'You get out of this house tonight, Sid Taylor or I'll. . . .'

Sid grasped the end of the crutch and pushed. Dan let out a strangled cry as he lost his balance, toppled over the top step and fell headlong down the stairs. Vicky screamed as her father tumbled down the steep flight of stairs, his head bumping sickeningly on every step. As he came to rest in a crumpled heap at the bottom, Vicky dropped to her knees beside him.

'*Dad!*' She was feeling for his pulse when Sid hurtled down the stairs and pushed roughly past her. Wrenching open the front door he ran out into the street. Vicky felt frantically but could feel nothing. She bent close to see if she could feel his breath on her cheek, desperately searching her mind for all the first aid she had ever learned. She knew it would not be wise to move him. But she must get help.

'Hello? Hello? Vicky, love?' Phyllis Thorne stood suddenly in the open doorway, her bulk blocking out the light. She took a step nearer and saw the old man lying at the foot of the stairs.

'Oh, my dear Lord,' she exclaimed. 'Is he dead?'

'I don't know. I need to go for help. Can you stay with him, Phyllis?'

'Of course I can.' Phyllis lowered herself painfully on to her knees and took the old man's wrist. 'Just you get off, duck, and be as quick as you can. There's a phone box on the corner of Cannon Street.'

Vicky ran out of the house in near panic. She was turning the corner of Artillery Street when she cannoned straight into a tall figure in a dark uniform.

'Hey! Steady on!' Two kindly brown eyes were smiling down at her whilst the policeman's firm hands grasped her shoulders. 'Where's the fire?'

'It – it's my dad,' she gasped. 'He had an accident, fell downstairs. I can't feel a pulse and I'm afraid – afraid. . . .'

'All right.' The brown eyes became serious at once. 'I'll come. Just lead the way.'

'It's 13 Artillery Street. I was going to ring for an ambulance.'

'OK. You do that. There's a box on the next corner. I'll go and take a look at him.'

When Vicky got back to the house the policeman was kneeling beside Dan, Phyllis looking on. He looked up. 'There is a pulse,' he told her. 'But it's very weak. I hope the ambulance won't be long.' He looked up at Phyllis. 'Were you here? What happened?'

'I was passing,' Phyllis said. 'I heard shoutin' and then a crash. Then before I could take another breath the door flew open and that Sid Taylor comes tearin' out as if the devil 'imself was after 'im! Nearly knocked me flyin'.'

The young policeman looked at Vicky. 'Sid Taylor?'

'He's our lodger.' She took a deep breath and tried to steady her voice. 'As you can see, Dad only has one leg. He was at the top of the stairs and he just lost his balance.'

He frowned. 'So, do you think Taylor went for help?'

'I doubt it. Sid always helps Dad upstairs. They were at the top, they were arguing. Dad just lost his balance.' Before she had time to continue they heard the clang of the ambulance bell as it came down the street and the next moment the ambulance men had taken charge. Examining Dan briefly, they got him on to a stretcher and into the ambulance. It seemed to Vicky that everyone in the street had come out to watch as she climbed in behind them. Leaning out she searched the crowd of onlookers for the policeman and saw him pushing his way towards the front.

'Thanks for your help, Constable. . . .'

'Blake,' he told her. 'P.C. Ian Blake. Good luck, Miss. . . .'

'Her name's Vicky,' Phyllis put in with a smile. 'Vicky Watts.'

'Good luck, Miss Watts. I hope your father's all right.'

The ambulance doors were closed and the driver began to move carefully off while the other ambulance man tended to Dan. They were about halfway to the hospital when he straightened up and tapped on the glass panel for the driver to stop. He bent over Dan again, his fingers against his neck for one long agonizing moment while Vicky held her breath. Then he turned to her, his face grave.

'I'm very sorry, love,' he said. 'He's gone. I'm afraid we've lost him.'

CHAPTER TWELVE

VICKY was all alone in the house. It felt eerily silent and empty. It had been over an hour since she had returned from the hospital but the shock of all that had happened still hadn't quite sunk in. Everything felt unreal, as though she was walking through a dream. The first thing she noticed when she got back was that the parlour door was open. Going inside she saw that all Sid's belongings were gone. He must have been back to collect them while she was at the hospital. It confirmed what she had always known, that he was a coward at heart.

Although she had no appetite she made herself something to eat, but the food tasted like ashes in her mouth and she left most of it uneaten.

It was about nine o'clock when there was a knock on the door. The sudden noise made her start violently and for a moment she sat rooted to the spot, her heart in her mouth. Could it be Sid, back again? She suddenly remembered that he had a key and the thought turned her blood to ice. He could walk in at any time and find her here alone. She was the only witness to what had happened. Would he come back to make sure she did not lay the blame on him? The knock came again and she got up and went into the hall, opening the door a crack. 'Who is it?'

A young man stood outside. He wore a tweed jacket and grey flannels. 'It's Ian Blake, Miss Watts. P.C. Blake,' he said. 'I'm off duty but I thought I'd call to see if you were all right.'

'Oh, how good of you.' Vicky sighed with relief and opened the door. The moment he had spoken she had recognized the voice and now that she found herself looking into his dark brown eyes again he seemed strangely like an old friend. 'Please come in.'

In the living-room he looked at the half-eaten food on the table. 'I'm sorry. I'm interrupting your meal.'

She shook her head. 'No. I don't want any more.' She looked at him. 'Dad died, I'm afraid – in the ambulance on the way to the hospital.'

'Yes.' He nodded. 'I heard. I'm so sorry.'

'They told me at the hospital that there will have to be a post mortem,' she told him. 'They think Dad had a heart attack as a result of the fall but they have to be sure before they can give me a certificate.'

He nodded. 'That's routine.' He looked around. 'Has your lodger come back yet?'

'No.' She bit her lip.

'You seem worried.'

'I am. He has a key and he could walk in at any time.'

'Does that bother you?' He frowned. 'Are you afraid of him, Miss Watts? Look, I'm off duty and I'm not here to question you but I get the impression that your father's fall wasn't really an accident.'

'I don't know. It's not for me to say.' Vicky sighed. 'They were having an argument. Dad was very angry; he didn't seem to know what he was doing when he raised his crutch. He was standing at the top of the stairs. Sid grabbed it and pushed and – and—' The breath caught in her throat. 'Dad didn't stand a chance.'

'You shouldn't really be alone at a time like this,' Ian said. 'Is there someone who could come and stay with you?'

Vicky shook her head. 'No. Not really.'

'Could you go somewhere? To a friend and stay for the night?'

'No. I have to stay here.' She was thinking about the money that was hidden somewhere in the house. If Sid came back and found the house empty he would ransack the place for it.

Ian was watching her closely. 'What are you so afraid of? There's more to this, isn't there?' He leaned forward. 'May I call you Vicky?' She nodded and he went on, 'Vicky, this is off the record, but the police will want all the details. It would be as well not to keep anything back. Have you told me everything?'

She sighed. 'Please, sit down.' It would be such a relief to tell someone. She hardly knew where to begin, but before she knew it she was telling him about the life she had led with her father, about Sid and how he had insinuated himself into their lives and tried to manipulate them. This young policeman seemed so trustworthy.

'The first thing to do is to get the locks changed,' Ian said when she had finished. 'This man is obviously ruthless and after what you've just told me there will be a warrant out for his arrest. If he pushed your father deliberately it could be manslaughter at the very least.'

Vicky bit her lip. 'Dad was trying to hit him with the crutch,' she said. 'He'll probably say it was self-defence.'

'A strong, able-bodied man against a cripple?' Ian raised an eyebrow. 'I doubt if any jury would be sympathetic with that.' He looked at her. 'Are you sure there isn't someone who would come and be with you? I don't like the thought of you being here alone.'

Again Vicky shook her head. 'Thanks, but there's no one.'

He thought for a moment. 'Look,' he said at last. 'My dad has a hardware shop. If I tell him it's an emergency he'll come and change the locks for you tonight. Would that be all right?'

She smiled at him. 'That would be marvellous. You're so kind, Constable.'

He winced. 'Ian, please,' he said. 'I'm off duty. What I'm doing and saying this evening is strictly off the record. There'll be an official visit in the morning from a couple of my colleagues. And by the way. . . .' He smiled wryly. 'When they do come I'd be grateful if you. . . .'

'Didn't mention that we've already talked about Dad's accident?' she finished for him.

He smiled. 'You've got it.' He stood up. 'Right. I'll go and get Dad and we'll see to those locks for you.'

Laura was walking again. Not well; not as she had done before, but at least she had the feeling and some of the use back in her legs. Each day she ventured a little further along the ward with the help of one of the nurses. Her back was healing well and so was the bullet wound in her right arm and this morning the doctor had told her that if she continued to make good progress she could go home the next week.

Peggy came to visit every afternoon and one afternoon she was accompanied by a smiling young woman. Peggy introduced her: 'This is Maureen Banks. Her two children, Bobby and Pam, were the children you saved in the raid and she's been waiting to see you.'

Maureen took Laura's hand. 'I've been looking forward so much to meeting you,' she said. 'I lost my husband two years ago. He was killed at Dunkirk. The children are so precious to me. If I'd lost them as well—' She broke off shaking her head. 'I can't bear to think about it, and I can't thank you enough.' She took a small package from her handbag. 'I want you to have this,' she said. 'The children and I put it together for you. We'd like you to think of it as a mark of our gratitude.'

Laura opened the carefully-wrapped package and found a box. Inside was the newspaper cutting with the story of the daylight raid and how she had saved the lives of Bobby and Pam. There was also a card expressing their gratitude, signed by the children and their mother. Then, at the bottom of the box, nestling on a bed of cotton wool, was a brooch in the shape of a lover's knot, set with garnets and pearls. Laura looked up at Maureen.

'I can't take this, Mrs Banks,' she protested. 'It looks valuable.'

'Not nearly as valuable as my children,' Maureen said. 'It's quite old. It was my grandmother's but I've never been one for wearing jewellery. It will suit you perfectly and I'd like to think of you wearing it and remembering the precious gift you gave me.' She leaned forward and kissed Laura's cheek. 'Thank you again.'

When she had gone Peggy opened her handbag. 'I've brought you something as well,' she said. 'Some notepaper and envelopes. I want you to promise me you'll write to your parents. Once you're out of here and well enough I really think you should go home.'

Laura smiled at her wryly. 'I see. You want to get rid of me, do you?'

Peggy squeezed her hand. 'You know that's not true. I'm going to make sure you're well enough before I let you on that train. But if I was your mother I'd want to take care of you myself.' She looked into Laura's eyes. 'It's up to you how much you tell them,' she said. 'That's none of my business, as long as you remember that you have nothing to be ashamed of.' She smiled. 'It's strange how things balance out, isn't it? Because you were on the promenade that day two children are still alive.' She picked up the little brooch. 'Wear this and be proud of the brave thing you did that day.'

Laura wrote to her parents the next day. She told them she had been on the Essex coast when she had been injured in a daylight hit and run raid. She left it to them to assume that this was the reason she had left the ENSA tour. She asked if she could come home to recuperate and by return of post she received a letter from her mother, asking her to come home as soon as possible. Meg's letter was full of news. David was home from North Africa and he and Moira had gone off on the honeymoon they had missed when they were first married. Vicky Watts's father had died in a fatal fall and her lodger, Sid Taylor, had been arrested and charged with manslaughter.

Poor Vicky will be called to give evidence when he comes to trial. The local papers were full of it, especially when it came out that Vicky Watts had owned the whole of Artillery Street. Ever since it all happened poor Vicky has been busy trying to sort everything out with the solicitor as her dad left no will. She hasn't been able to come to work at the shop since the tragedy but we are keeping her job open for her.

Meg ended the letter by sending everyone's love and saying how much they were all looking forward to seeing her. Reading all the news from home was a comfort to Laura. It was reassuring to know that they were looking forward to having her home but she wondered if she could ever go back to being the same Laura Nightingale she had been before. The events of the past months had changed her in so many ways.

It was three more weeks before she was well enough to make the journey from Balmford-on-Sea to Millborough. Peggy went with her to the station and saw her safely on to the train. Laura was still walking with the aid of a stick and by the time she arrived at Millborough after a long and difficult journey she was exhausted. Harry was waiting on the platform when she alighted from the train and the sight of his familiar face made her want to burst into tears.

'Laura, love. It's good to see you.' Harry hugged his daughter. 'Come on, lass. Mother's waiting with a nice hot meal. We'll see if we can get a taxi. You look all in.'

It felt strange to be home again. She was aware that everything was the same as before, and yet it was all somehow different. It was half-day closing so Meg had been busy cooking a celebration meal all afternoon. There was roast beef and Yorkshire pudding, followed by apple pie and by the time Laura had finished eating she was almost asleep on her feet. Her old bed felt warm and comfortable and within minutes she had fallen into a deep sleep.

Moira wakened her next morning with a cup of tea. 'Come on, sleepyhead!' she said, sitting down on the bed beside her. 'I must say you look better this morning. We were all worried about you last night. You looked so pale and peaky.' She plumped up Laura's pillow for her. 'Come on now. I want to hear all your news. It must have been terrifying, being injured in that raid. And you must have been so disappointed not to be able to continue with the ENSA tour.'

Laura shook her head. 'I was just glad to be alive.' Eager to change the subject she said, 'Anyway, you're the one with the news. What about this honeymoon? It must have been wonderful to have David home again.'

Moira sighed. 'Oh, Laura, it *was*. I can't tell you how wonderful. We went down to Bournemouth for a week. The weather was perfect and David looked so tanned and handsome. I'm so thankful to have him back safe and sound again. I really think we love each other more than ever.' She blushed and looked down at her hands.

'I'm so pleased for you,' Laura said. 'And Dad tells me you're back at school already.'

'That's right.' Moira looked at her watch. 'And I must go in a minute or I'll be late. The children only get four weeks' summer holiday now so that they can have two weeks off to do agricultural work in September. The farmers are so short of labour in spite of the Women's Land Army and the POWs.' She looked at her sister. 'So, will you go back to ENSA when your injuries are completely better?'

Laura shook her head. 'I don't think so.' She bit her lip. 'I don't think there's much call for crippled actresses.' Her eyes filled with tears and Moira quickly took her hand and squeezed it.

'*Don't*! Your back will heal and then you'll be fine, walking as well as you ever did. You're not to talk of being crippled.'

Laura lifted the sleeve of her nightdress to uncover her upper arm. 'Then there's this,' she said, displaying the livid scar where the bullet had torn her flesh. 'Not very pretty, is it?'

'But that will heal, too,' Moira assured her. 'It's early days. All your scars will fade with time. You'll be as good as new again.'

But Laura could think of one scar that would never fade; one that she was determined no one should ever know about. She would cope with it in her own way, alone. 'You know,' she said, looking at Moira. 'I can't believe how you and I used to squabble,' she said. 'I'm so glad we get on well now.'

Moira smiled. 'I think they call it growing up.' She took Laura's empty cup. 'Right, I'm off to school now and you are to settle down and get some more sleep. You've got a lot of it to catch up on.' She smiled. 'Mum's orders. More than my life's worth to disobey!'

Laura spent the next few days quietly resting at Meg's insistence. After that she was allowed to help in the shop for a few hours each day. The doctor at the hospital in Balmford had given her a letter for the local hospital and she spent a few hours each week in the physiotherapy department doing exercises to strengthen her legs. The summer days were long thanks to the double summertime that had been in place since the war began and sometimes Laura would walk round to Snape Street in the afternoon to meet Moira out of school. They would take a walk to the park or stroll down by the canal. Her legs were getting stronger every day and she could now manage without her stick.

'I think I'll soon have to start looking for a job,' she said one day.

Moira glanced at her. 'What kind of job?'

Laura gave her sister a wry smile. 'I might be reduced to going back to Maison Griggs and asking for my old job back.'

'You wouldn't, would you?' Moira said.

'Beggars can't be choosers,' Laura told her. 'My dreams of being a successful actress have vanished. I've had to come down to earth and I'm beginning to think that Mum and Dad were right when they used to hold you up as a shining example. I should have trained for a real profession.'

'Mum and Dad know now that you did right in pursuing what you were good at, and I keep telling you, you're going to be as good as new,' Moira insisted. 'You just need to give yourself time.' She looked at her sister. 'You haven't been to see Miss Seymour yet, have you?'

'No. I really must pay her a visit soon.'

The truth was that Laura had been putting off visiting her old friends. Everyone would want to know about her ENSA experiences and that was the last thing she wanted to talk about.

'Why don't you go round and see Vicky?' Moira suggested. 'She's had such a rough time lately and she always thought a lot of you.'

It seemed to Laura like a good idea and after lunch the following day she decided to go round to Artillery Street. The little row of terraced houses looked the same as ever, all the doorsteps scrubbed and whitened and the lace curtains snowy behind gleaming windows. Laura knocked on the door of number 13 and Vicky answered. She looked pale and thinner than Laura remembered, but her face lit up in a smile when she saw who her visitor was.

'Laura! How nice to see you.'

'I thought I'd pop round and see how you are,' Laura said.

'Oh, how kind of you,' Vicky said. 'I'm fine really. I feel bad at leaving your mother to manage alone.'

'Don't worry. She knows you have a lot to cope with at the moment. I'm helping until you're ready to come back.'

Vicky opened the door wider. 'What am I thinking about? Please come in. I was just going to make a pot of tea. You will stay and have a cup, won't you?'

The little house looked neat and clean. Vicky carried the tray of tea through to the parlour, which now held no trace of Sid. The truckle bed was back in the attic. The photographs were back on the mantelpiece and there were fresh flowers on the window sill. Laura was surprised to see the piano.

'Do you play?' she asked.

'A bit. The piano was Mum's. She taught me. It's horribly out of tune though and I've been trying to find someone to tune it. Listen.' She went to the instrument and played a snatch of a little Chopin waltz. Laura was impressed.

'Vicky! You're very good.'

'Very rusty, you mean, like the piano. Dad wouldn't let me play so I haven't had any practice for years.'

'I was sorry to hear about your father,' Laura said. 'Mum told me what happened.'

Vicky sighed. 'The police questioned me for hours. I was so thankful that Phyllis Thorne happened to be passing at the time and saw Sid running away. Without her all the blame could have fallen on me.'

'What happened to Sid Taylor?'

'He disappeared, but they eventually caught up with him. He's on remand at the moment, awaiting trial. I'm dreading having to give evidence.'

'Will he be tried for murder?' Laura shuddered, trying to imagine the horror that Vicky had faced over the past weeks.

'He's been charged with manslaughter,' Vicky told her. 'There's no proof that he actually meant to kill Dad.'

'What a terrible experience for you.'

Vicky looked at her. 'You've had your share too. Your mum told me that your friends were all lost when their ship was torpedoed.'

'The Moonlight Follies.' Laura sighed. 'Poor Maisie was looking forward so much to seeing Egypt. They were so good to me. I'll never forget them. I would have been with them if I hadn't got the chance to join the other tour.' Reluctant to pursue that particular subject she asked, 'What are your plans? You must have an awful lot to do and to think about.'

Vicky nodded. 'I have. People have been very kind. Your mum and dad – and especially Ian.'

'Ian?'

'P.C. Blake. He was the policeman who helped me that day. He even came round the same evening when he was off duty just to see that I was all right.'

Laura saw the warm colour flood Vicky's cheeks and drew her own conclusions. 'That was kind of him,' she said. 'Have you seen him since?'

Vicky nodded. 'He came to Dad's funeral. I was so grateful. There were only a few of the neighbours there.' She cleared her throat. 'Did your mum tell you that we owned all the property in this street?'

Laura nodded. 'It must have been a surprise?'

'It was more of a shock than a surprise.' Vicky looked at her. 'Mum inherited the property from her parents when they died. It was supposed to come to me when she died, but Dad kept that to himself. He always let me think we were really poor. He employed Sid to collect the rents and Dad was hiding the money here in the house.'

Laura was aghast. 'And you knew nothing about it?'

'Nothing at all at the time, but so much is clear now. That was the reason Sid was so keen to worm his way in with us – why he kept pestering me to marry him.'

'Oh, Vicky, how horrible!'

'He was swindling Dad too. He told the tenants the rent had gone up and kept the extra cash for himself.'

'I hope all this will come out at the trial,' Laura said. 'You must have been so frightened.'

'I was. He threatened me more than once. When he was still on the run I was terrified in case he came back to look for the money.'

'He still had a key?'

'Yes, but Ian had the locks changed for me. That made me feel safer.'

Laura smiled. 'Ian sounds like a real gem.'

Vicky blushed again. 'He's very kind.'

'So, did you find your dad's money?'

Vicky nodded. 'After Dad's funeral I decided to clear his room. I got rid of all his things: clothes, bedding, furniture – everything. When I took up the lino I found a loose board. Underneath I found hundreds of pounds worth of coins in brown paper bags – the rent money. It was so heavy it's a wonder it didn't fall through. I had to make several trips to the bank with it all.'

'So now you're a woman of property?'

'I suppose I will be once probate comes through. I won't know how much till then.'

'So what will you do?'

Vicky sighed. 'I don't know. I don't really want to go on living here; too many bad memories. But where do I go and what do I do with the rest of my life? I'm not used to being idle.'

Laura smiled. 'Perhaps P.C. Ian will have some suggestions,' she ventured. Vicky laughed, blushing bright pink. 'Laura Nightingale! What a thing to say!'

'There's always a job for you at the shop. Mum and Dad are very fond of you, but perhaps you won't want to come back now.'

'Oh, I will once everything is sorted out. I love working at the shop for your mum and dad.'

When Laura reached the end of Artillery Street that afternoon she paused, wondering which direction to take. She had promised to meet Moira later after school, but there was an hour before school came out. Should she go and see Rosa? Somehow the idea filled her with dismay. Rosa stood for everything she had left behind: all her hopes and dreams, now shattered and lying in ruins. Could she bear to be reminded? But the time had to come when she put all that behind her and maybe today was as good a day as any. She turned her face resolutely towards the park and Rosa's house.

After she had rung the front door bell Laura stood on the steps waiting for what seemed an eternity. She had just decided that Rosa must be out when the door opened and Rosa stood there, leaning heavily on her stick. She beamed with delight when she saw her former pupil.

'Laura! My dear girl, come in, how lovely to see you.'

Laura followed her into the familiar hallway, noticing as she did that Rosa was walking very slowly and seemed to be in pain. As though reading her thoughts Rosa said, 'Arthritis – as well as my other problems. I'm afraid I've had to cut down on the number of students I take, which is a pity. But you don't want to hear about all that. Come through to the studio and tell me all your news.'

Rosa had already heard of Laura's involvement in the daylight raid and her disappointment in having to miss the overseas ENSA tour. She asked if she was completely recovered from her injuries.

'It was my spine,' Laura explained. 'I still get very tired and my legs ache a lot but they're getting better every day. I'm helping Mum in the shop until Vicky can come back, but after that I'll be looking for a job.'

'How would you like to come and help me with some acting classes?' Rosa asked. 'You could do the evening ones if you like. You're qualified to teach and it might even help your recovery.'

Laura brightened. 'Oh, Rosa. I'd love that.'

'Then, as soon as you feel strong enough we'll arrange it.' The older woman looked thoughtful. 'I've had an idea. It might help you to have some dancing lessons with Frances. It would help get the strength back in your legs.' She shook her head. 'Poor Frances. You won't have heard that she lost her husband at Tripoli. They'd only been married a few months.' She shook her head. 'This damned war. It seems sometimes that it will never end. Everyone is so weary of it.'

'Dad says the tide is turning,' Laura said.

Rosa sighed. 'I do hope he's right, darling. I do hope and pray he's right.'

When Moira came out of school she could see that Laura was tired so she suggested that they go straight home. As they walked Moira listened as her sister talked about Vicky and Rosa's idea that she should take on some of her classes.

'I knew it would do you good to see your old friends,' she said, tucking her arm through Laura's. 'The old sparkle is back in your eyes. But you mustn't overdo it, you know. It's early days yet.'

At Jessop Street Meg and Harry were busy in the shop sorting out the evening papers and the girls went upstairs to the flat. Moira instructed her sister to put her feet up on the settee. 'I'll put the kettle on,' she said. 'Do you want a magazine or something to read?'

'I've got a library book.' Laura made to get up but Moira held up her hand.

'I'll get it. Where is it?'

'Thanks. It's in the drawer of the bedside table.'

Moira was some time returning to the living-room and when she did she was holding, not Laura's library book, but a small box – one which Laura instantly recognized.

'I'm sorry, I couldn't help seeing it,' Moira said. 'I shouldn't have looked inside and I'm sorry, but. . . .'

Laura sprang up, her heart beating fast. 'You had no right!'

'I know and I'm sorry but I've read the card and the cutting. Laura, what you did was. . . .'

'It was nothing! Give that to me!' As Laura snatched the box the lid came off and the contents spilled out on to the settee: the card from the children and their mother, the lover's knot brooch and the newspaper cutting. Moira bent and picked up the newspaper clipping.

The German hit and run raid on the promenade at Balmford-on-Sea yesterday caused five deaths, three of them children. Thirteen seriously injured casualties were taken to hospital. Not least of these was heroine of the day, Laura Nightingale, the brave young hairdresser who saved the lives of nine-year-old Bobby Banks and his seven-year-old sister, Pamela, by shielding them with her own body as machine-gun bullets rained down on them. Laura sustained bullet wounds to her arm and back from which she is making a good recovery.

'Why on earth didn't you tell us?' Moira asked quietly.

'I don't want to remember that day.'

'Mum and Dad will be so proud of you when they know.'

'No! Don't tell them – please, Moira. I want to forget about it.'

Moira was shocked to see Laura's lip beginning to tremble. 'All right. Don't get upset. I won't tell anyone if you don't want me to. Come here.' She put her arms around Laura. 'Whatever you say I think what you did was wonderful, but why does it describe you as a hairdresser? I thought you were in Essex with ENSA.' She felt Laura's body trembling and looked into her eyes. 'Laura – what is it? There's more, isn't there? What's upsetting you so? Tell me.'

There was a long pause before Laura began to speak. 'I had to leave the company,' she whispered. 'Because, because I was pregnant.' Her voice was so low that Moira could scarcely hear her. 'I was going to have a baby – Max Higham's baby. He didn't want me once he knew about it and I had to leave.'

Moira shook her head angrily. 'What a rat! So, what about the. . . ?'

'I lost the baby. It was the raid – my injuries.'

For a moment Moira said nothing, just held her sister close while she wept. At last she took out her handkerchief and dried Laura's tears.

'Oh my God, Laura,' she said softly. 'How could you have kept this to yourself all this time? Does he – does this Max Higham know?'

'No.' Laura shook her head. 'He wouldn't want to know. He wouldn't care. I thought we were in love, Moira. I thought we'd be married when he knew about the baby but – but he was. . . .'

'Already married?' Moira drew her sister's head down on to her shoulder. 'Oh, Laura. I'm so sorry. Don't cry. He isn't worth it.'

'I know. It's just that I feel so – so worthless.'

'Don't you dare say that!' Moira picked up the lover's knot brooch and pinned it on to Laura's blouse. 'There,' she said. 'They didn't think you were worthless when you saved their lives. Just remember that.'

The girls talked long after the light was out that night. Never before had Laura confided so much in her sister and it was such a relief to pour it all out. It must have been two o'clock in the morning when Moira suddenly sat up.

'Laura – there's something I'd like to tell you. This is probably the wrong time and just for the moment I'd like you to keep it to yourself, but I think I might be having a baby. I haven't said anything to anyone yet, not even David. It must have happened that week in Bournemouth. It isn't what we planned; it isn't the best of times to be bringing a child into the world. We haven't even got a home of our own yet and in a few months I'll have to give up my job. By rights it should be worrying me to death but – but if it's really true, if it's really going to happen I know we're both going to be thrilled to bits.'

Laura's eyes were luminous with tears as she hugged her sister. 'Oh, Moira,' she whispered. 'Of course it's the right time to tell me. I'm so pleased for you. You've no idea how much better it makes me feel.'

What she didn't tell Moira – and would never be able to bring herself to tell anyone, was what the doctor had told her the day before she was discharged from the hospital. The words he spoke that morning were burned into her memory like a brand.

'I'm so sorry to have to tell you this, Laura, but owing to your injuries and the surgery we had to perform in order to save your life, it is unlikely that you will ever be able to have another child.'

CHAPTER THIRTEEN

Vicky was back at work behind the counter in Nightingale's shop. The ordeal of Sid Taylor's trial was over and she was trying hard to pick up the pieces of her life and work out what direction to take. It was such a relief to be living something resembling a normal life again.

Sid's trial had been a terrible experience. The pathologist's report showed that Dan had died of a heart attack brought about by shock. There were also signs of a brain haemorrhage caused by repeated bumps to the head as he fell down the stairs. When Vicky's turn came to give evidence she had spoken as clearly as she could, though her voice had shaken with nerves and more than once the judge had to ask her to speak up.

Sid had ranted from the dock that it was all her fault. He accused her of wanting her father dead and of urging him to cause an accident, promising to marry him and share in the proceeds as a reward. Fortunately Phyllis Thorne spoke up for her stoutly. Giving evidence as the only witness to Dan's fall on the day he died, she told the jury that since coming to lodge with the Watts, Sid had behaved in a tyrannical way. He had taken it upon himself to put up the rents and threatened tenants who fell behind with their payments with eviction. She described Vicky as a patient and caring daughter who had looked after her father loyally since losing her mother at an early age.

Ian was called to give evidence as the policeman who had been first on the scene. He told how he had found Vicky running down the street in a distressed state, trying to find a telephone box, and how Phyllis, who had stayed with Dan had told him how Sid had almost knocked her over in his hurry to get out of the house.

As they sat in the waiting-room for the jury to deliver their verdict Vicky trembled with apprehension. Seeing how upset she was, Ian moved across to sit beside her.

'If Sid is found innocent and acquitted he'll be after me,' she said. 'He'll want his revenge.'

Ian shook his head. 'All the evidence is stacked against him. I don't think there's much doubt about how this will go.' He looked at her. 'Anyway, you've got me to protect you now, haven't you?'

She looked at him in surprise, but before she could speak the clerk of the court arrived to call them back into court. The jury was ready to deliver the verdict.

As well as manslaughter Sid had been charged with theft and extortion. As the foreman of the jury stood up Vicky held her breath and when the verdict of 'guilty on all counts' was pronounced her head swam dizzily, the tears welled up and began to trickle down her cheeks. The court listened in silence as the judge sentenced Sid to twelve years' imprisonment.

It was over. The dark cloud that had hung over Vicky's life for so long had lifted at last. Sid was to go to prison. With luck she would never have to see him again. She could scarcely take it in.

Outside the court Ian was waiting for her. 'Vicky. Are you all right?' His brown eyes were concerned as he saw her tears.

'I'm fine,' she told him. 'It's just the relief. I can't believe it's all over.'

He touched her arm. 'I've been thinking. Now that it's over I'll have no more excuses to come round,' he said. 'But I'd still like to see you as a – as a. . . .' He flushed slightly. 'Well, as a girl-friend, I suppose I'm trying to say.' He looked at her. 'Would that be all right with you?'

Vicky's heart was beating so fast she could hardly speak. This had to be the best day of her life. 'Of course it is, Ian,' she told him. 'I'd like that very much.'

A wide grin spread over his face. 'Smashing! The pictures then? Saturday night? I'll pick you up about seven. All right?'

She smiled back. 'All right. I'll look forward to it.'

Daydreaming behind the counter Vicky remembered that first date with Ian. When Laura had heard about it she had suggested a new outfit. Vicky hadn't had any new clothes for ages. She'd been used to making over her old clothes the best she could, so when Laura suggested that they go shopping together she jumped at the offer. Together they chose a smart blue skirt and jacket and, as Vicky still had all her clothing coupons, she was able to get a pair of blue and white shoes to go with them.

Laura had looked at her in the fitting-room. 'Would you be offended if I offered to do your hair for you?' she asked tentatively.

Vicky blushed. In the past she had always cut her own hair and worn it tied back. There had never been any money for professional hairdressing. 'Oh, Laura, would you really?'

With her hair curling softly on her shoulders and the blue suit set off by a white blouse and a dash of lipstick, Vicky was transformed and Ian gave a gasp of delight when he called for her that Saturday evening.

'Oh, Vicky! You look lovely!' he'd exclaimed. Vicky smiled to herself at the memory.

'A packet of Woodbines, please, duck, and an evening paper when you've done dreaming!'

She came down to earth with a bump and looked at the man grinning at her across the counter. '*Oh*! I'm sorry. I was miles away.'

'You're telling me!' He laughed. 'Reckon you're in love duck. By the look on your face you were somewhere a bloomin' sight better than Millborough.'

'Oh no,' Vicky said under her breath as the man left the shop. 'Millborough's like heaven for me as long as Ian's here.'

Moira's baby daughter was born in April. The little girl, whom she named Diana, showed signs of imminent arrival at two o'clock on a Sunday morning and was born only an hour after Harry rushed Moira to hospital in a taxi. David, now stationed on the south coast, was given a brief forty-eight hours' compassionate leave to be with his wife and daughter. Normally it would have been more but he confided to Harry that there was 'something in the air' and that it was on the cards that he would be sent abroad again quite soon. His suspicions proved right when just a few weeks later the Allies made a successful landing in Normandy. The much heralded and longed-for 'second front' had begun and was immediately code-named D-Day. It was only a few days later that London once again became terrorized by bombing; this time from Hitler's new weapon, the V1 rocket. Harry called it Hitler's last stand.

Everywhere in Europe the Germans seemed to be on the run. In July the Allies took Normandy and in August the news broke that Paris had been liberated. Harry watched the news and read the papers avidly. He worried a little at the appalling loss of lives the Allies were suffering. Two of his friends in the ARP had lost sons after the Normandy landing and although he said nothing to his wife and daughters he worried for his son-in-law.

Greatly heartening for everyone was the decision to lift the blackout. 'Thank goodness we shall have the street lights back on next winter,' Meg said with a sigh of relief. 'Fumbling about, looking for the kerb with my torch was enough to make me want to hibernate!'

In spite of her father's stoic optimism Moira worried all the time about David. He'd landed in Normandy with the British Expeditionary Forces on D-Day and since then next to nothing had been heard from him. Laura and she talked about their concerns and their suspended lives long into the small hours after the lights were out in their shared bedroom.

'Suppose he doesn't come home?' Moira would whisper in her bleakest hours. 'Bringing Diana up without a father will be so hard.'

'You're not even to think about that,' Laura said into the darkness. 'David will be home. I know it. Just knowing that you and

Diana need him will be enough to bring him through.' But she said the words with a conviction she didn't feel. Although it seemed that victory was in sight the papers constantly reported the heavy loss of life the war was costing. At the cinema the newsreels showed some of the horrific conditions the troops were having to contend with. For her sister's sake, she too prayed that David would be safe.

Laura had fallen in love with her new niece on sight. She thought that Diana was the most beautiful baby she had ever seen and never missed an opportunity to cuddle her. She was now working at what had been Maison Griggs but had now been passed on to Ada's niece, Jean Martin, who had renamed the place Jeannette's. Jean had been pleased to employ Laura, as Shirley was about to marry her American boyfriend Carl, whose baby she was expecting in a few months.

'Mum and Dad went barmy when they first knew,' Shirley confided. 'But when the war is over I'll be going back to America with Carl. He's a sergeant in the Eighth Air Force and he comes from just outside Los Angeles. That's in California, right near Hollywood, so I'll be rubbing shoulders with all the stars.' She buttoned her smock over her expanding waistline and tossed back her curls. 'I think it was the best thing that could have happened, the Americans coming over here,' she announced. 'Carl's dad has a farm and they grow oranges. Can't you just picture me, sitting under a tree eating oranges all day? I don't know when we last saw oranges piled up on the market stalls, but I've got a green ration book now so I'm entitled when the green-grocer gets a few in. Not that Carl doesn't bring me anything I want,' she added with a smug little smile. 'Do you know, they've got everything at that base, stuff we haven't seen since before the war: tinned fruit, ice cream, all the booze you can knock back.' She looked at Laura with a hint of triumph in her eyes. 'Just shows, don't it? All that studyin' and passin' exams never got you half what I'm gettin', did it?'

'*Shirley*,' Jean put her head round the door. 'Mrs Hodgkiss is waiting for her shampoo and set. She's been sitting there for at least ten minutes.'

Shirley pulled a face at Laura through the mirror. 'Can't wait to get over to LA and away from this dump,' she said. 'No more Mrs Hodgkiss and all that mob. Can't wait. I can't tell you how sick I am of women's flippin' 'eads!'

Hairdressing wasn't exactly Laura's ideal job either. It felt depressingly like a step backwards and she wondered if she would ever get another chance to achieve her dream of being an actress. But at least she knew that she was good at it and she did get some satisfaction from her customers' pleasure when they saw her finished work in the mirror.

She gave classes at Rosa's on two evenings a week, teaching speech and drama to ten to fourteen-year-olds. She loved working with the children and found it rewarding. On two other evenings she joined Frances's ballet class and found that Rosa had been right. The movement and exercise strengthened her legs and helped keep her fit and supple. In September when the children had started the winter term she suggested to Rosa that they produce a Christmas show. At first Rosa was sceptical, wondering if the young first-year students were up to it, but Laura knew that taking part in a show would be good for the children's confidence and they would certainly find it enjoyable. Their enthusiasm would more than make up for their lack of experience, as she pointed out to Rosa. And of course the parents would love it and would make a ready-made audience. At last the older woman agreed and after that most of Laura's evenings were taken up with rehearsals. Knowing that Vicky needed something to take her mind off what she had been through she suggested that she might like to play the piano for rehearsals. Vicky agreed happily and the arrangement was working out well. Life was full and busy once again and Laura was grateful for it. It was one Saturday afternoon in late October that Ethel Radcliffe suddenly put in an appearance at Jeanette's asking breathlessly for Laura.

'I had to come and tell you at once,' she said when Laura came out of the cubicle where she was working.

Laura noticed the older woman's flushed face and animated

manner. 'Tell me what?' she asked. 'What's happened?'

'It's Peter!' Ethel took a deep breath and swallowed hard. 'I heard this morning. He's a prisoner of war in Germany. The Red Cross have only just located him. It seems he's tried to escape more than once and he's been moved around a lot. He's at a place called Stalag something or other now. Apparently it's a camp where they put the troublesome ones,' she added proudly.

Laura's head was spinning sickeningly and she reached out a hand to steady herself. 'Peter! Is – is he all right?' she asked.

'I haven't had all the details yet but when I know any more I'll let you know.' Ethel reached for Laura and hugged her hard. 'I always told you I'd never give up, didn't I?' she said. 'We're going to get our Peter back, Laura! I have to keep pinching myself to make sure I'm not dreaming.'

Jean looked out from the cubicle where she was working and cleared her throat meaningfully. Laura steered Ethel towards the door. 'I'll come round and see you as soon as I can,' she said. 'Thank you for coming to tell me, Ethel.'

For the rest of the day she could not get the news out of her mind. It didn't seem real. Peter was alive. He would be coming home again. And if her father was right it would not be long before the war was over now that the Allies were swinging things their way. But how could she look him in the face again after all that had happened? When he went away they had both been mere children. Now they were two different people. Everything had changed. Nothing could ever be the same again for either of them.

She tried to examine her feelings. She still loved Peter. She realized now that she had never really stopped loving him. What she had felt for Max was not love; she recognized now that it was something else, a fever – a kind of madness. But what she had felt for him and all that had happened to her as a result had changed her enough to make her question everything she felt and did now.

On Monday evening she went round to see Ethel who had now been sent a bundle of letters from Peter which had never reached her. He had written of the way his plane had come down and the injuries he had received, his capture and imprisonment. They were heavily censored but there was enough information in them to prove that his experiences had been tough and often extremely harrowing.

'Do you think they'll repatriate him?' Ethel asked hopefully.

Laura shook her head. 'I think it's only the sick or very badly-injured prisoners who get repatriated,' she said, remembering the cinema newsreels of severely disabled men arriving back in England. 'I think we have to hope that he doesn't qualify for that.'

'I want him back so much,' Ethel said. 'I don't *care* what he's like. I just want to have him home where I can see him and touch him; where I can nurse him better again and keep him safe.'

Laura felt a lump in her throat as she looked at the older woman and heard the passion in her voice. 'You've been so brave, Ethel,' she said. 'And now that we know he's alive we can wait a little bit longer, can't we?'

At Jessop Street, sharing a room with Moira and baby Diana wasn't easy. The baby no longer needed her night feeds but she had begun to cut her teeth now and was often restless in the night. Even though Moira took her through to the living-room, Laura's sleep was broken. Lying awake all her thoughts were of Peter. It was a miracle that he was alive. She still couldn't quite take it in, but in many ways she dreaded the day when they would meet again. She knew for certain that she had changed and Peter must be a different person too. The boy who went away, declaring his love for her was now a man; a man who had seen untold horrors and looked death in the face. They were both scarred, physically and mentally. Was it possible that there could ever be a second chance for them? Would Peter even want a second chance once they met again, especially when he knew she had betrayed him so disloyally? More than that, he deserved the chance to settle down with a girl who could give him children. It would never be possible for them to regain what they had once had and it was foolish to pretend it would be.

Christmas came. Diana, now an engaging nine months old,

was sitting up in her high chair and thoroughly enjoying the brightly coloured decorations and the tree with its lights. The delight on her face when she saw her new dolly and the wooden pull-along duck lovingly carved for her by Harry, made them all laugh.

'By the time David sees her she'll be walking and talking,' Meg said with a wistful sigh. 'I think it's a crying shame, him having to miss all her lovely little baby ways.'

Harry saw Moira's lip tremble and said quickly, 'It's the same for so many new dads. We're not going to talk about that today, Mother.' He rubbed his hands together and gave a jovial laugh. 'Now, where are those mince pies you were making last night? I'll crack open that bottle of sherry I've been saving.'

Laura had bought tickets for all her family to see the drama school show. Meg and Harry were to attend the first night of *Snowflakes* which was to be staged on Boxing Day night and the two nights following. Moira was going on the second night. Outside St Mary's Hall was a large poster advertising the show:

SNOWFLAKES
A Christmas entertainment
performed by the first year students of the
Rosa Seymour School of Dramatic Art,
Dances choreographed by Frances Grey.
Produced and directed by Laura Nightingale.

It made the butterflies flutter in Laura's stomach just looking at it but she tried hard not to let the children see her nervousness. They were buzzing with excitement backstage as they put on their costumes and were made up by Rosa in the large dressing-room at St Mary's Hall.

Laura had designed the show in the form of a revue, with sketches and musical numbers choreographed by Frances. There was a one-act comedy play to end the first half and a grand finale on which she and Frances had collaborated. Vicky had proved such an able pianist at rehearsals that Laura had asked her to take on the role of musical director, an offer which Vicky had blushingly accepted. Even Ian had been roped in to help with building and painting scenery and later he had persuaded two of his friends to work as electrician and stage manager.

When it was almost time for curtain up Laura wished everyone good luck and slipped away to join Harry and Meg in the front row, her heart drumming with nerves and excitement. The curtains parted on the opening number, 'White Christmas'. The children danced and sang in their red fur-trimmed costumes with a background of white gauze spangled with silver sequins donated by Meg who had found them in her sewing box. Skilfully lit by Ian's friend the effect was stunning and the children performed the number perfectly. Laura heaved a sigh of relief and glowed with pleasure at the applause that followed.

The rest of the show went smoothly. There were one or two moments when Laura held her breath, but she was the only one to notice the slight hitches. When the children had taken their fmal bow Rosa walked on to join them. She looked elegant in her black pre-war velvet evening gown and thanked the audience graciously for coming and all the back-stage workers who had put in so much of their own time. She brought on a smiling Frances, congratulating her on her choreography, and praised the children, pointing out that it was their first year at the school. Finally she looked directly down at Laura where she sat in the front row. 'Last but by no means least I want to give a big thank you to Laura Nightingale who has worked so hard to make *Snowflakes* a success,' she said. 'If it hadn't been for her faith in her young students and her hard work and dedication, the show would never have happened.' She held out her hand. 'Laura, please come up and join us. This is where you belong.'

After a moment's hesitation and a sharp jab in the ribs from Meg, Laura stood up and joined Rosa and the children on stage. The applause was deafening. Then from the wings came Ian bearing a huge bouquet of flowers which he put into a surprised Laura's arms.

Rosa whispered, 'The children clubbed together to buy them for you.'

As she took a bow Laura felt tears prick her eyelids. She blinked them away and smiled at her students and their audience. For the first time in many months she knew what it was to feel happy and fulfilled.

Rosa gave a party afterwards for everyone connected with the show. It was the perfect way to relax and wind down and it was almost midnight when Laura, Meg and Harry made their way home through the frosty streets.

Inside the door to the flat Harry stopped in his tracks, his eyes wide with surprise. An army greatcoat was slung over the banisters and at the bottom of the stairs a large khaki kit bag lay where it had been hastily dropped. Harry turned to his wife and daughter. 'Thank God!' he said huskily. 'Oh, thank God! It looks as if our lad has come home.'

Upstairs Meg opened the door of the living-room and peered tentatively round it. 'Moira?'

Moira stood by the kitchen door, a freshly-brewed pot of tea in her hands. She held a finger to her lips and pointed. David lay on the settee, the buttons of his tunic undone and his boots off. He looked pale and haggard but in his sleep his lips were curved in a smile.

'He's home, Mum.' Moira said. 'My David's home again. Safe and sound. Isn't it wonderful?'

CHAPTER FOURTEEN

DURING the Christmas holidays Laura learned that the school had received a flood of applications. Knowing that Rosa was planning to cut down the number of students she took, Laura wondered if she would agree to her taking the two extra classes that would be necessary if they were all to be accepted. She was quite prepared for her to refuse the new applicants. But when Rosa invited her in to talk about it she was to be surprised.

'I've been giving it a lot of thought,' Rosa said as they sat over a pot of strong tea and ginger biscuits in the basement kitchen. 'It would be a great pity to turn people away. The Christmas show was such a success and this new spurt of interest is all down to you. I believe we could have run the show for a week and still sold out.'

'I know you want to retire,' Laura said. 'You've worked hard all your life and you deserve to. I wouldn't like to think I was the cause of you having to rethink your plans.'

'Well, as I said, I've thought it over and I want you to take the school over.'

Laura stared at her, a biscuit halfway to her mouth. '*Me?*'

'Yes, my darling. You. You're qualified to teach and you're clearly very good at it. You have a wonderful way with the children. Even I was surprised at what you'd achieved with them in one term.'

Laura was still trying to take Rosa's suggestion in. 'But – what about you?'

'It's time I moved to a smaller place,' Rosa said. 'This house is too large for me and the stairs are becoming difficult. I've seen a nice little bungalow not far from here but I've been putting it off because I can't bear to part with the old house. Now. . . .' She leaned forward with a smile. 'To my way of thinking the perfect solution would be for you to move into my flat upstairs and take over the running of the school.'

'Oh, Rosa! Do you really mean it?' Laura's eyes were full of tears.

'You'd be doing me a favour, darling. I was dreading having to sell this old house and give up the work I love.'

'You'd still come in to teach then?'

'No. I thought I'd do one-to-one coaching for exams – at home, in my own place. As I said, it's not far from here.' She leaned back with a sigh. 'So – what do you think?'

'It sounds marvellous,' Laura said. 'I don't have to think about it. It's a dream come true.'

Rosa leaned forward and laid her hand on Laura's arm. 'You remind me so much of myself at your age,' she said. 'Especially since your bad luck with your injury. My heart almost stopped that day when I saw you walking with a stick. It was like history repeating itself. Thank God that modern medicine has saved you from ending up cripple like me.' She cleared her throat. 'Of cours, we'll have to see a solicitor and get all the business side of things tied up properly,' Rosa said. 'And while we're there I might as well tell you that I'm planning to leave the house and the business to you in my will.' She held up her hand as Laura began to protest. 'No! I've quite made up my mind. I've no family; no one else to leave it to and you deserve it, so we'll hear no more about it if you don't mind.' The old twinkle came back into her eyes. 'And anyway, I have every intention of living to be a very old lady indeed so it's a long way off.'

Laura laughed and hugged her. 'Amen to that! Rosa, I can't tell you what this means to me. I'm thrilled.'

Rosa patted her shoulder. 'Good. That's all settled then.' She held up the sheaf of applications and adjusted her glasses. 'I'll write and invite the little dears to come in for auditions then, shall I?'

As the first green shoots of spring began to show it seemed that the whole world was beginning to awake from a nightmare. Just as the winter was loosening its hold the war was in its final stages. At the end of March the Allies crossed the Rhine, Mussolini was captured and executed and finally, on the last day of April, as the Allies stormed into Berlin, Hitler took his own life. Harry was ecstatic. As the news was announced on the wireless he grabbed his wife and danced her round the room.

'Harry Nightingale, let me go this instant!' a flushed Meg demanded, pushing him away and patting her hair. 'Fancy getting excited about someone's suicide. It's not Christian!'

'Neither was he,' Harry said. 'Nearly six years of hellish suffering he's put the world through. After the misery and destruction he's caused it's no more than he deserves.' He sat down again with a sigh. 'This poor battered old world is gonna take a lot of rebuilding and no mistake, but at least now we can make a start on it.'

Moira was thrilled. 'To think David and I can start to make a life of our own at last,' she said to Laura. 'I'm going to start looking for a flat for us right away; something small to begin with, till David gets on his feet again. His old job will be there for him as soon as he's demobbed so that won't be a problem.' She looked at her daughter, happily playing in her playpen. 'I keep hoping she won't start walking till he comes home for good. I want him to be there when she takes her first step.'

Vicky was still working in the shop. Laura went to see her one evening to tell her that she was to take over Rosa's drama school and ask her if she would like to play for them regularly in the future. Vicky agreed happily and they sat chatting over cups of coffee. Laura saw a change in the other girL The dowdy, downtrodden look had gone. She seemed much more relaxed. Her hair and her grey eyes shone with health and there was colour in her cheeks. Probate on Dan's estate had taken a long time to come through, but she was now the legal owner of Artillery Street as well as a sizeable bank account but, as she confided to Laura, she had no idea where her future was going.

'Ian and I are getting along so well. I'm scared it might spoil things when he knows just how much money and property Dad left,' she said.

Laura looked at her. 'When you say that you and Ian are "getting along well", what do you actually mean?'

Vicky blushed. 'Well, I suppose I – er. . . .'

'Love him?' Laura prompted. 'It's nothing to be ashamed of, Vicky. Do you?'

Vicky bit her lip. 'Yes – very much.'

'And does he love you too?'

'He says so. I never thought anyone would fall in love with me, Laura. Sometimes I have to pinch myself to make sure I'm not dreaming.' She took a sip of her coffee and looked shyly at Laura over the rim of the cup. 'He's asked me to marry him.'

'*Vicky*! That's lovely. Congratulations! You have said yes, haven't you?'

'I've said I'll think about it.'

'But if you love him what is there to think about?'

'I'm afraid that when he knows exactly how much I've inherited he'll think he's not good enough or something silly.'

'Well, I think you should tell him at once,' Laura said. 'After all, he's already asked you to marry him so he can't be accused of being a fortune hunter, can he?'

'Oh, no! I know he'd never be that anyway.'

'And it's not good to have secrets from each other, is it?'

'N-no.'

Laura sensed that Vicky was uncomfortable talking about Ian's proposal so she changed the subject. 'What are you going to do about the houses?'

'I've had an offer from an estate agent,' Vicky told her. 'He said that with the men coming home there'd be a demand for houses. He'll take them all off my hands at a competitive price. It sounds like an awful lot of money and he says it will save me a lot of worry.'

'Mmm. Are you sure that's the best you can do?' Laura asked.

'I did ask your dad,' Vicky said. 'He said to hang on because the government will pull down all the old properties and use the land to build flats. He said he'd read it in the paper. I could name my own price if I hung on for a while.'

'So, why don't you? I daresay that's what this estate agent has in mind anyway.'

Vicky nodded. 'Some of those people have lived there all their lives,' she said. 'I won't have them evicted, so I've decided to offer the present tenants the houses they live in at a reduced price first. Then the government will have to buy them back if they want them.'

Laura smiled. 'That's very selfless, Vicky. You've really thought it through, haven't you?'

'I know what it's like to be poor,' Vicky said. 'I'll never forget that, whatever happens.'

'And Ian?'

Vicky smiled with a new spark of confidence. 'Don't worry. I won't let him go,' she said. 'I'll think of a way.'

Laura's official takeover of the school was planned for the beginning of the next school year in September. All the legalities were tied up. At Rosa's request the school was to retain its name during her lifetime. She suggested that the prospectus should be headed, *The Rosa Seymour School of Dramatic Art. Under the direction of Laura Nightingale.* Laura was more than happy with this.

Rosa bought her little bungalow and planned to move in as soon as she could. She suggested that Laura might like to move into her vacated flat as soon as she had moved, making room for David when he came out of the army.

During the spring term Laura struggled to keep on her job at Jeannette's as well as the classes, which now took up most of her evenings. Meg complained that she was running herself ragged and urged her to give in her notice. 'It's not so long ago that you couldn't walk without a stick,' she pointed out. 'All that standing can't be doing your back any good.'

Laura knew that she was right and at last she was obliged to give in her notice at the hairdresser's. Jean was devastated. 'You've built up such a good clientele,' she said. 'And now that Shirley's left we're going to be really short-staffed.'

Shirley's baby had been born on Christmas Day, a pretty little girl she had named Peggy-Louise. She and Carl had been married just before he was shipped home with his unit and she was waiting for her sailing orders along with all the other GI brides in Millborough.

Laura felt guilty for letting Jean down but she knew she could not hold down two jobs any longer. 'The girls will be coming out of the services soon,' she pointed out. 'There'll be plenty of women looking for work before long. But until you find someone I'll come in and work on Saturdays if you like.'

Jean sighed. 'Oh, don't put yourself out,' she said with a sniff. 'We can't have that, can we?'

On 7 May the war was officially at an end but for several weeks prior to that Meg had been busy planning a Victory party. She had enlisted the help of all her Women's Institute friends including Ethel Radcliffe and they had formed a committee. At first they had thought of having a street party but in the end they had decided to have it in St Mary's Hall, just in case of bad weather. The official date for Millborough's victory celebrations was set for Saturday 19 May. Meg was constantly busy with endless lists and lobbied all the housewives to donate food – whatever they could manage on the day.

On the day, Meg and her band of helpers were up bright and early. The men were enlisted too, to help erect trestle tables in the hall and hang up bunting and flags. By mid-morning the hall looked festive and patriotic and the food had started to arrive. The housewives of Millborough had come up trumps. Meg couldn't help wondering where some of the women had managed to find such treats, but everything was received gratefully and without question.

By three o'clock all was ready and by half past the eager residents had begun to arrive, all dressed in their best. After tea there was to be a fancy dress contest for the children, a raffle, the proceeds of which would go to Mrs Churchill's Aid to Russia Fund and then, when the children had gone home to bed, there was to be dancing, played for by Ted Willis's band.

The long trestles groaned with the array of sandwiches and home-made cakes, jellies, fruit and trifles bedecked with brightly coloured 'hundreds and thousands'. To Meg's dismay one enthusiastic housewife had made an outsized trifle in a washing-up bowl. 'I do hope she gave it a good scrub,' she said as she tried to disguise the enamelled rim with a crepe-paper frill.

The children tucked in with gusto. One or two of them had to be taken home with tummyache but on the whole, everyone was in the best of spirits.

Laura and Moira spent most of the time in the kitchen, filling and refilling the enormous enamelled teapots from the hissing urn and washing up. Neither of them felt much like a marathon feed. Moira had heard that morning that David would have to wait another three months for his discharge and she was a little disappointed. She had been to see several flats but her initial enthusiasm had been eroded as one disappointment followed another.

'That last one was no better than an attic with three families sharing the same bathroom,' she said despondently as she and Laura washed up together. 'And nowhere under cover to put the pram. Others won't allow children at all. What are we supposed to do?'

'Never mind, you'll find something suitable soon,' Laura assured her. 'And I'll be moving into Rosa's before long so you and David will be able to have our room at Jessop Street to yourself.'

They were just putting the last of the dishes away when Ethel came into the kitchen. She was flushed and her eyes were sparkling with excitement.

'One of the neighbours came to tell me I had a visitor in the middle of serving tea,' she said. 'I thought, what a nuisance, having to leave just when the party was getting under way.' She paused to take a deep breath and reached out to take Laura's hand. 'When I got home who do you think was waiting for me on the step?'

'Oh, Ethel. . . .' Laura's heart began to beat faster. 'Not – not. . . ?'

'Yes, *Peter!*' Ethel gave a little giggle of excitement. 'I brought him back with me and he's out there now, in the hall. He wants to see you, Laura. I thought I'd better come and warn you first though.'

Moira looked at her sister. 'Well? What are you waiting for, standing there like a lemon?' As Laura moved towards the door she called out, 'Take your apron off first though, glamour-puss!' Laura pulled off the offending apron and threw it to her sister who caught it, smiling at Ethel.

The main hall was buzzing with people. The fancy dress contest was over and the children were now playing blind man's bluff. She searched the sea of faces but could not see Peter or anyone who looked remotely like him. For a moment she wondered wildly if Ethel had dreamt the whole thing. Then a voice spoke at her shoulder. 'Hello, stranger.'

She spun round and her heart jumped into her mouth as she found herself looking at the tall figure in RAF uniform. He seemed taller and he had certainly lost weight. His uniform hung loosely on him and his face looked thin and angular. There were fine lines around his eyes and mouth that hadn't been there before, but in spite of everything, when he smiled he was the old Peter, just as she remembered him. Her heart turned over and a huge lump in her throat prevented her from speaking. He opened his arms and she went into them.

'It – it's been such a long time,' she said. 'I thought I'd never see you again.'

'Can't get rid of me that easily.' He held her away from him. 'You look wonderful. The same as ever.'

The children's game ended and as someone suggested it was time for lemonade, a collective yell went up. Peter glanced around at the crowd of over-excited young people and grimaced, 'Can you get away for a while?' he shouted. 'Can't hear myself think in here.'

Laura nodded. 'I'll get my coat.'

Outside it was comparatively quiet. There were other celebrations going on. Numerous street parties and the formal civic party for the councillors at the Town Hall left the streets almost empty. The shops were decked with bunting and Union Jacks and as they turned in at the park gates they heard the strains of Millborough's town band coming from the bandstand.

Peter grinned. 'William Tell. They haven't widened their repertoire then? Nothing much changes, thank goodness. I can't tell you how many times I've dreamt of being here like this with you.'

They found a bench in a quiet corner and sat down. Peter took a deep breath as he looked around at the blossoming trees and the green grass. 'Believe me, there was many a time when I thought I'd never see home again.'

'It must have been terrible,' Laura said. 'All you've been through.'

He took her hand and held it tightly. 'It was, but I don't want to talk about that now. I want to hear all about you. What have you been doing? Mum said you'd been away with ENSA and that you were shot in a hit and run raid.' He looked at her with concern. 'Are you all right now?'

'Yes. I'm fine.'

'I did write to you,' he said. 'We never knew whether the letters actually got home or not and I expect you've heard that I made a break a couple of times, but I did try and get word home to let you know I was still around.'

'I didn't get any letters,' Laura said. 'Your mum only got hers after she knew you were a prisoner. We thought the worst, Peter. The telegram Ethel got said "missing believed killed".'

'I know. Poor Mum.'

'She's been marvellous,' Laura told him. 'She never stopped believing that you'd come home again.'

'And you?' He slipped an arm around her shoulders and drew her close.

She hid her face against his shoulder. 'I wasn't nearly as brave.'

His arm tightened around her. 'I still can't believe I'm home and it's all actually over – that I'm sitting here with you, breathing English air again. I could sit here like this for ever. I never want to let you go again.' He looked down at her. 'The good news is that we're being discharged almost at once, so it won't be long before we can begin to live again. I've missed you so much, Laura. I'm going to have to start looking for a job to begin with of course, and then. . . .' He peered into her eyes. 'What is it? Why are you crying?'

She shook her head, fumbling in her pocket for a handkerchief. 'I've missed you too. So much has happened. The war affected everyone and – and. . . .'

He cupped her face and kissed her. 'Never mind all that. We might have lost a few years but we've got the rest of our lives. We can make up for it, can't we?' He tipped her chin up and looked into her eyes. 'We *can*, can't we? You do still feel the same? I mean, if you'd met someone else it would hardly be surprising and I would understand. After all, you did think I'd gone for good and. . . .'

'*Please* – please, don't!' She put her fingers against his lips and swallowed hard at the lump in her throat. 'There's no one else, Peter. We have to put these horrible years behind us now, try to forget them.'

'So – so you're still my girl?' he asked her softly.

She looked into his eyes, the eyes she loved and remembered so well and nodded. 'We ought to be getting back now,' she said. 'Your mum will want you to spend this evening with her. I think she deserves that.'

'You haven't answered my question.'

'Yes, Peter, I'm still your girl.'

But later, long after she was in bed and Moira slept soundly beside her she wondered if she was still Peter's girl – if she ever could be again. He would have to decide whether he still wanted her when he knew how thoroughly she had betrayed him with another man. It was terrifying to think that if Max had proved trustworthy she would have been married to him by now, the mother of his child. It was what she'd wanted at the time – at least what she *thought* she had wanted. If Max hadn't abandoned her she would never have gone to Balmford-on-Sea. She would never have been injured in the raid and lost the baby. She would not have ended up damaged, flawed, unworthy of Peter's love – unable to give him a child. He would have to know all this if they were to pick up the threads of their relationship. She turned over, burying her face in the pillow so that Moira would not hear her crying. She knew without a doubt that she couldn't tell him, couldn't bear to see the look of disgust and disappointment on his face when he knew that she wasn't the girl he'd left behind, and never could be again.

Over the weeks that followed life was busy for Laura. Most evenings were taken up with classes and helping Rosa to pack and move into her bungalow. Peter had returned to his squadron to await demobilisation so the confession she dreaded so much could be postponed for now.

Moira was openly envious of Laura's flat. 'To think you're going to have three whole rooms and a bathroom all to yourself,' she complained. 'While David, Diana and I still have to squeeze into a poky bedroom here with Mum and Dad!'

Laura felt guilty. 'I'd willingly change places with you,' she said. 'But until it's signed and sealed the flat still belongs to Rosa.'

'I'm sorry.' Moira shook her head. 'I wasn't trying to make you feel bad,' she said. 'It's just that I'm so desperate for us to find a place of our own. Beginning married life cramped up like this isn't what I wanted at all.'

Then, out of the blue the solution came. Shortly before David's demob came through Derek Harriman, the owner of the men's outfitter's shop where David was to take over as manager, offered them the flat above the shop as he and his wife were moving to a house in the suburbs. Moira was almost beside herself with delight when she came back from viewing it.

'There are two bedrooms,' she said, her eyes shining. 'A lovely big sitting-room overlooking the high street, a kitchen and a little bathroom. It's *perfect*!'

'I've got some curtains you can have,' Meg said. 'Tell you what, we'll go round there and measure up. If they need altering I can do it on the machine.'

'Hold on a minute.' Harry held up his hand. 'How much rent are they stinging you for? Better make sure you can afford it before you start making curtains.'

Moira smiled. 'That's the best bit, Dad. Ten bob a week, including gas and electricity. Mr Harriman says he'll feel better having someone living on the premises for security's sake.'

'Oh, well, that's all right then.' Harry looked at his wife. 'Right then. Seems to me that this is as good a time as any to tell the girls our plans, Mother,' he said.

Meg nodded. 'Now that we know you're both going to be settled we can go ahead,' she said.

The girls looked at each other. 'Go ahead with what, Mum?' Moira asked.

'Your mother and I are thinking of retiring,' Harry said. 'We're getting on a bit now and we're both tired. The war has taken its toll on us – all the paperwork and red tape with the rationing and everything, we've had enough and we'd like to spend whatever time we've got left relaxing.'

'Good for you,' Laura said. 'But what does that mean? Will you be selling the shop or putting in someone to manage it?'

'We'll sell,' Harry said. 'We want to buy a little place in the country. Not too far out, a village perhaps; on a bus route so that we can get in and out to the shops and to you girls, of course.'

'Somewhere where we can have a little garden and grow some nice flowers,' Meg said.

'And veg,' Harry added. 'Nothing like home-grown veg. So you see we'll need to sell this place to afford that.'

'It won't seem the same without the two of you here in the shop,' Moira said wistfully.

'But think how Diana will love a trip into the country to see

Grandma and Grandpa,' Laura said.

'Yes. I'll put up a swing for her in the garden,' Harry added. He looked at his wife. 'We can't wait, can we, Mother?' He rubbed his hands together. 'So – now that you girls know, we can put Nightingale's on the market. I reckon it'll be snapped up in no time with the fellas coming home from the war.'

CHAPTER FIFTEEN

'Have you always wanted to be a policeman?'

Vicky and Ian were walking in the park. It was a gloriously warm Sunday afternoon in late June. Ian was off duty and wore the tweed sports jacket that Vicky liked to see him in.

'Ever since I was old enough,' he said. 'It was Dad's idea. He was in the force till he was in his forties. That was when he came out and bought the hardware shop. He always wanted me to follow in his footsteps and I suppose I thought it was better than working in a factory or being stuck in some office.' He sighed. 'I regretted it when the war came though. I'd rather have gone off to fight like all my mates did, but I was led to believe that this job was just as important.'

Vicky shuddered. 'I'm glad you didn't go.' She slipped her arm through his and hugged it. 'I like having you here, safe and sound.'

'Everyone thought we'd be bombed like the cities,' Ian said. 'But we never were so I might as well have joined the army.'

'Have you thought that if you had we might never have met?'

He smiled. 'That's right. Anyway, it's all water under the bridge now,' he said. 'By the way, I've put in for my sergeant's exams. It'll mean a lot of studying but I'll get more money if I pass.' He glanced at her. 'Ready for when you say "yes". You *are* going to say yes one of these days, aren't you, Vicky?'

Vicky took a deep breath. 'Ian, come and sit down. There's something I have to tell you.' She drew him over towards a bench

208

under the trees and sat down, patting the seat beside her. 'Don't look so worried,' she said. 'It's nothing horrible.'

After a moment's hesitation he sat down beside her. 'I don't like the sound of this. Better get it over with quick.'

'Ian, you already know that Dad owned the houses in Artillery Street.'

'*You* did, you mean,' he pointed out. 'They should have been yours.'

'Well, they are now that everything's sorted out. I had an offer for them from a local estate agent. It was a good offer but I turned it down. I've heard that the council might pull the houses down eventually to build new flats.'

'A compulsory purchase order, you mean?'

'Yes, so I've offered the sitting tenants the chance to buy their houses at a low price. More than half of them have managed to get mortgages and they've accepted, which means that they'll get their money back and maybe a bit more besides when and if that happens.'

He looked at her with concern. 'It's none of my business, Vicky. I mean, it's your money, but you'd have been better off to wait for an offer from the council.'

'I like this way better,' she told him. 'I want the tenants to benefit. After all, they had to suffer Sid's bullying and threats and I feel partly responsible for that.'

He slipped an arm round her. 'I love you, Vicky Watts. Thanks for telling me your plans, but it's your business, not mine.'

'I wanted you to know and to – approve,' she said. 'They're not just *my* plans and it's not as unselfish as you might think. I've got money in the bank besides the property, you see . . . quite a lot of money. Dad never parted with a penny if he could help it.'

Ian frowned. 'Honestly, you don't need to tell me all this, Vicky.'

'But I do. The reason I haven't talked to you before is that I thought it might put you off me if you knew I had a lot of money.'

'Of course it wouldn't—' He stopped in mid-sentence. 'Oh! Because of what people might say, you mean?'

'It doesn't matter to me what people say, but it might matter to you.' As he opened his mouth to protest she held up her hand. 'Don't say anything yet. I haven't finished. I don't want to stay on at number 13. The place holds too many bad memories. I've had an idea that will mean spending most of the money and I'd like to know what you think of it.'

He smiled. 'Well, as I said, it's nothing to do with me what you do with your money, but fire away if you insist.'

But Vicky's face was deadly serious. 'I've been working for Mr and Mrs Nightingale at the shop for ages now and I've loved it from the very first day. A couple of weeks ago I thought it was all coming to an end when Mrs Nightingale told me they were going to sell up and go and live in the country. At first I was really upset and disappointed, then I had this exciting idea.'

Ian frowned. 'Yes?'

'I want to know what you think of me offering to buy the shop.' She held her breath. There, she'd said it. She'd told him everything in one fell swoop. Now it was up to him.

He shrugged. 'It's your decision, Vicky.'

She shook her head. 'What I'm really asking you is – how do you fancy being the joint owner of a newsagent's shop?'

He blinked. 'Me?'

'Yes, you – *us*. There's a lovely flat over the shop too.' When he still sat there with his mouth slightly open she nudged him. 'Ian Blake, I'm trying to say yes – *yes, I'll marry you*. If you still want me, that is.'

'Want you! Of course I want you, you silly girl. All I want to know now is *when*?'

'So you agree that we share everything?' she asked. 'If I buy the shop I won't have much of Dad's money left so I need to know that you approve.'

'I want you to do whatever makes you happy,' he said. 'But I'd like to stay with the police if that's OK with you. I'd still like to think of myself as the breadwinner.'

'Of course, whatever you want,' she told him. 'So, is that all right?'

'You bet it is!' He pulled her to him and kissed her soundly. 'But I have to say that it's the daftest acceptance of a proposal I've ever heard of. More like a business deal!' He looked into her eyes. 'But don't you think you can take it back, Vicky Watts. It's been taken down and it'll be used in evidence!'

'So. . . .' She laughed shakily. 'So we're – engaged then, are we?'

'You bet we are,' Ian said.

All the Nightingale family were invited to Vicky and Ian's wedding. It was a quiet affair with the ceremony at St Mary's and a small buffet reception afterwards at Ian's parents' house. The couple were to spend a week at the seaside and move into the flat in Jessop Street on their return, taking over the shop the following Monday. Vicky was so excited about it all as she told Laura. 'On that first day when I started working for your mum I never dreamed I'd one day own the shop,' she said, her eyes shining. She glanced across to where Ian was talking to David and Moira. 'I never thought I'd meet someone like Ian either,' she said, blushing, 'let alone marry him. I have to keep pinching myself to make sure it's all really happening.'

Laura hugged her. 'No one deserves it more than you, Vicky. It's lovely to think that you'll be taking the shop over instead of some stranger. I know Mum and Dad are thrilled about it too.'

Since the war in Europe ended so many changes had begun to take place. Laura had moved into Rosa's flat as soon as she had vacated it, so as to make room for David at Jessop Street, but by September all the family would have moved on. Meg and Harry retired to the pretty little cottage five miles out of town in Benningford village, and Moira, David and baby Diana, now an active toddler, moved into their new apartment over Harriman's Outfitters. The prospect of post-war life should have been exciting and challenging, but for Laura it was overshadowed by a dark cloud.

Peter had received his discharge from the RAF at the beginning of June and was back living with his mother who was enjoying nursing him back to his former health. He had found a job at Shearing's as assistant chief engineer and began working there at the beginning of July. Laura saw him gradually blossoming into his former self, putting on weight and regaining some healthy colour in his face. But the more he looked like the Peter she remembered, the more she feared confessing the changes that had taken place in her. She had been busy with classes at the school and redecorating her flat and she latched on to these things to make repeated excuses when Peter asked her out.

'Surely you can't be *that* busy,' he said exasperatedly when she turned down his suggestion that they spend a Sunday together by the sea. 'The weather is perfect for a day by the sea. I've even got the use of a car. You're working too hard, Laura.'

She bit her lip. It was the third time in a week that she had turned down his invitations and she could see that he was deeply hurt by her refusal. She knew she should face up to it and tell him the truth. Remembering her own words to Vicky she felt like a hypocrite. *It's not good to have secrets from each other*, she had told her. It was all too easy, advising others. Why couldn't she take her own advice? But the thought of Peter's hurt reaction and the prospect of losing his love and respect made her into a coward. They hadn't come through a war, Peter's imprisonment and years of being apart for it to end like this. Much better to let him think that they had outgrown their teenage romance. Except that she knew they hadn't.

In the end she agreed to the day by the sea and Peter picked her up at eight o'clock the following Sunday morning. He'd borrowed a car from an uncle who had a petrol allowance for his business and he looked so happy and carefree when he arrived that it made her heart ache to look at him.

It was a bright, clear morning as they drove to the coast with a heat haze dancing on the road ahead. Peter urged her to sing with him as they used to. 'Remember that song we used to like, "Smoke Gets in Your Eyes"?' he asked her. He began to hum the tune in the gentle baritone voice that tugged at her heart strings. She hadn't heard the song for a long time but snatches of the evocative words came back to her. *They say, someday you will find, all who love are blind – when the lovely flame dies – smoke gets in your eyes.* Without warning the tears welled up in her eyes and began to fall.

'*Don't!*' she said abruptly. 'Stop it, Peter.'

He turned to look at her. 'Darling! What is it? What's the matter?'

She shook her head. 'Nothing. I just can't – that song. It's. . . .'

He pulled the car off the road and switched off the engine. 'I think you'd better tell me what's wrong,' he said softly, handing her a clean handkerchief. 'I've known ever since I first came home that there was something – something not quite right between us.' He touched her shoulder. 'There was someone else, wasn't there?' He touched the lover's knot brooch she wore on her jacket. 'You always wear this. I don't remember it. Did he give it to you?'

She shook her head. 'No.'

'What happened, Laura? Was he killed? Does it still hurt? Is it that you're still grieving for him?'

'No! It was nothing like that.'

'Then what?'

She swallowed back the tears, dabbed her eyes and gave him back his handkerchief. 'It's all in the past. I don't want – I *can't* talk about it. Please, Peter, let's just forget it, shall we?'

'You obviously can't.' His face hardened with hurt and rejection and he switched on the ignition again. 'This isn't working, is it?'

'Not really.'

'Do you still want to go to the sea or do you want me to take you home?'

'I – I think I'd rather go home, please.'

Inwardly she chastized herself. She'd had her chance and she'd let it go. She was the worst kind of coward and she hated herself. She told herself it was better like this. She didn't deserve his love. Once he knew what she had done he would hate her and she couldn't bear that. She remained silent on the drive home but her mind was in turmoil. When he drew up outside the house and she made to get out he reached across and stopped her.

'Laura, please. I can't let you go like this. Can we go inside and talk?'

'*No!*' Her heart thudded with panic. 'Really, Peter, I can't, not at the moment.'

For a long moment his eyes held hers then he sighed. 'All right. If that's what you want. Can I ring you in a few days' time?'

'Of course. I'm sorry, Peter.' She stood on the steps and watched as he drove away, hating herself and wishing she'd had the courage to tell him everything. Either that or finish it for good. Perhaps if he knew it wasn't his fault he wouldn't be so hurt. Upstairs in the flat she curled up in a chair and sobbed until her heart ached.

It was the following evening as she was seeing the last of her class out when a familiar figure began walking up the steps. Laura's heart missed a beat. 'Ethel!'

The older woman smiled. 'You haven't been to see me for so long, Laura. I've missed you and I said to myself this evening, well, if Mohammed won't come to the mountain. . . .' She looked at the departing children. 'Is this a bad time?'

'No, I've finished for this evening. Come up to the flat and have a cup of tea.'

Upstairs in the flat Ethel looked round. 'This is nice. Plenty of room. Are you going to live here all on your own?'

The implication was plain and Laura blushed. This was going to be really difficult. 'For the moment, yes.' She went into the kitchen and Ethel followed her.

'I'll come straight to the point, dear. I know it's none of my business but is there something wrong between you and Peter?'

Laura filled the kettle, keeping her face averted. 'Whatever makes you think that?' She knew even as she spoke that it was going to be useless trying to pull the wool over Ethel's eyes. They had known each other far too long for that. She turned to look at her. 'Don't worry. I daresay it will work itself out eventually,' she said.

In the living-room she poured the tea and handed Ethel a cup. The older woman sipped her tea slowly, studying Laura's face. 'You're looking peaky dear, if you don't mind me saying so. Peter isn't himself either. In fact I'd go as far as to say that he's eating his heart out over something. He tries to keep it from me but I know my boy and I can see how unhappy he is.' She put her cup down. 'Laura – I've got to say this. If you don't love him any more I think you should tell him. It really isn't fair to keep him hanging on like this. He's been through too much to be punished like this.'

Laura was appalled at Ethel's choice of words. 'I'm not trying to punish him, Ethel. I do still love him, very much. It's just – just that when I was away there was someone else and—'

'No!' Ethel held up her hand. 'No, don't go on, Laura. I don't want to hear it. It's none of my business. I didn't come here to pry or to judge you. You don't have to tell me anything, but please, dear, for pity's sake, tell *him*. Get it out in the open and put him out of his misery.'

'I will,' Laura said quietly. 'I will, I promise.'

Downstairs as Laura was seeing her out Ethel turned to her. 'Look, I shouldn't tell you this but Peter was planning a surprise for your birthday next week. He's got tickets for the Theatre Royal on Wednesday evening. It's a touring company. They're doing *Daddy Longlegs*. Remember when you were in it with the Millborough Players before the war and Peter was working backstage? He thought it would be fun to see it again together. Let him take you, Laura. Don't spoil his surprise. And maybe afterwards you could tell him whatever it is that's bothering you.' She looked at Laura pleadingly. 'There's no one I'd rather have as a daughter-in-law than you, Laura. It's always been my dream to see the two of you married. And please believe me, I'm not interfering. Peter would be furious if he knew I was here, so don't tell him, will you?'

'Of course I won't.'

'I just want to see you both happy.' Ethel put her arms around Laura and hugged her. 'I'll say goodnight then, dear. No ill feeling?'

'Of course not. Thanks for coming, Ethel.'

When Peter rang a few days later and asked her out on the following Wednesday she accepted. Getting ready on the night she was nervous. There could be no more stalling. She had promised Ethel. Tonight she had reached the point of no return. By the time the evening was over Peter would know everything and their future together would hang in the balance.

He picked her up as arranged. When she opened the door to him he wished her a happy birthday and pressed a small box into her hand. When she opened it she found a string of pearls inside.

'Thank you.' She kissed his cheek. 'They're lovely, Peter, but you shouldn't have. I don't—'

'Don't what?' he asked. 'Don't you like pearls?'

'Of course I do. I was going to say that I don't deserve such an expensive present.'

'I think you do.'

But she couldn't bring herself to put the necklace on and as they walked the short distance to the theatre the strain between them was almost tangible. Inside Peter bought a programme and they took their seats. The auditorium gradually filled up and when it was almost time for curtain-up Laura opened the programme on her lap. Without taking in what she was looking at she read the advertisements, but it was when she turned the page and came to the cast list that a name jumped off the page at her, almost making her heart stop. *Director: Max Higham.* She half-rose from her seat, but Peter put out his hand.

'Don't go now. It's about to start.'

The lights were dimming and the curtain rose for act one. Reluctantly she sat down again. Somehow she managed to get through the first act; her heart frozen, she neither saw nor heard any of it and the moment the curtain came down for the interval she began to get up.

'I'm sorry – I won't be long.'

He looked up at her with concern. 'What the matter? Aren't you feeling well?'

'It's all right. I'm fine.' She put her hand on his shoulder. 'You stay here. I won't be long.'

She drew indignant looks as she pushed her way through the throng of people heading for the bar. To her relief the foyer was almost empty and as she stepped out into the street she gulped in a deep breath of fresh air and began to walk briskly. It was only then that she realized that in her hurry to leave she had left her jacket and handbag on her seat. There was no way she was going back for them. For the first time she acknowledged the fact that she was running away and she hated herself for letting Peter down so shabbily. Tonight she'd had such good intentions. She'd meant to do the right thing whatever the consequences. But the sight of Max's name on the programme was enough to set her nerves jangling and send waves of panic washing over her. All the pain he had caused her came surging back and as long as there was the slightest chance of seeing him while she was with Peter she had to leave – to put as much distance as she could between them.

The air was warm and heavy with the scents of summer, a beautiful evening, but to Laura the street might as well have been shrouded in November fog. All she wanted was to get home and close the door – shut out the memories and the pain.

She turned the corner to take a short cut past the Crown and Anchor but when she saw the illuminated sign 'Stage Door' a few yards down the street she turned abruptly to retrace her steps. At that moment the door suddenly opened and Max came out. Catching her breath, she flattened herself against the wall, hoping he wouldn't see her as he stepped towards the kerb. He was about to cross the road when he turned and his eyes widened in astonishment as he caught sight of her.

'*Laura!* Well, well, what a surprise.' He walked towards her. 'What are you doing here?' As she made to turn away his hand shot out and grasped her arm. 'Hey! Don't run away. I was just popping across to the pub for a drink. Why don't you join me? We've got a hell of a lot of catching up to do.'

She pulled her arm away, aware from his breath and slightly slurred speech that he had already been drinking heavily. 'No,

Max. I don't want to talk to you – now or ever.'

He frowned. 'Oh, come on, Laura. That's not like you. I know we parted on difficult terms but I'm divorced now.' He chuckled. 'Footloose and fancy free as they say. Maybe we could meet again one evening while I'm here. Pick up the threads, talk about old times.'

'*No!*'

His fingers grasped her arm again and he pushed his face close to hers. 'Laura, darling – just for the record, what did you have, a boy or a girl? Do I have a son or a daughter?'

'Leave me alone, Max. I didn't – there is no—'

'Oh, I see. Came to your senses and got rid of it, did you? What a pity you didn't listen to me in the first place? Things could have been different.'

'Let me go!'

'Why? What's your hurry?'

'Let me go – *please*!' She tried to wrench her arm from his grasp but the more she pulled the harder his fingers gripped. He laughed. 'Why the panic? I'm only trying to be friendly.'

'I think the lady asked you to let her go.'

Laura turned, her heart jumping as she saw Peter standing there, her jacket and bag over his arm and his face as white and hard as stone.

'I don't know who the hell you are,' he said to Max. 'But I suggest you go before I get the police.'

Max attempted to draw himself up, swaying a little on his heels. 'The lady, is it? I can assure you she's no lady, old boy. And if you're thinking of taking up with the little trollop I feel sorry for you.'

Peter took a step towards him and grasped him by the lapels, pushing him hard against the wall. 'If you weren't so disgustingly drunk I'd knock you down for that,' he said. 'Be on your way and don't bother Laura again or you'll have me to reckon with.' He let Max go with a push that almost sent him sprawling.

Regaining his balance, he straightened his collar, looking Peter up and down with a sneer. 'Steady on old chap or you might drop your handbag!' He walked away in the direction of the pub, weaving a little as he crossed the road.

Stony-faced, Peter took her arm. 'Come on, I'll take you home.'

They crossed the park to Rosa's house in silence. Laura took out her key and made no attempt to stop Peter as he followed her up the stairs to the flat. As she closed the door she turned to look at him. 'I don't know why you're still here. You must have heard what he said. And before you ask, it's all true.'

Without replying he took her arm and steered her to the living-room. 'There are two sides to every story,' he said. 'I want to hear yours. I think you owe me that.'

She took a deep breath, feeling strangely calm now that the moment had come. Soon it would be over and she could lay the whole miserable episode to rest and be free of the agony. She told herself that the promise of peace of mind was almost worth the sacrifice she was about to make.

'Max was in the same ENSA company as me,' she began. 'We toured with a play. I fell in love with him – or thought I did. When I realized I was expecting his child he told me he was married and threw me out of the company.'

Peter muttered something under his breath and she saw his hands clench into fists. 'Was it true what he said?' he asked quietly. 'Did you *get rid of it*, as he so delicately put it?'

She shook her head. 'No. I could never bring myself to do something like that.' Her knees suddenly threatened to buckle and she sat down, staring down at her hands. 'I knew I couldn't bring that kind of disgrace home so I went to stay in a little seaside town called Balmford-on-Sea. I got a job there in a hairdresser's and I meant to have the baby, to bring it up on my own somehow. Then one day I was on the promenade when the German planes flew in and I took those two bullets. One in my arm and the other in my back. I lost the baby as a result.'

He sat down beside her and touched her hand, his eyes dark with hurt and compassion. 'Oh God, Laura!' He made her look at him. 'I have to ask you. In spite of everything, do you still love him?'

She shook her head. 'I know now that I never did. Not in the true sense. I was young and naïve – infatuated. He was older, more experienced. He—'

'Seduced you.' He nodded towards her jacket draped over the back of the chair, the lover's knot brooch still pinned to the lapel. 'Yet you still wear that.'

Laura turned to look at the brooch in surprise. 'Max didn't give me that.'

'Then who did?'

'That day at Balmford, the day of the raid – it was swift and unexpected. The school children had just broken up for the holidays. The seafront was crowded with them. When they began to machine-gun us all there was no time to think. I threw myself to the ground over two of them, a little boy and a girl.'

'And the bullets hit you instead of them?'

'It wasn't bravery – only a kind of instinct. It just happened. Later, when I was in hospital, their mother came to see me. She gave me the brooch. It had been her grandmother's. It was given to me in gratitude for her children's lives.'

There was a moment's silence then Peter reached out and put his arms around her. 'Oh, Laura. Why have you kept all this to yourself?'

'I was ashamed,' she said. 'Moira is the only other person who knows and she found out by accident.' She raised her face to look at him. 'I couldn't wear the brooch for a long time, because of its associations, because I felt I didn't really deserve to.' She looked into his eyes for the first time. 'I thought you were dead, Peter. I know that's no excuse but—'

'Shh.' He put his fingers over her lips. 'The war has messed up so many lives. We all have scars, memories that will haunt us for the rest of our lives. I'm no exception.' He took her hand in both of his. 'Now I want you to hear my story. The last time I tried to escape there were three of us. We got as far as France but we split up when we had a narrow escape. We were shot at and two of us were hit. Mine was only a flesh wound in my shoulder but it got infected and I started to feel groggy. I sheltered in a barn one night, delirious and out of my head. The following morning I was discovered by a girl. At first we were each as scared as each other, but once she knew who I was she decided to help me. She explained that her brother was away fighting and she was trying to keep the little farm going till he came home. The Germans had shot both her parents for sheltering an escaped POW, but in spite of that she hid me and cared for me for two weeks, sharing what little food she had and dressing my wound. She put me in touch with a man from the village who gave me a map and some clothes. I would have been on my way the following morning but the Germans must have been tipped off that she was hiding someone. She saw them coming and stalled them while I got away. From a copse of trees on the hillside nearby I saw them shoot her. Saw her fall in a hail of bullets.'

'Oh, God, how terrible.' Laura squeezed his hand. 'You loved her?'

He sighed. 'It was wartime. She was kind and gentle. We comforted each other. She gave her life for me and I'll feel guilty about it for the rest of my life.' He looked at her. 'So you see, I'm in no position to judge anyone else. We're both victims of circumstance – of the war.'

'I thought you'd hate me when you knew,' she whispered.

He stared at her. 'Hate you! It was only the thought of you that kept me going.' He touched her hair. 'How could I ever hate you, Laura?'

'There's something else,' she said. 'Before I left the hospital the doctor told me that because of the surgery they'd had to perform it was unlikely that I'd be able to conceive again.' She looked at him. 'I couldn't give you a child, Peter. I'd understand if you. . . .'

He pulled her close. 'We have each other, Laura,' he whispered against her cheek. 'It's so much more than many people have. I've never wanted anyone but you and we should be thankful for the miracle that has brought us together again.'

Early on the morning of 10 August, Harry bent his head close to the crackling wireless set as he listened to the report on the dropping of the atom bomb on Hiroshima. 'Thank God the Germans never got their hands on a weapon like that first,' he told Meg. He rubbed his hands together in satisfaction. 'Well, thanks to the Yanks the war's got to be well and truly over now and no mistake.'

'Those poor people,' Meg said. 'A whole city wiped out, razed to the ground.'

'*Vaporized*, it said,' Harry put in. 'No country can stand up to a threat like that. They're sure to surrender now.'

'All those innocent civilians – women and children,' Meg said with a shudder. But Harry was shaking his head.

'Plenty of innocent civilians died in this country too, remember, Mother. That's war for you.' He got up and looked out of the window at the garden he was slowly getting back into shape. 'I do believe those roses will give us a good show next summer thanks to my pruning,' he said with satisfaction. 'And how about a nice little vegetable patch down there near the shed come the spring?'

Meg nodded. 'That'd be lovely.'

'I reckon that old apple tree is tough enough to take a swing for little Diana too. I think I'll make a start on that this morning.'

Hearing him whistling in the kitchen as he put on his boots she gave a sigh of satisfaction. She and Harry had always dreamed of retiring to a cottage in the country and now here they were. True, the cottage needed a fair bit of work, which was why they had got it cheap. It had stood empty for most of the war. The garden had been a wilderness when they first moved in. But Harry was good with his hands and he'd already made a clearing. He had mended the fences and the creaky gate and he was enjoying himself planning the garden while she was gradually decorating the rooms. She began to clear the breakfast table, remembering the life they had left behind. No more getting up at five for the papers every morning, thank goodness, or sorting out all those sweet coupons and filling in the returns. It had been such a headache, the shortages and the restrictions, the blackout and the fear of bombing. But they'd still managed to make a little profit